XENI

A MARRIAGE OF INCONVENIENCE

REBEKAH WEATHERSPOON

REBEKAH WEATHERSPOON PRESENTS

and it was informative and entertaining, and it was funny." - Carrie S, *Smart Bitches Trashy Books*

TREASURE

"This story is rich yet beguiling, magnificent yet down to earth, and intriguing yet heartwarmingly human." – J.J., *Rainbow Book Reviews*

For Sunny. And the moon.

CONTENT WARNINGS

Below you'll find just a few notes about the goings-on of this story. If you consider such warnings to be spoilers, please do skip ahead. xoxo - Rebekah

- Death of a family member before the story begins.
- Bisexual adult with an unsupportive parent.
- Discussion of abortion in a character's past.
- Brief mention of miscarriage in a character's past.
- A pregnant supporting character.
- Graphic Sex Scenes.

September

The stream behind St. Michael's Episcopal Church was a lovely place for a memorial service.

It was a Tuesday, late in the morning and only a select few had gathered. Xeni Everly-Wilkins stood a few feet from the water's edge holding a small portion of her Aunt Sable's ashes. The rest had already been sent back to California at her Aunt Alice's request. Xeni had been escorted by Lucy Pummel to the beautiful spot, shaded by tall trees and buzzing with the sounds of nature thriving in the extended summer heat. The elderly, dark-skinned Black woman stood beside her still, and beside his wife was the Reverend Pummel. They were joined by her aunt's other close friend Bess Thompson and her daughter Maya, who Xeni guessed, like her, was also in her early to mid-thirties.

"We're just waiting on Mason McInroy. He's providing the music," the Reverend said, breaking the silence.

"Thank you," Xeni replied with a smile she knew the

Reverend would understand. He reminded her of her Uncle Rand. A serene, older, Black man who always knew what to say and when.

Xeni had already attended one homegoing celebration for her beloved aunt the week before. Sable Junette Everly was survived by her seven sisters and too many nieces and nephews to name on a program. She'd lived a full life, bursting with love and laughter and, most importantly, music. Xeni had done her job that day. She'd woken up early and sent texts to her cousins, Anton and Rosia, and made sure they were ready to help her wrangle their many family members. She'd held her mother's hand, let her step-father hold them both. She'd sat through hours and hours of stories and laughs, recounting the life of the former R&B singer who was also one of the only people in Xeni's life who truly knew her.

Xeni had doled out hugs of comfort, accepted condolences and bit her tongue as each and every member of their community told her just how much they loved her Aunt Sable and how much they envied the bond and the amazing life she'd shared with her sisters. Xeni hadn't said a word about how her mother and her other aunts had been fighting with Sable since before Xeni was born.

Xeni kept quiet about the Thanksgiving dinners and Easter Sundays that had come to a grinding halt when one of the Everly sisters would bring up Sable refusing to do a tribute show, or how Sable wouldn't have missed a birth, graduation or birthday if she would just try to think about someone other than herself for a minute. She didn't mention how suddenly, when Xeni was twelve, Aunt Sable had thought it was best to finally put three thousand miles between herself and her sisters.

She'd kept Xeni close. Phone calls. Quiet trips. Gifts. So many gifts, but it wasn't the same. Xeni knew how stubborn Everly women could be, but in all those years she still wished that just once her mother and her sisters could put their petty beef aside and be a family again.

Now Sable was gone.

When all of the plates and all of the leftovers were wrapped up and divided, Xeni had handed her part of the emotional responsibility for her mother off to her step-dad and boarded a plane alone. Her aunt had made her final wishes very clear. After she was gone, she only wanted Xeni in her home. She only wanted Xeni going through her things. She'd left money for everyone in the will, all her sisters and all the kids, but she didn't want twenty-plus people tromping through her house, fighting over her stuff. She'd put it in writing so it was nice and legal, and then called Xeni to make sure she heard it directly. Any help Xeni needed was welcome, whether friends or an assistant, but she did not want her sisters anywhere near Kinderack, New York.

Xeni had known for sure there were three things waiting for her when she got there. A thirty-five hundred square foot colonial filled with the remnants of Sable Everly's life, a will and, from the way her aunt had left things with her family, probably a whole heap of other bullshit that Xeni didn't want to deal with. Maybe a secret husband somewhere in her Aunt Sable's past. Definitely the jewelry she'd stolen from her sisters in a petty squabble. Or something worse, like proof she and her sisters were covering up a murder.

It had all crossed her mind, but every time she asked her mom about any piece of Sable's life, Xeni had found herself in the middle of another argument. If she asked one of her other aunts, they'd tell her to stay out of grown folks' busi-

3

ness, as if thirty-five wasn't grown. Thirty-five hundred square feet was a lot to tackle on her own, but she knew going it alone was for the best.

She'd already spent one night in the sprawling colonial and, though it felt cold and already untouched, Aunt Sable was in every corner. Xeni could hear her voice, hear her deep laugh. The scent of her favorite perfume lingered everywhere. They deserved more time together, but that wasn't the way life—or death—worked.

She glanced around their small gathering again and almost shook her head. Her aunt had moved to the smallest, mostly White, town she could find in the middle of nowhere New York, but still managed to befriend every Black person in shouting distance. A moment later, she heard the sound of footsteps rushing through the trees.

"I know, baby. After, we'll get ice cream. I promise," she heard a woman say. A child responded, but Xeni couldn't make out what they said. A moment later, another Black woman, carrying a toddler on her hip, and this White dude who was larger than any human being had the right to be, came hurrying up the path.

"It's my fault," the man announced. "Apologies." By the look of the bagpipes tucked under his arm, the kilt and the thick Scottish accent, Xeni guessed this was Mason McInroy. Of course her aunt would want a bagpiper to commemorate her final send off. Xeni ignored how lusciously thick everything about him was. His beard, his wide shoulders, his arms, the massive legs emerging from the perfectly hanging plaid, even his neck—she ignored all of that and smiled at the woman instead.

"Xeni, this is Mason and his cousin Liz," Reverend Pummel said. "And that's little Palila."

4

"Hello."

"My husband, Silas, couldn't make it, but he sends his regards. He loved your aunt very much. We all did." Liz said, breathing heavy. She wasn't a small woman, either. Easily six feet tall and pregnant. Very pregnant. Xeni was pretty sure her husband ran one of the busy apple orchards in the next town over. Whatever he did, eleven a.m. on a Tuesday wasn't the ideal time for anyone to step away from work, and according to her aunt's final wishes, that was the point. She didn't want the whole town to show up. Just the people who mattered to her most.

"Well, I'm glad you could make it. I know this isn't an ideal time. How are you, sweetheart?" Xeni asked the little girl. She buried her face in her mother's shoulder in reply.

"Sorry. Selective shyness is the thing these days."

"It's okay," Xeni replied.

"I think this is everyone," Bess started to say when they all turned at the crunching of leaves coming from down stream. Three teenage girls came tromping through the trees.

Xeni looked over as Bess's hands went right to her hips. She cocked her head at the short Black girl in the group. "Shouldn't you be in school?"

The girl's mouth opened, then shut again. Xeni knew the look on her face. She was considering her words very carefully. "Yes, grandma. We should, but we didn't want to miss this."

"My mom said I should come, since she couldn't close the restaurant for lunch," the tall Asian girl blurted out.

"And you, Miss Vargas?"

"I'm—I'm ditching, but if it weren't for Ms. Everly, I wouldn't already have the lead in *Oklahoma*. Imagine me. A little Dominican girl playing Laurey. This part will help me get into drama school. I owe Miss Sable my life."

"As soon as we're done here, I'm taking all three of you back to school."

"Yes, ma'am," they all said.

"Xeni, this is my granddaughter, Sydney. My son, Christopher's, daughter. Her friends, Mari Vargas and Emma Chen. Say hello to Ms. Sable's niece."

"Hi," they all said.

"Nice to meet you," Xeni replied, mustering another smile. "It's been nice meeting all of you."

Reverend Pummel stepped forward then and the moment he cleared his throat, the distractions from the late arrivals faded away. They were all gathered by the stream for a reason. Though her hands were sweating, Xeni gripped the small gold jar tightly.

"When our friend Sable told me what she wanted today, she made herself very clear. She told me to keep it short and sweet," the Reverend said. "She asked that we all say one nice thing about her before we send her on her way." Xeni tried not to laugh, but a little snort managed to escape. All their disagreements aside, the Everly women had one thing in common: they loved constant, over-the-top praise.

"She asked that Mason play one song and that we truly say goodbye. Again, her words, she didn't want any of us hanging on to any ole bullshit. She didn't have time to haunt anybody. She was too damn tired."

Xeni choked, a burst of laughter sputtering out of her, bringing a couple of fat tears with it. A few of the others joined her, trying to chuckle under their breath. She hadn't had the cathartic cry she needed yet, the true release, but from time to time, a few tears would escape on reflex.

"Who would like to go first?" the reverend asked.

Lucy Pummel spoke up. "Ooh, there's a lot I could say, but I think most importantly, Sable taught me that I am never too old to make new friends."

"She's been there for us ever since my dad died. Like, she's been a really good friend to my grandma. And she taught me how to drive. She didn't yell at me once, even when I almost crashed her car. She—yeah. Ms. Everly was the best," Sydney said.

"I think, maybe, she filled that void for all of us. She collected wayward souls in need of her warming glow," Liz added, tears lining her eyes. "Some of you know I lost my parents way too soon. Then I moved here and thought Maya and Silas were the only Brown faces for two hundred miles, but Miss Sable, and Mrs. Pummel, Bess, Mrs. Chen, Maya. You let me in to your little coven. You were all there for me through two pregnancies and I'm so sad that she won't be here to meet this little."

"She helped me come out to my mom," Maya said. Xeni watched as she reached over and gave Bess's hand a squeeze. "I'm going to miss her courage and the way she shared that courage around. God knows she had more than enough to share with all of us."

Bess smiled at her daughter, then let her gaze drift back to the ground. "She cheated at cards and had the audacity to be offended whenever she got caught. And every time it made me laugh. I will miss laughing with her every day."

Mason took a step forward then and adjusted the bagpipes in the crook of his arm. "The day before she passed, she told me I was single because I refused to shave my neck." More laughter erupted around their tight circle. Even through his thick accent, Mason was able to convey her aunt's blunt delivery. "I thought it was my numerous attempts to prove myself as an amateur magician. I'm not one that thrives on insults, but Ms. Everly just wanted the best for me. She wanted me to be happy. She didn't want that for just anybody."

"No, she didn't," Bess said through a tearful smile.

Xeni shook her head in agreement. Her aunt hated a lot of people.

"I was shaving my neck for her approval when I got the call from Maya here. I'm sure if Ms. Everly were still with us, she would have me turn my head this way and that. Tell me to crouch down. 'Couldn't expect someone at sea level to examine the top of a mountain.' And then she'd tell me I did a good job and now I just needed to work on my wardrobe. She wanted me to be my best me and I am grateful for that. Also, one time I was there to witness her calling Marle Langsby an ashy-lipped demon who was filled with nothing but hate," Mason chuckled a bit. "You have to admire a woman who speaks her mind."

It was Xeni's turn then. She'd had more than enough time to find the words to join this parting chorus. So many things ran through her mind. How much her aunt had meant to her, the things her aunt had done for her, how complicated her aunts and her mother had made her life with their constant fighting, just how much she'd miss her. But Xeni kept all those things to herself, like she had done for most of her life. She swallowed the lump in her throat and said what she knew this particular group of people needed to hear.

"I want to thank you all for being here. I come from a family of singers, actors, public speakers, community organizers, and one thing I think we've perfected is the show. Everlys know how to perform and command a crowd, and my aunt was no exception. But I think when you're so good at being on, a lot of people don't get a chance to know the real you. My aunt was very intentional when it came to who she let into her life and how. It makes me very happy to know that she had you all and that she loved you all enough to let you in. As she would say, to be loved by Sable Everly was to be truly blessed."

"Amen," Lucy said.

"She lived an amazing life and all I want for her now is rest and joy." Heat rushed up Xeni's neck with the sudden, panicked realization that she'd been putting off for nearly three weeks. Her aunt was gone.

She didn't wait for Reverend Pummel's cue or whatever music Mason was going to play. She used the little bit of energy and composure she had left and slowly made her way to the very edge of the stream. She thought about the finality of it all. There was nothing anyone could do or say. No magic trick, no spell at the height of the new moon. No affirmation. Sable Everly had passed on and it was time for Xeni to let her go.

Xeni unscrewed the gold lid and carefully tipped the ashes into the swiftly flowing water. The small bits of grey and white and black were swallowed up and whisked away. Maybe they'd make their way out to sea, but Xeni hoped some forest creature like a deer or a bird that only sang in the early hours of the morning would drink them up and a piece of aunt Sable would live again.

She didn't realize the ground was damp until she'd let her weight settle into the grass, and she couldn't bring herself to care. She couldn't be bothered with the small group of mourners who were watching her lose her shit. Xeni pulled her knees to her chest and then stared at the water. She wanted to cry, desperately needed to, but her body refused. Still, she needed just a moment to try and take it all in. She had about three seconds to pretend her pain was private before the unmistakable drone of bagpipe music rose behind her. Xeni had forgotten how fucking loud the bagpipes were. She closed her eyes against the sound and forced herself to breathe.

It was another ten seconds or so before Xeni realized what song he was playing. "Another One Bites the Dust" was a hilarious selection for a send off, but maybe not the most appropriate. Her head turned automatically. For some reason, she didn't expect to see Mason looking back at her, his large brown eyes rimmed red. He continued to play even as she raised an eyebrow at him, questioning what exactly the fuck was going on, but all he did was shrug and roll his eyes, the sadness on his face disappearing for just a moment. Right. It wasn't his song choice. He played about a quarter of the song Xeni hadn't intentionally listened to since she was gifted Jock Jams on CD before shifting with shocking ease to "Let You Go."

Xeni squeezed her eyes shut as the air left her lungs. She could hear her mom plain as day singing that song while she worked in the kitchen. Her Aunt Alice belting it out at a family reunion. She remembered the exact look on her Aunt Sable's face when she found the notebook that contained her original lyrics. A love so strong, lost forever. The first hit that had landed the Everly Sisters at the top of the charts. They'd never sing it together again.

Mason played the final notes as Xeni continued to watch the flowing water, her breathing struggling to even out. She heard the sounds of footsteps heading back down the wooded path. After a while, she felt a warm hand on her shoulder. She turned and looked up at the kind and patient expression on Bess Thompson's face.

"This is your place, for as long as you need it. Okay?"

Xeni nodded, then let out a deep, shaky breath. The breath carried a layer of pain with it. She'd miss her aunt for the rest of her life, but this was the way she wanted to say goodbye. This was the quiet moment she craved, away from the noise of her family. She knew the peace she felt was Aunt Sable herself, saying her goodbye, letting Xeni ago. She was still devastated, but grateful all at the same time.

She watched the water for a few minutes more, then she turned to Bess. "I'm starving,"

"Lucky for you, McInroy's Cafe is open today and Mason is a good cook. Come on."

Xeni stood and dusted off the seat of her pants. The damp spots would dry soon enough. She let Bess link their arms together and lead the two of them out of the forest.

2

"I don't like that you're there alone," Xeni's mother, Joyce, yelled through the phone. She didn't quite grasp the concept of the car's Bluetooth function. She didn't need to raise her voice just because she was in the car.

"You could have come with me. I told you that."

"No, I couldn't. Knowing Sable, she'd have the locals waiting with shot guns at the town line just to keep us away."

Xeni couldn't stop her eyes from rolling. "There were no guns for me. Just a man with two goats. I had to answer his riddles three before he was willing to get me to the town square. There, two witches with four goats waited for me. I—"

"Yeah, okay. That's enough."

"Everyone has been very nice and her friend Bess has been very accommodating."

"At least someone has some kindness and common sense left in them."

"What are you and Daddy doing tonight?" Xeni asked, changing the subject.

"Oh nothing. I'm on my way to pick him up from urgent care."

"Is he okay?"

"Oh yeah, his shoulder is just acting up. I keep telling him he's too old to be climbing up on roofs." Xeni had to agree. Her step-dad was fit for his age, but he wasn't young anymore. Roofing was tough work. A picture of her aunt's house popped into her mind again. If she could sell it for enough, maybe her step-dad could afford to retire a little early. Or maybe they could keep it and use the rental income. She breathed out the compound guilt gnawing at her. She'd figure it out.

"That's smart. Tell him to rest. I'll call him later and nudge him to take it easy."

"Please. He'll listen to you. You find your grandma's brooch yet?"

"No," Xeni sighed. "I haven't, and if I do, you'll be the first to know."

"There's no if. I know she has it. Your grandmother told Hazel she could have it and—"

"Mommy, I know. As soon as I find it, I'll let you know. I should go."

"Okay. I love you. And remember, don't feel guilty about whatever she's left you. The house, a little bit of money. Your cousins already got their checks. I talked to Rosia before I left the house. I know your aunt left you a little more and the house and that's yours. You do what you want with it."

"I will."

"But your grandmother's jewelry—"

"Okay, I'm going!"

"Okay, okay. Call me when you're done."

"I will." She ended the call before her mom could go on another tear.

After she let out another deep breath, Xeni glanced up at the white, weather-beaten sign jutting out over the street. Bart Barber, Attorney at Law. Bess had already headed inside, but there were still a few minutes before their meeting with Mr. Barber began. She looked back down at her phone and opened the LetsChat app. She'd silenced notifications from the chattiest group in her phone, but she couldn't miss the "36" backlit in bright blue next to the words INTERSECTIONAL FEMINISTS OF BENETTON.

Her thumb hovered above the screen for a few moments as she reconsidered jumping back into the conversation. Even though the girls were at work now, she knew it would only take a few moments before one of them responded. She wasn't ready to do the catch-up and the debrief. She slipped her phone back in her bag and walked up the few worn stone steps into the brick Colonial. Inside, the only thing that made it seem like a converted office space was the furniture. Bess was sitting in one of the few chairs making up a small waiting area against the wall. An older White woman with dyed black hair sat behind a massive, cluttered desk next to a fireplace that looked like it had been built some time in the late seventeen hundreds.

"Martha, this is Xeni," Bess said, motioning between them.

"Absolutely." The woman stood, offering a bright smile. "Ms. Everly told me you were beautiful, but she undersold it. You are just lovely. And your hair!"

"Thank you," Xeni said, sidestepping the woman's curious grasp. She ignored the pained look on Martha's face and waited.

"Yeah, well. Um, why don't you have a seat and I'll let Bart know you're here."

"Thank you." Xeni lowered herself into a creaky wooden chair next to Bess. She looked around the office space, taking in the photos and the news clippings on the walls, and the old-timey maps of the town center. When she'd had enough of L.A., a quick trip to Palm Springs or Santa Barbara was usually enough to hit her reset button. Xeni couldn't imagine moving to a small town like this, so far away from her friends and family.

"Martha's harmless enough. They just—" Bess started to whisper.

"No, I get it. I get the same thing back home. I was in line at Whole Foods last week and this woman picked up her daughter and told her to feel my hair." Xeni hadn't done much beyond trim her ends in ten years. As a result, she had a gorgeous mane of long, thick natural hair. Fools from all walks of life were drawn to it.

Bess's eyes sprang wide. "Mercy."

"Used it as a teachable moment for the child, which her mother didn't like. If you're not going to tell your kids that human petting zoos are a thing of the past, I will."

Bess chuckled quietly and patted Xeni's knee. "I think Martha got the message."

Martha reappeared a moment later, her bright smile refreshed. "Come on in, ladies. Bart will see you. Can I get you water or coffee?"

"I'm fine. Thank you, sweetie."

"No, thank you," Xeni added. She was already on edge. Lunch had provided the recharge she needed, but on the short drive back into the center of town, the gravity of part two of all of this finally hit her. She'd lost people before. Her grandparents, friends who had slipped away too soon. But she'd never been responsible for any part of the *after*.

She knew she could handle it. She was an Everly. She could handle anything. All she had to do was sit down with this Bart Barber and find out exactly what her aunt had left her. Then she was off to sit down with the realtor. Next came the biggest job, cleaning out the house and deciding what to do with it.

She tried not to think about work. The Whippoorwill School where she taught kindergarten had agreed to a three-week leave. She could negotiate longer if she needed, but beyond two months she would have to sit out the rest of the academic year. She couldn't afford to do that and she didn't want to. She needed to wrap things up here in New York, get back to her students, her family and friends, and get on with the rest of her life. It was how she coped with any level of extreme stress, looking forward and pressing on. She could and absolutely would do it. One step at a time.

She followed Bess and Martha down the hall into a conference room dominated by a large table. There was barely enough room for the twelve wooden chairs crammed around it. A pitcher of water and glasses were at the far end. Xeni took a seat next to Bess, both of them facing the door.

"Thank you again. I'm pretty overwhelmed right now." Xeni said quietly.

"No need to thank me. Sable was always there when I needed her. And now I'm gonna be here for you."

An older White man and a White woman in her late forties entered the room a few moments later.

"Mrs. Thompson. One day I'll get you in here for the right reasons," Bart Barber said. His tone was dry, but Xeni wasn't entirely sure he was joking. Whatever was happening though, Bess was in on it.

"I'm not leaving my husband for you, Bart."

"Yet. Miss Everly? This is Mora Jordan."

"Your aunt's financial advisor," Ms. Jordan tacked on.

"Hello." Xeni stood and shook both their hands.

"It's nice to meet you. I'm sorry you had to witness the old folks flirting," Mr. Barber said.

"I'll allow it until Bess tells me otherwise," she replied.

He shot her a firm nod before taking his own seat on the other side of the table beside Ms. Jordan. "We're just waiting on one more person," he said, "and then we'll get started." Almost on cue, Xeni noticed the atmospheric change of the front door opening. A second later she heard Mason McInroy's voice.

"Been running late all day."

"Don't worry, sweetheart," Martha replied. "Right this way."

The moment she saw Mason's giant frame fill the doorway, the wave of confusion that suddenly hit her was joined by another feeling she couldn't explain. She watched as Mason actually had to duck and turn to squeeze into the conference room. She swallowed a weird pinch of anxiety and focused on *why* he was there.

"My apologies. Just had to get Shelby settled after the lunch rush. Didn't mean to keep you waiting. Oh—" Xeni felt his gaze land on her. He seemed just as confused. "Should I come back?"

"Nope. We were just getting started. Have a seat," Mr. Barber said.

Mason grabbed the back of the closest chair, then clearly

had second thoughts as he pushed it back in. The width of the chair's arms were not enough for him to sit comfortably. And that was if he could fit his legs under the table.

"I'll stand if you don't mind."

"Fine by me," Mr. Barber said as he nodded in Xeni's direction.

She cleared her throat, a frown clouding her face. "Is there somewhere we can go where Mason can sit?"

"Oh, um," Mr. Barber froze. The town was smaller than a gnat. Xeni doubted that he hadn't seen Mason around, at the very least. He should have known that the cramped conference room wouldn't accommodate him.

"Don't worry about it, love. I'm fine. Plenty of headroom up here." Xeni noted the high ceilings, but it still didn't make it okay.

"Whatever makes you comfortable."

Mason dipped his chin, then crossed his arms over his broad chest. The muscles of his forearms were kind of distracting, but she forced her eyes back in Mr. Barber's direction.

"Right. We have a lot to cover, so I don't want to say this won't take long. I just want to clarify that. Ms. Everly asked that we speak to you both at the same time. We are here to clearly express her wishes and answer any questions you may have. Do either of you have any questions before we begin?"

Xeni had several dozen, but she knew it was best to let Mr. Barber get started. "No, I'm fine. Please go on." Mason shook his head as well, then motioned toward the files Mr. Barber and Ms. Jordan had set out on the conference table.

Ms. Jordan began. "Ms. Everly had what most would

consider to be a sizable estate. Mr. McInroy, she's leaving to you a gift of one hundred thousand dollars."

The air was immediately sucked out of the room, most of it going right to Xeni's lungs, if the sudden tightness in her chest was any indicator. She glanced over at Mason and quickly discovered he had no poker face to speak of. One of his eyebrows was nearly in his hairline and his cheeks and neck were turning a stark shade of red. Both of them kept their mouths shut and let Ms. Jordan go on.

"Ms. Everly is leaving her daughter, Xeni Everly-Wilkins, the remainder of her estate. The property at Fifty-Four Maple Court in Kinderack, New York, a Mercedes E-class sedan, a Toyota 4-Runner, the property at seventy-three Terry Lane in Oak Bluffs, Massachusetts. There are additional assets all valued at twenty-three million dollars. The properties are held in a trust. That means—"

"I'm sorry." Xeni paused, struggling like hell to gather her thoughts. "How much? All of this is worth how much?"

"Twenty-three million dollars," Ms. Jordan replied calmly, like that wasn't a metric shit-ton of money to just drop on someone. And what was this about another house? "There is more. If you—"

"I—there has to be a mistake. I know my aunt has a little bit of money, but not that much. And she never mentioned a house in Massachusetts."

"Miss Everly, I've been working with your aunt for nearly ten years now and my father was her advisor for the twenty years before I came on. I can assure you that this is an accurate accounting of Ms. Everly's estate and we spoke at length about exactly what she wanted passed on to you."

"Well, something isn't right. You have me down as her

daughter. I don't know if there's some legal loophole that says only her kids are entitled to all of this stuff, but I'm definitely not claiming that kind of money just to get caught up in some fraud charges."

Ms. Jordan fell silent for a moment before she glanced over at Mr. Barber, but it was Bess that covered Xeni's hand with her own.

"That part is also true," Bess said.

"What are you talking about?" Xeni asked. She looked up as Mr. Barber stood and held out a piece of paper. It was a birth certificate. She looked it over and all the information looked right. Her name. Her place of birth, the right hospital. The spot for her father's name was blank like it had always been. Her birthday was the same, February ninth. But one thing was off. Joyce Everly wasn't listed as her mother. She blinked and focused harder on the dark ink. The name Sable Everly stared back at her.

"No. My mom is Joyce Everly, Sable's older sister. And I have my birth certificate at home. This is wrong." Xeni's eyes scanned the paper again as the silence hung heavy in the room. Something else was different. The time of her birth. She was born at 8:30 a.m.. Not 12:55 a.m.. She could feel more than one pair of eyes on her, willing her to accept this fake birth certificate as the truth, but she couldn't. Not for any amount of money. "What does the law say about this?" she asked Mr. Barber.

"What do you mean?" he replied.

"Like, how much trouble could we all get in if I accept this forgery and take the estate? I won't say my family couldn't use the money, I just—"

"Xeni, it's not fake," Bess said. "I was there. I drove Sable to the hospital."

"I thought you two met when she moved here."

"We reconnected. We were old friends."

"No, this doesn't make sense. Joyce is my mom. My dad was a studio bassist named Orlando Powers. I was an accident, but my mom decided to keep me and that's why the Everly Sisters broke up and my aunt went solo. I—"

"Why don't we let Mr. Barber and Ms. Jordan finish," Bess suggested. "And then we can answer as many of your questions as possible."

Xeni's jaw clenched as she tried to process Bess's calm aura. She didn't know the woman well, but Xeni could read people better than most. Bess wasn't lying, but someone in this room or in her life was. She closed her eyes for a long moment, then let out a deep breath. "Please. Go ahead."

"Um, there's more in the form of stocks, investment properties. We can go over those a little later," Ms. Jordan said. "After we discuss the conditions."

"Oh my god," Xeni groaned quietly. "What now? What conditions?"

Ms. Jordan sat back a bit, turning her attention to Mr. Barber. He stood and handed Xeni and Mason each an envelope. Xeni's name was written on the front, but Mr. Barber kept going before she could open it.

"In order for either of you to claim any of this, Ms. Everly asked that you two be married. To each other."

"Bloody hell," Mason said as he slammed the back of his head into the door jamb.

"Is this some kind of joke? What does the letter say?"

"Your aunt only agreed to release the estate if you and Mr. McInroy agreed to marry each other. The marriage must be legal and last no less than thirty days. She explains why in the letters. Why don't we give you two a moment."

Xeni was too fucked up to respond. Her aunt was leaving her more money than she could comprehend and all she had to do was marry some dude she'd never met. Was that even legal? She couldn't begin to wrap her mind around the other shit. There was no way Sable was her mother. It just didn't make sense.

As Bess stood to leave, Xeni tore open the envelope. Sure enough, there was a letter inside. She recognized her aunt's handwriting from the dozens of birthday and holiday cards and notes she'd sent over the years.

My Dearest Xendria, If you're reading this I know you have spoken to Mr. Barber and you've been given your fair share of shocking news. I know you, so I'll stick to the facts. You are mine. My sisters made the decision that I wouldn't be the one to raise you and through the years they forbid me from telling you who you really belong to. Now that I'm gone, there's nothing stopping me from telling you the truth. You are my daughter. I carried you. I gave birth to you. I gave you your name.

You're probably wondering why I'm making it so difficult to claim what's rightfully yours as my daughter and my only child. I know you've closed yourself off to love. Don't try to deny it. I didn't forget the conversations we had or any of the things you told me. From the moment I met Mason, I knew there was something different about him. He's one of the good ones, Xeni. Marry him and you'll see.

You'll have more questions than I can answer, but I want you to know without any doubt that I have always loved you like you were my own, because you are. As for the rest, ask my sisters. They know the truth and they have been the ones who've kept it from you for all of these years. I love you and my only regret in life was not fighting harder for you. Take my last bit of advice. Take the blessings that have been laid out in front of you and give Mason a chance. You deserve the amount of love he's carrying around in that kind heart of his. If you ever feel lost, trust the moon. I love you.

Your mother, Sable

P.S. Don't let my sisters touch our mother's jewelry until they tell you the whole truth.

Xeni reread the letter twice before she realized she was shaking. What in the whole fresh fuck? It was really something to have the foundation of your life ripped out from underneath you while being shamed for your selective single status all at once. Maybe Sable was her real mother. Who else could guilt her from beyond the grave with such a level of drama?

She swiped at the tears of rage gathering at the corners of her eyes before she glanced up at Mason. The redness had spread all the way up to his hairline and she wasn't sure if he had tears of sadness or tears that matched the anger she felt lining her eyes. All she wanted to do was put her aunt's spirit to rest. She didn't want a new tax bracket. She didn't want two new properties to manage. She didn't want a husband.

"Do you want to read my letter?" Mason asked.

Xeni stared at him for a moment before she jumped up from her chair. Maybe his letter made a lick of sense. She made her way around the room and took the slip of paper from his hand. His letter was much shorter.

I know what you said, but just take the money. Take care of her and let her take care of you.

3

M ason was having a hard time breathing. Ms. Sable's passing had been a blow he wasn't prepared for. From the moment they met, she'd taken him under her wing, convinced him to open up and be honest about the complete disaster his life had become. He'd miss her dearly, but at the moment he wondered what in the world she'd been thinking. Mr. Barber could have dropped the news of Xeni's apparently eventful birth on her in private. Why would Ms. Sable want him here for that? He looked down at Xeni. Her niece? Daughter? Christ, Xeni was right. There must be some kind of mistake.

"Here." Xeni thrust his letter back in his hands, seemingly disappointed with what she'd just read.

"Does that help?" he asked.

"Not even close."

"Can I have a look at your letter?" he asked.

"I'd rather you didn't. There's more... personal stuff in mine. It's much longer."

"Okay, then. That's fair."

"Okay, okay. Jesus." Xeni stepped in to the corner across from the door, the only space in the room that wasn't occupied by the table or chairs. She started pacing back and forth. "Okay. Do you need the money?"

"I could use it, yeah."

"What do you need the money for? Drugs? Gambling debt? A hundred grand is a lot of money."

"Erm, I need it to cover some student loans, basically. I got a bad interest rate."

"Right. Okay. Clearing up your student loans would make anyone's life easier. And my… aunt was big on education. I can see why she'd want to help you with that. Okay. Do I need the money?" she said to herself as her eyes darted to the floor. "Do I want the money? You're hurt and you're angry, but you'd be a fool to turn down that type of cash. Okay." Her eyes settled back on him. They really were gorgeous brown eyes. Mason had tried not to notice, but he couldn't help himself. Xeni Everly-Wilkins was one of the most beautiful women he'd ever seen.

Under normal circumstances he'd be too nervous to ask her out. Probably tell her a few jokes, show her a terrible magic trick or his skills on the fife, and ultimately friendzone himself in under five minutes flat. Not that there was anything wrong being friends with someone you find attractive, but one day—

Mason shook his head a bit and forced himself to focus on the issue at hand. This was not about the persistent pathetic state of his love life. His dear friend was gone and she had left him in quite a jam. He needed that hundred thousand dollars. He wasn't exactly sure walking down the aisle with a woman he'd just met was the best way to get it.

"Can you even do this? I mean you're a White male. You

can do whatever you want. But this will take months to sort out, right? You're Scottish, right? You're not a citizen."

"I am."

"You are?" He'd gotten the same shocked response before.

"Dual citizenship. My mother was born in Cleveland."

"Oh, okay. So we have to do this, right? I have to do this."

"I'm not going to make that call," Mason replied. "Our stakes are not the same."

"Did she say *anything* to you about this?"

"She told me she was going to find me a wife, but I thought she was taking the piss. I didn't think she was serious. I take it from your reaction she didn't mention anything about this either?"

"No. No, she didn't." Mason watched Xeni as she sighed and leaned against the wall. "So what's your deal? You work at the cafe?"

"Yes. My cousin Silas owns the farm and I run the food services there."

"Mmm, and you play the bagpipes."

"Yes, I guess I fancy myself a bit of a musician. What about you? Your aunt did mention to me that you're a teacher."

"I teach kindergarten, yeah. So you at least knew I existed."

"Your au—Ms. Sable talked about you a lot. She seemed very proud of you."

Xeni's eyes rolled toward the ceiling. Mason couldn't miss the few fat tears that ran down her cheeks. His gaze darted to the box of tissues at the center of the table. He reached for them, then shuffled around the edge of the table. She took a few, then wiped her cheeks.

"Thank you." She let out another deep breath and seemed

to gather her focus. A clarity came to her eyes, like she'd made a decision. "Mr. Barber didn't say how long we had to stay married, did he? No, he did. Thirty days, but he didn't say we had to live together. We can get married. You can pay off your debt. If Ms. Jordan is as smart as I think she is, she can help me. I don't know. How the fuck do rich people move money around? She can help me figure something out so I can keep this money and then we get a divorce. Right?"

Mason immediately thought of his parents and what they would think of this scheme. Different types of disappointment was all that came to mind. His mother being let down once again that he was no closer to the real thing and his father... The decision was simple. He wouldn't tell them. He'd swear Silas and Liz to secrecy, even though he'd been the one to blab to his aunt about Silas's sudden love match. He could count on them to keep this new development on this side of the pond if they decided to go through with it.

"People get divorced all the time. Shall we invite them back in, just to make sure? The way things are going, I wouldn't be surprised if this wasn't the first of ten elaborate tasks we have to complete. First we marry, then we visit the village witch who's the third born of the first born. Then—" Mason said.

A little laugh sputtered out of Xeni. The sound of it made Mason smile. "What?"

"Nothing. I said basically the same thing to my mom on the phone. Yeah, okay. Let's get all the information and then we'll figure out what to do next."

Mason nodded, then poked his head back into the claustrophobic hallway. Mr. Barber was talking to Bess in the reception area. "We're ready," he told them.

A few moments later, everyone had reassembled in the

conference room. Mason stayed by the door. He was on his feet from dawn to dusk most days, so a little while longer wouldn't hurt. Ms. Jordan picked up where she'd left off, and she and Mr. Barber went on for nearly another hour, breaking down the rest of Ms. Sable's estate, pausing every so often to answer Xeni's questions. Not that he had any doubt, but Xeni sure was bright. She was two steps ahead of his every thought, asking follow-up after follow-up question. And she wasn't afraid to tell Ms. Jordan when she had no idea what she was talking about.

Mason learned a lot in that hour. He was also reminded of just how much money he didn't have and how long it was going to take to finish paying off his father if he and Xeni decided they couldn't go through with Ms. Sable's absurd scheme. It also didn't take long for Mason to remember that there would be no twenty-four hour quickie divorce. If she decided to claim this inheritance and they filed for divorce after thirty days, it seemed like it would be months before she would have everything sorted out. This was a bad idea. Still, Mason's mind was made up. This was too much money for Xeni to walk away from. If she needed him to marry her so she could claim what was rightfully hers, he would.

"How long do we have to decide?" Mason asked.

"Um, I wouldn't wait very long. I wouldn't advise you leave either property unattended and—"

"So no time. I got it," Xeni said. Mason lungs felt like they were collapsing on themselves when she looked over at him again. That resolve was back in her eyes, but so was the pain. She hated this. "I need a day. I need to—I need to talk to my parents. I have a lot to think about."

"I think that's a good idea," Bess reassured her.

"Why don't we regroup on Friday and if you and Mr.

McInroy are married, we'll take care of all of the paperwork," Mr. Barber said.

"Wait, we can get married that quickly?" Xeni asked the question that was right on the tip of Mason's tongue.

"If you head to town clerk's office now, you can be married by this time on Thursday."

"Jesus," Xeni said with a deep breath. The same overwhelming feeling bounced around in his own head. This was a whole lot to process in such a short amount of time. "Okay. So we'll meet right back here, Friday."

"That works for me," Ms. Jordan said.

Martha would contact everyone with an exact time. With that decided, their meeting was adjourned. Mason left first and headed outside to wait. He slipped his baseball cap on to block his eyes from the sun, even though the clouds were beginning to roll in. He could smell it in the air. The rain was coming.

A few moments later, Xeni and Bess came walking down the stone steps.

"Oh good, I thought you'd taken off," Xeni said.

"No, just stepped out for a bit of air," Mason replied.

"Hmm. Do you need to get back to the farm right now?"

"No, they can handle things without me a little bit longer."

"Maybe you could drive me back to the house. We should probably talk."

"That's a good idea," Bess said. "You have my number?"

"Yes, thank you. I'll give you a call if I need anything."

Mason watched as Bess gave Xeni's hand a light squeeze before she turned and crossed the street toward her own car.

"I'm just over here," he said, pointing to his beat-up

Suburban a ways down the street. "I know the way to her house."

"Okay."

Mason didn't miss how exhausted Xeni sounded. The quiet thank you she offered him as he held her door open and helped her up into the cab was the last thing she said before they arrived at Ms. Sable's house. She lived about fifteen minutes outside of the town center. When they pulled in the tree-shaded driveway, a large lump formed in Mason's throat. He half expected Ms. Sable to walk out the front door and offer them a big wave like she'd done so many times before. He brought his truck to a stop and waited. She let out a small sigh, then scratched her jaw. Mason watched as a small, angry welt raised on her skin.

"Your—your face."

"Oh." She touched the spot. "It's this weird skin condition. It's a stress thing. I get these welts if I scratch myself. It's fine. Why don't you give me your number? Then you can call me or text me later and let me know when's a good time to go to the town clerk's office tomorrow."

"We don't have to do this," Mason replied.

"Yes we—I mean, I do. Sorry. I'm absolutely all in my head." She turned to him. That clarity was back in her eyes. Like she'd made a decision. "Will you marry me?"

Mason knew what his answer should be. No. A firm no. He wanted to try to talk her out of it. He wanted to come up with some sort of reasonable alternative, but he had none. Ms. Sable's wishes were legal and binding.

"Might as well," he said, giving in.

"Great. I'll ask Mr. Barber about a pre-nup or a post-nup or whatever. Shit. I'll call him when I get inside. I'm sorry I just can't give you half of everything whenever we finally dissolve this thing. And you seem nice and all, but it's a lot and you might decide you'd like your inconvenience fees to the tune of ten million dollars, and nah. That's not happening."

"I don't want your money."

"Now. But as you can see, money makes people do stupid things. We saw proof of that just this afternoon."

They exchanged numbers, then Xeni climbed down from the truck. "I'll try and make this as quick and painless as possible. I promise your next proposal will be more romantic."

She closed the door and hurried inside.

Mason stared after her, his mouth hanging open. What the hell had he just agreed to?

Xeni walked into her aunt's newly remodeled kitchen and set her stuff down. She looked around, her eyes focusing on the mug she'd set by the sink that morning. She looked over at the fancy new fridge, covered in photos and Christmas cards that were nearly a year old. Her high school graduation portrait was there, right in the center of it all. She stared at it, concentrated on its placement until her vision started to blur.

She blinked, then reached for her phone. More alerts were lighting up her LetsChat app. A few missed calls. She opened her contacts and called her Aunt Alice. The oldest of the Everly sisters, she'd had her own issues with Sable, but Xeni had at least witnessed her efforts to play peace maker. That always turned to the role of referee when she sent Xeni's mom and her other sisters back to their respective corners to cool off. The phone rang and rang, but the voice-mail kicked in. Xeni ended the call and dialed her step-dad.

She knew she should put the phone away and calm down. Take another deep breath, maybe a few dozen more. Gather her thoughts before she talked to anyone about any of this, but no. She wanted fucking answers.

"Hey Peanut," Dante's cheery voice came through after the fourth ring.

"I have to ask you something and you have to tell me the truth."

"Okay. What's going on?"

"Did you know that Sable was my real mother?"

Dante was silent for a moment too long before he spoke. "Peanut, I told your mother I was going to stay out of this—"

"So you knew. Thank you. That's all I wanted to know."

"Your mom is with me right now. Why don't you talk to her."

"I can't. I have to go." Xeni hit the bright red button at the bottom of the screen.

———

It was nearly ten p.m. when Xeni took a moment to count the different rooms she'd disassociated in over the last several hours. Four. She'd spent some time in the kitchen, just staring out the window, coming in and out of awareness, considering how much lying to someone for their whole life was worth. Millions and a house on Martha's Vineyard maybe? She'd managed to draft one text to her mother.

> *Just really upset right now.*
> *Can't talk.*

She was a fool to think that would work. After ignoring a dozen or so calls from her mother, she forced herself to eat something with the bottle of Chardonnay she'd cracked open. She'd come back to herself sitting at her aunt's piano, cheese and cracker crumbs on her shirt.

She moved to the T.V. room and envisioned the conversation her mom had had with Dante all those years ago, while Jeopardy played in the background. She thought of what she had told him when she explained she was raising her little sister's baby. She wondered how easy it was for him to keep that a secret. She wondered just how many of the fights her family had had over the years were about her. Mostly she wondered why.

When a commercial broke into some terrible family sitcom, she realized she wasn't even watching the T.V. so she went upstairs to the newly renovated master bathroom. It was hers now right? Or it would be after a quick trip to the town clerk's office and an emotionless walk down the aisle. Might as well take the massive soaker tub for a test drive. She filled it with piping hot water, remembering where she was just as the water came dangerously close to spilling over the edge.

She undressed and slid into the water, that *why* beating at the backs of her eyes, begging her to cry so she could release some of the tension. But the tears weren't coming. They might, eventually, but for now she chose numb over weepy.

She sat in the water, her body warm and wet, and still as tense as before. What was she going to tell her family about the money? Not a damn fucking thing. The angry part of her had a point. Why should she tell them shit? If they could lie to her about her whole existence, she could lie to them about millions of dollars.

She ran her finger over the rim of the tub and asked herself who the fuck she thought she was kidding. She was smart and knew how to keep her cards to her chest, but she wasn't a liar and, unlike every other Everly woman she knew, she wasn't selfish.

Her phone rang again and she ignored it. If she weren't waiting to hear from Mason, she'd let it die and never charge it again. God, Mason. She'd meant to hit him with the important questions. Was he a murderer? Did he have a criminal record? Where did he stand on Brexit and *The Great British Baking Show*? But what did it matter? This would be the sham marriage to end all sham marriages. She didn't need to get to know him. She just needed him to say I do.

Xeni finally pulled herself out of the tub, lotioned up and got ready for bed in the guest room. She risked a look at her phone. More missed calls from her parents, texts from the girls checking in, a voicemail from her cousin Rosia. She glanced at the transcript, saw the words "your mom wanted me to call" and immediately switched to LetsChat.

All her girls were home from work, texting up a storm. She was three hundred messages behind. Her brain couldn't do the catch up.

Heeeeeey!

Meegan: *Xeni!*
Shae: *Hey boo, I was just thinking about you.*
Joanna: *How did the service go? Are you okay?*
Sarah: *Yeah, how'd it go?*
Sloan: *Xeni-boo! Twins about to murder each other. Brb, but I wanna hear it all. Love you!*
Keira: *Do you need anything?*

Xeni thought about how surreal her day had been, the madness that she knew had just begun to unfold. The lies and the secrets. My god, the lies. The sounds of those damn bagpipes popped in her head as her thumb hovered over the screen. Xeni didn't have the energy to get into it, not with all of them at once. And the superstitious part of her knew not speak on certain things until they were concrete and sure, especially when it came to money.

When she was ready, she could tell Sarah. She'd mastered the art of the tempered response. Then she could tell Keira and Shae and Joanna. And Sloan when she had time. When she was ready to laugh about it, she would tell Meegan. At the moment, she couldn't feel the slightest bit of humor in the situation. So in her aunt's dying words, she did the only thing she could do and stuck to the facts.

The service was lovely.

4

X eni hoped sleep and a shower would help her find some clarity and peace with her current situation. Instead of a refreshed calm and the joy that came with the potential of a new day, she felt like she hadn't slept in weeks. Her REM cycles had been filed with dreams that could only be described as stressful as fuck. She woke up dehydrated and, worst of all, angry. Her sour mood hung around as she got dressed and made sense of the hair she hadn't wrapped before falling into bed. It followed her as she struggled to get the coffee maker working and seemed to triple when she finally checked her phone.

She could only fake it with the girls for so long. She read about Sloan's kids and Meegan and Sarah caught her up on the most recent drama at school, but it didn't take much for her thoughts to battle their way back to the surface and push the comfort she could only get from her closest friends to the side. She didn't tell the girls she had to meet Mason first thing in the morning. She didn't mention his name at all. She didn't mention that she was saving as much energy as possible for the conversation she was going to eventually have with her mother. Instead she carefully directed the conversation back to their lives, claiming she needed the distraction. Soon. She'd tell them the truth soon.

After a while though, even their distractions weren't enough. She wanted to know more about the new flavors Shae was introducing at her bakery, Sweet Creams, but Xeni knew if she stayed in the chat she'd say something. No, she'd blurt it all out. And then one of them would try to soften the blow and she'd snap at them because none of them had ever been in this situation. They would never understand. So she bowed out, claiming the jet lag and the emotion of laying a loved one to rest after such a long struggle. All that factored in, but those were things she'd expected and prepared herself to handle. Xeni didn't expect to be the likely cause of a family drama that spanned three decades. Yeah, the sour taste of that was thick enough to survive the night.

She glanced at her phone and like magic it started vibrating in her hand. MOMMY. She hit decline, then switched over to the last text message she'd sent her mother. Her mother had jammed up the stream with texts that followed every phone call Xeni had ignored. She ignored those texts too. She'd keep calling and texting, and if Xeni didn't answer or respond eventually, Joyce Everly-Wilkins would show up. That was the last thing Xeni wanted or needed.

> *I'm fine.*
> *Please just give me some space.*
> *XP*

Kisses, Peanut. The sign off Xeni used when everything was okay. Her mother responded immediately, even though it was barely five a.m. on the West Coast.

Call me back tonight or
I'm coming out there.
You need to talk to me. XM

Kisses, mom.

"See?" she muttered to herself. Xeni slipped her phone into the pocket of her dress, then stopped in her tracks. She stood still for the few moments she needed to remember what she had been doing before her phone rang, then she walked into her aunt's study. It only took her a couple of minutes to spot exactly what she was looking for on the bottom of a cluttered bookshelf. She plucked an empty manila folder off the top of a full box and wiped the dust on her thigh. She regretted that move for a moment, before looking down and realizing she could barely see the dust on her skirt.

She sat on the arm of a large wooden chair and pulled out her phone. She had a text chain going with Mason now. He'd checked in twice already, confirming the time when they'd meet at the Kinderack Town Clerk office and then again, asking if she'd had anything to eat. She appreciated the consideration, but holy hell did she want to be left alone, just for a little while. She made a promise to the universe that she'd be nice to him the minute the exasperated thought crossed her mind. She knew she could get bitey when she

39

was stressed and she didn't want to bite Mason. He was the only other innocent victim in this absurd plot.

Xeni just wanted a little more time before she had to turn off the rage and go back to being a polite, considerate person. She sighed and started typing, reminding herself that he was definitely was not at fault here. It was those damned Everly Sisters.

Hey just checking in.
Do you have the proper documentation?

She added the wikiHow link with its cut-to-the-chase descriptions of what they needed to apply for a marriage license in New York, then hit send. She slipped her phone back in her pocket and went to look for the keys to her aunt's car. Those were easy to find too, hanging on a hook right next to the kitchen door. She grabbed them and went to the garage. She was leaving nothing to chance. Knowing her luck, she'd find the keys to twenty different cars and the garage would be empty. She'd have to marry someone else just to get the location of her aunt's real carport, then she'd have to have three children of her own to get the combination to another locked door.

Xeni let out a sigh of relief when she found both cars were where they should be. She pressed the open padlock button on the Mercedes key. The single beep of the alarm, the click of the doors unlocking and flashing of the lights was the first bit of comfort she'd had all day. She just hoped it didn't explode when she put the thing in drive.

Another wave of sadness washed over her as she turned the key over in her hand. Why was her aunt doing this? Her mother? What the fuck was she even supposed to call her now? Knowing she didn't have time for this, she pushed the feelings down again. Numb was definitely the way to be for the foreseeable future and thinking about every detail of her family's odd betrayal would only make Xeni feel anything but. She walked back into the house to grab her purse and her phone vibrated in her pocket.

A response from Mason.

Yes, I do.
Just thought I'd ask again.
Do ya need a lift to town?

> *No thank you.*
> *I'll meet you there.*

Grand. See ya soon.

There was no reason to wait. Xeni grabbed her things and drove into town.

The Kinderack Town Hall was easy to find. It was less than two blocks from Mr. Barber's law office and circus of lies. Xeni found a parking space easily and made her way up the stone steps into a brick building that looked like it might have been a church at one point. Inside, the wood floors were unevenly worn, giving the main entrance a sense of history, but the bright fluorescent lights sucked all the warmth out of the place. Xeni looked at the directory on the wall and found the number for the clerk's office just as the door opened and Mason McInroy stepped inside.

"Hello," he said as he took off a Yankees baseball cap. A strange heat rose in Xeni's chest at the sound of his voice. It was just an accent, but something about that accent made her want to do things. His general thickness didn't help either. She looked him up and down, more closely this time. This was a man who did not skip leg day or a meal. The round-ness of his belly and his broad chest seemed to bend the McInroy Farm t-shirt to his body's will in a strangely appealing way.

She had to ignore the sudden way her clit seemed to spark to life at the thought of his body. Xeni was focusing on staying numb. Numbness and crisp efficiency. She didn't have the time or the emotional bandwidth to find her poten-tial husband attractive. She glanced at the manila envelope tucked under his arm.

"How're you faring this morning?" he asked.

"I've had better days, not gonna lie. Ready?"

"After you. And I have to say, you look very beautiful today. I like your dress."

"Oh. Thank you. You look very handsome as well. I like what your beard is doing," she said motioning in the general direction of his face.

"I spend my days in a messy apron. Seems like a good idea to at least have my face in order."

"Well, you're doing a bang up job," Xeni said, reminding herself instantly why she'd sworn off men. She always sounded like a complete bonehead whenever she engaged with them. Mason took pity on her though and nodded down the hall.

"Let's get on with this."

"Right." Xeni turned on her heels and led the way, suddenly very aware of the mass of energy following behind her. They entered the town clerk's office and started a line behind an elderly White man in a red cap. Xeni almost turned around and walked right out, but when he turned and gave them both a friendly nod, she saw that his hat said MAKE ME YOUNG AGAIN.

It was cute and all, but people really needed to rethink their novelty apparel. He grabbed what he needed and then it was their turn. A woman with greying blonde hair who wore her two-pack-a-day habit all over her skin waved them over.

"Hi. We'd like to apply for a marriage license," Xeni said. "And is there any way we can expedite it?"

The woman's eyes narrowed for a moment as she considered Xeni, then Mason.

"One moment." She sat down at her desk, pressed a couple keys on her keyboard, then slid back in her chair and pulled open a filing cabinet. Her fingers shuffled with frightening speed. There was something terrifying about competent and confident government employees. Her eyes scanned the piece of paper in her hand before she slid her chair back to the counter.

"Just fill in that information there. And I need to see some ID." Xeni took the application form and saw her and Mason's names and addresses already filled in under Spouse A and B.

"Wait. Why—"

"Sable Everly's your aunt. She came by a couple of weeks ago and told me you two would be in for a license. It's all paid for."

"What?!" Xeni shouted in something that could only be described as a hysterical laugh.

"I just need to see your birth certificates and your IDs and we'll get this taken care of for you."

"I'm—I'm sorry." Xeni was positive she was having a stroke. "What was your name?"

"Deborah. Deborah Billings."

"Nice to meet you, Deborah. Could you excuse us for a moment?"

"Sure. Take your time."

"Thank you." Xeni turned to Mason and pointed toward the hallway. "Follow me this way. Just for a second."

"Excuse us." He shot Deborah a polite smile and then motioned for Xeni to lead the way. They waited for a woman and a small child to squeeze by toward the exit. Then Xeni stepped into a doorway marked MAINTENANCE. She appreciated that Mason ducked his head so he could hear her whisper. She ignored the heat that came with their sudden closeness.

"Is it just me or does this feel like we're a part of some elaborate prank?" she said quietly.

"No, that sounds about right."

"I'm kinda over it. So here's what I'm thinking."

"Mmmhmm, tell me."

"We own this. We have to get married if we want this money. So let's get fucking married. You're a cook right? And I saw a whole bakery over at the farm. We pull together some good eats, some low-quality booze. Ask your cousin to donate some apples for some party games. You invite your friends, 'cause we need witnesses. I'll invite Bess, the only person I know in this town. Maybe we invite Deborah, she seems fun. We have a fucking wedding."

"You might be onto something. I almost did this whole bride and groom thing once before, but it didn't quite go off the way I'd planned," he said, like he'd finally found someone to dump this hot goss on.

Xeni felt her eyebrows go up. "Oh really?"

"A tale for another time. Nothing sinister. All I'm saying is that I wouldn't hate another crack at doing it properly, on my terms. I'll get the refreshments and you—you get a dress."

"Yesss," Xeni lightly slapped his shoulder with the back of her hand. She actually smiled when she heard his throaty laugh. "We'll do this part of it our way. At least we'll enjoy ourselves for a few hours and then we'll go back to getting jerked around by my aunt from beyond the grave."

"Let's go back in there and have a chat with Deborah."

Back in the office, it only took a few minutes to get their paperwork in order.

"You can come pick this up before five. We'll have everything ready for you and then you just have to wait twenty-four hours before you can perform the ceremony. License is good for ninety days if you decide to wait."

"I can come back this afternoon," Xeni suggested. "You probably have to get back to work."

"I do have a wedding to plan." Mason's enthusiasm reassured her a bit. When she made up her mind about something, she committed and often that lead to her going it alone. It felt nice to have at least one person on her side in what was starting to feel like a never-ending shit show. There was nothing else Deborah needed from them, but Xeni needed to ask about something that Deborah said when they first arrived.

"Deborah, question. What else did my aunt say to you, exactly?" Deb didn't seem to be keeping any secrets. If she knew about the money, Xeni was confident that she would have made a comment about it already, but Deborah was definitely more in the know than Xeni had expected the Kinderack town clerk to be. If her aunt had shared more than the contents of that letter, Xeni wanted to know.

"Well, we talked about a lot of things. We had a real good poker game going down at the Senior Center. None of us are ready to pick it up without her." A cloud of emotion passed over Deborah's face and Xeni was quickly reminded that Sable Everly had lived in this small town for over twenty years. She'd had a very specific list for her memorial, but she was an Everly and if one thing is true about Everly women, they knew how to make friends wherever they went. Sure, she and Deborah may not have been super tight, but they spent enough time together for Sable to share her plans.

"She said there was a complicated situation with her sisters and with you. The long and short of it was basically that she was finally getting some of the say she was owed in your life. She said she missed everything. The least she could do was pick out a good husband for you."

"I'm not sure if that's sweet or deranged," Xeni said.

"A little of both, maybe. I'm not sure if I should be flattered or deathly frightened. Elaborate prank or century-old curse. Only time will tell." Mason tacked on a wink for added effect.

"My husband and I go to McInroy's every Saturday for lunch. So at least you know he can cook," Deborah said, nodding toward Mason.

"Mmm, I guess that's a plus."

Deborah tapped her knuckles on the counter. She was done with this conversation. "Four o'clock."

"Thanks." They headed back toward the main entrance.

"You alright?" Mason asked as he held open the door. Xeni must have checked out again as they were walking through the building.

"Yeah. Do you have to get back to work?"

"I don't have to. I can hang around a bit, if you need me."

"And, what? Let you see my wedding dress before the big day?"

"Yeah, let's keep as much bad luck as possible at bay. You have my number."

"I'll text you if I need anything."

Mason nodded, then turned and walked to his beat-up SUV parked across the street. Xeni didn't realize she was watching him until she felt her head tilt a bit to the side. She was definitely checking out his ass and he definitely glanced back over his shoulder and caught her.

"It's okay to admire the view," he called out. "It'll be all yours tomorrow after four."

"Okay, okay. Relax," Xeni shouted back. She was still miserable and numb. Super numb and full of rage, but that didn't change the smile that lingered on her face as he drove away. Her future husband was kind of funny.

5

Mason gripped the edge of the steel counter to stop himself from pacing. In the time it took him to text his friends and his cousins and get back to the farm, the anxiety over Ms. Sable's ultimatum had transformed into something he could only describe as giddiness. It was probably still anxiety, but Mason could feel it was edged with excitement. He'd been in the States for seven years, an exile firmly imposed by his father. Now that he and Xeni were one step closer to receiving their portions of the inheritance, he could finally put that part of his life behind him. At the rate he'd been going, it would have taken him another ten years to fix what he'd fucked up. Now he could feel the crushing pressure in his chest finally starting to ease.

There was no joy in losing Sable. He knew he would miss her every day for the rest of his life, but he couldn't thank her enough for lifting this burden off his back. Only a handful of people knew the real reason he'd come to run the cafe on Silas's farm, not that anyone needed to know. But when he'd finally shared the truth with Ms. Sable a few years ago as they bonded over their shared love of seventies funk, she'd offered the first real bit of comfort he'd felt since moving into the room above the cannery.

He thought back to the night she'd invited him over so they could talk tunes. He'd explained his initial interest in becoming a piper, and how after he'd mastered his first song, he'd finally felt like he'd given his father a reason to be proud of him. Ms. Sable had been so easy to get on with, he'd found himself sharing the dirty details about his whole fucked-up situation. The guilt and the shame were still fresh at the time, but she'd told him the only thing he needed to hear and for once he actually felt heard.

He loved his cousin Silas. Still, he wasn't much for conversation. Plus, he'd had his own family drama to worry about. And then Liz arrived. She was fantastic, a real great girl, and as time went by she became a true friend to Mason. Maya and her wife, Ginny, were great pals too, but they traded exclusively in sarcasm and barbs. And they had each other, which is really what he'd been looking for. Someone who finally understood him. He found that friendship in Ms. Sable and even though she was gone, she had tried to help him out one last time. He could admit that he'd been a little pissed off with her overly involved plan, but if Xeni was on board, he wasn't going to say no. And like she'd said, they were going to do things their way. For Mason, it felt like a second chance.

His first wedding had been a nonstarter. His first fiancée, a mistake. He and Xeni were strangers. They definitely weren't in love, but this time he got to choose. Xeni seemed like a damn good choice.

Mason looked up, arching an eyebrow at Ginny as she let out a dramatic sigh. There wouldn't be much activity in the cannery until the afternoon, but she and Maya had plenty of jam, sauce and honey to make. The smell of fresh lavender honey filled the space. He knew he was interrupting their day.

"Just tell us now," Ginny said. "You can debrief Silas later."

"Let me tell you all at once. Don't worry, I won't take up too much of your time."

Just then, the back door to the kitchen opened, bringing a gust of heat and his cousins with it. Liz's pregnant belly entered first and she was talking to Silas over her shoulder.

"I just want to stick to my birth plan this time."

"I just want to be there this time," Silas replied. "But talk to Dianda again. You hired her for a reason."

"Yeah, I'll call her tonight. Sorry. More baby business," Liz said offering a warm smile. "Hi, hi, hi. We got your text. What's going on?"

Mason stood his full height and pulled his confidence together. "I need help planning a wedding. By tomorrow."

Maya blinked several times. "Uh, whose wedding?"

"Mine. To Ms. Sable's—to Xeni Everly."

"Uh…" Ginny echoed everyone else's confusion.

"Yeah. Uh is right. Spill it," Liz said.

Mason laid out select details of what Mr. Barber and Ms. Jordan had shared with him and Xeni. How much money and the conditions he'd have to fulfill to get it. He made sure to leave out the bits that belonged to Xeni and Xeni alone. What he had to share was more than enough to process before the lunch rush.

"That's what she left you in her will?" Liz said, the shock still clear in her voice. "I thought it was going to be her piano or something."

"No. She's offering to clear up my debt, essentially."

"But... you have to marry someone you don't know."

"I'm not worried about that. Xeni and I have spoken and we're on the same page. We fulfill the terms of the will, we both get what has been left to us. I pay off my father and we live happily ever after."

"Does this mean—" Ginny stopped herself, her gaze drifting over to Maya.

"What?"

"Does this mean you're leaving?" Maya said. "Like, going back to Edinburgh? You won't owe your dad anymore. You could go back."

"Oh nah," Mason said confidently. "I miss home, but I really like it here. This will make it easy to go home and see my mum, for a visit, but no. No plans to move back just yet."

"Okay," Maya replied, though she didn't sound so sure.

"This is a good thing. And I thought you all loved a party. It'll be slapdash to say the least, but I think we can pull together a pretty fun party to celebrate these legally binding nuptials."

"We can and you're right. This is good for you," Liz said.

"Look, mates. I'm fully understanding that I am coming off this side of downright ecstatic, but can we all admit that things have been depressing as fuck around here lately, and me doing something stupid and impulsive with a woman I just met might be the thing we all need? Shake things up a bit."

"I don't think it's stupid. If I had the money to help you pay off your dad, I would have given it to you years ago," Liz replied.

"Yeah, same," Ginny said.

"I mean, I think Xeni's hot as fuck and my mom's only had good things to say about her," Maya added. "Real wedding for a fake marriage that leads to real money that'll get you off the hook with your dad? Go for that."

"Wow," Ginny suddenly said.

"What?"

"I mean, wow. Really babe? Hot as fuck?"

"Oh, come on. When you saw her in the diner yesterday, *you* said you didn't expect her to be that pretty."

"But hot as fuck? Wow."

"I'll wow you."

"You two, please. Not in front of the jam," Mason interjected. He looked over at Silas, who hadn't said a single thing. "You've been awfully quiet."

"Just listening. I'll talk to you after."

"Okay."

"Tell us what you need," Liz said, getting them back on track like always.

"I need to figure out where to do this. And I'm gonna need some makeshift rings. I'm not finding anything to fit around these sausages in twenty-four hours."

They bounced around ideas and in no time they'd figured out a pretty decent plan. Unless Xeni objected, they were getting married the following night there on McInroy's Farm.

"I have to head back to the barn," Silas announced once everything had been sorted. "Come talk to me for a sec."

"Yeah." Mason followed his cousin out into the lingering heat that didn't seem to give a damn that it was already fall. Their red Irish Setter, Honeycrisp, was waiting at a nearby tree for Liz to finish her day.

"What's on your mind?" he asked when they reached Silas's red pick-up truck.

"I'm wondering what you're going to tell your dad. He's going to wonder where the money came from."

"The way I see it, it's none of his business. He made up his mind about me and he named his terms. If he wants to complain about how I paid back the money he insisted on giving me for things I didn't want, then so be it."

"We shouldn't tell our parents about Xeni at all then."

"I agree."

Liz had literally been on the run from a dangerous former client when she came into their lives. She and Silas had created a whole web of lies to keep her safe. When Mason slipped and mentioned Silas's new girlfriend to his mom and his aunt, shit had really hit the fan. It didn't help that Silas's dickhead twin, Scott, was also in love with Liz. In the end, it all worked out. His aunt and uncle finally knew the truth and they had welcomed Liz into the family with open arms. He was pretty certain Scott had gotten over his crush.

But his aunt and uncle weren't like his parents. When Silas finally shared his suspicions that he had undiagnosed autism, they backed off their corporate dreams for him. He had the farm now and even though Scott had bailed on running it with him, Silas was happy and that was more than enough for his parents.

In Mason's case, he was an ongoing source of disappointment. His mother would have questions, but Mason knew she'd understand in the end. The truth of this would just give his father more reason to berate him. He wasn't telling them a thing.

"I want the wedding to be fun for Xeni. She's having a tough time of it. And she has to deal with her own family."

"I get it. One day off from the stress is what you need."

"Exactly what we need."

"See if you can get Joe-Joe to work a double tomorrow and we'll make it happen."

"Thank you."

"Hell, Palila would love to be a flower girl and this one will do anything Liz tells her," he said motioning to Honeysuckle, who was still snoozing away. "I'm sure she'll jump in as ring bearer."

"I don't even know if Xeni likes dogs. I should probably ask her."

"Probably. You're good?"

"Yeah, I think. I'm alright."

"What Maya said... Is she really good looking?"

"I've been trying not to think about it, given the circumstances, but yeah. She's a stunner. An absolute stunner."

"Well then you have to marry her."

"Seems like the smart thing to do."

Xeni sat in the car, staring at her phone again. She and Mason had given themselves permission to enjoy the next twenty-four hours, before the reality of what they were doing would hit them with a force that Xeni knew she wasn't prepared for. The only way that was going to happen was if Xeni bit the bullet and called her mother. The line rang and rang. Xeni let out a deep breath and prepared herself to leave a voicemail when her mom answered.

"Hey sweetie," she said with an upbeat calm that immediately set Xeni on edge. She knew what was coming, but she hoped her mother wouldn't pull this shit right now. Not with her, not about this.

"I'm calling you back."

"Good. I was worried. How did things go with the lawyers?" Still calm. Still cool. Too casual.

"Are we really doing this?"

"Doing what?"

"I know Daddy told you. I know. I just want to know when you were going to tell me."

"Tell you what? What did Daddy tell me?" Xeni closed her eyes, her jaw clenching. She knew by her tone that her mother really had decided to play stupid. She didn't do it very often, only when she knew she was dead wrong and wanted to be right.

"So you weren't going to tell me that Sable was my mother."

"Oh that?" she said. "No. I wasn't going to tell you that. And Sable wasn't supposed to tell you that. Is that what the lawyers told you? Laying all our business out there when our sister's not here to explain herself. Let me tell you something, when Sable needed my help, I stepped up and I did more than just help. I did the one thing she didn't want to do." She was starting to shout. Xeni began to shut down. She didn't have to force the numbness. It took over on its own.

"What was that? What didn't she want to do?" Xeni asked. Her voice felt dead in her throat.

"I am your mother!"

"Why are you yelling at me?"

"I'm not yelling at you," she yelled. "My selfish little sister put her career before her family and then wanted to take that family back whenever it damn well suited her. She had no right to tell you. She had no right to tell you *like this*. And of course she waited until she was gone. Just like Sable. Always trying to have things her way, any way. I raised you right and

55

now she wants to take that away from me when I don't get a say."

The rest of Xeni's questions died on the tip of her tongue. She couldn't talk to her mother about this. Not now.

"I should go."

"Are you saying I didn't do right by you?"

"No, I'm saying I have to go," Xeni said, keeping calm. "We need to talk about this, but right now you're not listening. I can only talk to you if you're going to listen to me. So, I'm going to go."

"Wait, when are you coming home?"

"I don't know. I've barely touched the house."

"Did you find the jewelry yet?"

"I'll let you know when I book my flight back. Tell Daddy I love him."

And just like that, the switch flipped back. "Okay, I will. I love you, honey."

"I love you too." Xeni ended the call, then set her phone in her purse on the passenger seat. Once, she didn't talk to her mother for more than five minutes for two months. It was over grad school. A stupid fight about loans and staying in state. Xeni had a plan, a good plan, but her mother was so set on her own plans for Xeni's future that she wouldn't listen to anything she had to say. This was bigger, more consuming, and hurt in a way that Xeni couldn't understand. She had a right to know what happened. She didn't care who was wrong or who had made the best decisions, she just wanted details. She wanted at least some version of the truth, without someone screaming at her.

Xeni closed her eyes and tried to breathe. No tears still. She was too angry to cry real tears. Too frustrated, but she could feel the anxiety rising. The stress pulling at her heart in that very specific way. She needed to tell someone. She needed to talk to someone she could trust. She reached for her phone again, then jumped when it started ringing in her hand.

An unfamiliar New York number scrolled across the screen. Thinking it might be Ms. Jordan, she answered.

"Hi. This is Xeni."

"Hi Xeni. It's Liz. I'm Mason's cousin. The one who's seventeen months pregnant."

"Oh, hi. How are you?"

"I was just calling to ask you the same thing."

"I'm fine," Xeni chuckled a little. Astronauts could see that was a lie from space. "Thank you. I'm guessing Mason told you our amazing plan?"

"Yeah, I'm looped in. He gave us our to-do list. But it occurred to me that you don't exactly have a girl squad to help with last-minute bachelorette duties. A bride needs her clique. What can I help you with?"

"Oh no. It's okay. It's the middle of the week. I know you guys are busy. And you have your kids, born and unborn."

Liz laughed. "P's at daycare until five and the other one goes where I go for a few more weeks and then like five years after that. The bakery is covered and I'm going to whip up a cake tomorrow morning. Oh, that reminds me. Do you have any food allergies?"

"No, but I am somewhat of a vegetarian. I eat seafood, and I'll eat chicken if I have no other option, but I prefer not to."

"Okay great. Veggie options on the menu. I make a mean apple cake with vanilla cinnamon frosting. Perfect for a fall wedding. Sound good?"

Xeni's stomach actually started growling. "That sounds amazing."

"Perfect. What else do you need?"

Xeni didn't want to bother Liz or any of Mason's friends with things she could handle on her own, but... "Actually, yeah. I was going to find some place to get an inexpensive dress. I'd love some recommendations."

"How about this? I finish up around two and I can come with you."

"Sure. That would be great."

"And listen, I know this all seems like a lot, but Mason is a good guy. If you need a man that comes with terms and conditions, you couldn't find anyone better than him."

"You know, in all this, he's actually the least of my worries," Xeni said and she wasn't at all shocked that she meant it. So far, dealing with Mason had been the easy part. She ended her call with Liz then drove back to her aunt's house to start looking for that fucking jewelry.

6

A quiet chuckle slipped from Xeni's lips as she pulled around the front of Kinderack's local Target. Liz was waiting, sitting on one of the red concrete orbs by the entrance. She spotted Xeni and waved. Xeni pulled into one of the many empty parking spaces, then quickly walked across the lot to meet her shopping companion.

"Thanks for meeting me."

"It's my pleasure. I'd hug you, but..." Liz motioned toward her large belly.

"It's all good. When are you due?" Xeni asked as they headed through the sliding double doors. A security guard that couldn't have been more than eighteen smiled and nodded at them.

"In a few weeks. This kid is ready now, though. I can feel it."

"I can't imagine what that must feel like." Xeni had been pregnant twice before, each time for a whole hot second, but she'd never reached the point where the woes of the third trimester were even close to a thing.

They walked further into the store, passed the remains of a back-to-school display and stopped in the women's clothing section. "I say that like this isn't the easy part. Once they come out, you realize you've made a terrible mistake and you have a whole ass human to take care of. I'm kidding. I love my daughter so much."

"Oh, I do get that part. I teach kindergarten."

"Oh okay. So you do get it," Liz laughed. "*That* I can't imagine. I'm terrible with other people's kids. Dealing with a few dozen of them at once? No way. P is like the weirdest kid, but she's my weirdo."

"No, that totally makes sense. Every school year, it takes a little while to get the kids settled in the classroom, get them used to being away from home, from their parents, their nannies. But once things are rolling, those kids are my favorites. They become my babies. Last year I wanted to fight the kids across the hall. Sass mouthing me every day at recess."

Liz let out a high pitched "Ha!"

"Can't fight toddlers, but you think about it from time to time." Xeni let a wistful sigh. Thoughts of all the start-of-school drama she was missing at that very moment made her chest feel a little tight. She pushed the feelings down and turned to a rack of corduroy, spaghetti-strap dresses.

"So what are we looking for? How can I help?" Liz asked. "I suggested Target because you give off a pretty chill vibe, but not like pottery-instructor-who-thinks-they're-woke-but-belongs-to-the-local-country-club. A lot of the boutiques in town are like that. Old White lady expensive in this very particular way. Plus, they never have my size."

Xeni didn't have a hard time believing that. Liz had to be close to six feet tall and, even without the baby who was currently renting her womb, she was rocking some serious curves. Xeni knew what it was like being Black and trying to shop in certain parts of L.A.. She imagined Liz had enough awkward, slightly racist stories to tell.

"Probably smart to come to a big chain store too. Small town. Small stores. Lots of questions."

"Oh, you think you're going to escape the questions? If that's what you're hoping for, you should probably leave town now," Liz teased.

"Ugh. Too much to ask for? Can't just swoop in, marry someone, claim an inheritance and leave?"

"Uh, no. I arrived here on textbook shady circumstances and my husband, Silas, basically just drove me around the first day and introduced me to everyone to get all the speculation out of the way. He knew people would start showing up at the farm to meet me and after we got engaged, they did."

Xeni chuckled a little. "What were the shady circumstances?"

"I used to be in corporate litigation and a former client tried to have me killed." She said it all calm and cool, like she hadn't just mentioned attempted murder. "Silas's brother stashed me here until things blew over. Well—until that client blackmailed me and had me fired."

"Whoa. Whoa, whoa, whoa. Honey, that's beyond shady. I'm just going through drama with my mom and my aunties. Someone tried to kill you?"

Liz stepped close and dramatically took Xeni's hand between her warm palms. "That's why I came with you today," she said, her tone only half joking. "If anyone knows what it's like to find themselves, a city bitch through and through, in Kinderack County married to a half Scotsman who's bigger than barn, it's me."

"So you're not from here?"

Liz dropped her hands and turned back to the racks. "Girl, no. I'm from the Bronx. Been here over three years and my sister still hasn't forgiven me. She hates driving up here."

"Well, I'm not staying, but if for some reason I bump my head and decide farm living is the life for me, you're the first person I'm talking to."

"I don't know. It didn't take that much persuading for me. Let me stop lying. Silas didn't even have to ask. Moving up here was my idea."

"Yeah, but it sounds like you're pretty in love and from the looks of things," Xeni shot a meaningful look toward her Liz's pregnant belly, "making the most of it."

"Okay, I'll give you that. It took me a whole hot three days to start falling for Silas, but if there's one thing those McInroy boys have in common, it's their big hearts. I'm not saying you're gonna wanna make this for real, but Mason will get in there, right in the center of your chest and make himself nice and comfortable. He's a real sweetie."

"Does the giant *everything* run in the fam?"

"Well, I don't know if Mason's packing *everything*, but yeah."

"Sorry. I wasn't talking dick size. I just meant, I didn't know if Mason's overall dimensions were an anomaly. I take it Silas is a big man too."

"Both their dads and their moms are not small people. Silas has a twin. Not as swole, but just as tall." Liz took out her phone and showed her a family photo from their wedding. Yeah, her husband and his brother were pretty large. Pretty hot too. Xeni swallowed, not sure what to make of the fact that Mason was bigger than them both. And how that fact made her a little warm between her legs.

"Oh yeah, okay. Definitely a family thing."

"Makes me worry about Palila," Liz said, slipping her phone back in her purse. "At this rate, she'll be pushing seven feet before she hits middle school."

"She's a cute kid."

"Thank you. Okay, let's shop. What do you want?"

"Good question. I'm guessing this is all happening at the farm?"

"I suggested we just do it at our house. We're right on the property and we just finished the downstairs remodel. We have a huge porch and you can look out over the apple orchards. All very Instagrammable if you want us to take pictures."

"Shit yeah, I want pictures. I told Mason, if we have to do this, we're doing it right. There will definitely be digital documentation."

"Are you doing okay though? Like, with all of this? Mason was pretty jumpy when he told us the news."

"Oh yeah?"

"Yeah. He's kind of excited, I think? He really needs this money."

"Listen. Student loans are a bitch. There's just way more shit on my end, but if this whole circus can help clean up his student loan debt, I can be a temporary wife for that," Xeni said. She glanced over at Liz and caught the way her smile faded. "Is it not student loans?"

"No, it is. In a way. I think if you ask Mason, he'll tell you."

"But it's nothing, like bad, is it?"

Liz looked up at the ceiling. "Umm, bad in the it's-shittyhe's-going-through-this-crap kind of way, but no, he didn't do anything bad. He doesn't owe the mob or anything."

"Okay, good."

"It's just a situation. I'm sure he'll tell you. Just ask."

"I will." Sure, she and Mason had just met and she believed Liz that he wasn't in any kind of trouble that would land him in cement shoes, but she still wanted to know. She wanted to enjoy their sham wedding and, for now, she was fucking done with secrets.

"Oh, how about this?" Xeni stood back and looked at the dress Liz had pulled off the rack.

"Okay, yeah. That's perfect."

After she'd purchased all her last-minute wedding necessities, Xeni and Liz had plopped down at the Starbucks kiosk and continued to get to know each other. Xeni liked Liz a lot. They were getting along so well, they lost track of time and they both had to rush back into town, Liz to pick up her daughter and Xeni to get their marriage license. The town clerk's office was oddly busy when she arrived. She took a seat and waited for her turn to see Deborah.

While she waited, she pulled up her group chat with the girls again. Damn this time difference. They were all still at work. At least her afternoon with Liz had shaken her out of her funk. Oh, she was still plenty pissed at her mom and she couldn't get a handle on what she was feeling toward her aunt at the moment, but she wasn't feeling so cold and closed off. She wanted to tell her friends what was going on, she just didn't know how.

Missing you hos.

No one responded right away, but then a text alert from Sloan popped up. Xeni had hard and fast rules about not befriending the parents of students that attended Whippoorwill, but she was so glad she'd opened herself to hanging with Sloan when she'd moved to L.A.. Sloan was busy with her family and her career in medicine, but she always made time for Xeni. She was a good friend.

Hey foxy lady!
How are you doing?
Everything okay?

Yeah, I'm doing okay.
A little hectic around here,
but I'll get through it.

I bet. Moving is the worst.
I can't imagine trying to "move"
while grieving and then it's not even your stuff.
I wish I was there to help you.

Yeah that, Xeni thought. So far, she'd managed to move everything in her aunt's bedroom around in search of her grandmother's jewelry, but she hadn't actually sorted anything. She had to wait because something in her gut told her now wasn't the time for actually cleaning and sorting. Not yet.

It's a lot, but I'll get it sorted out.
I miss you.
How are Rowan and the girls?

A picture of her friend's husband holding their adorable four-month-old popped up on the screen. The daughters from her marriage to her douchebag ex were in the bottom of the frame, trying to get the baby's attention. Xeni chest warmed as she clicked on the photo and let it take up the whole screen. She loved Sloan and she loved Sloan's family. Seeing them together gave her hope. The hubby, three kids and a house with a pool in Westwood life was not for her, but they were good people who filled their house with love and that gave Xeni hope for humankind.

She minimized the picture, then pulled up her most recent emojis. Just then her phone started to vibrate. The screen went black and Mason's name scrolled across it.

Xeni stepped into the hallway and hit ACCEPT. "Hey. I'm picking up the license right now."

"Excellent. We've run into a small snag. I just spoke to Mrs. Pummel and the Reverend left this morning to officiate a wedding in Vermont. He won't be back until Monday."

"Crap. Do you know anyone else?"

"Not really a churchgoing man, but I'll put the feelers out."

"I'll call Bess. She might know someone."

"Okay, you do that."

"Thanks for giving Liz my number. We had a great time."

"That's good to hear. I didn't want you to have to go it alone."

Xeni's cheeks started to warm out of nowhere, but she ignored it. It wasn't important. "I appreciate that."

"Erm, do you maybe want to come by the farm for dinner tonight? No reason for you to be alone at Ms. Sable's house."

"Thanks for the invite, but I have to find something for my mom and I kinda want to see if I can do it tonight so I don't have to think about it tomorrow. It'll be our wedding day after all. Wanna get this off my plate so I can focus on you and that dreamy accent all day long." Xeni smacked herself in the forehead as soon as the words left her mouth. THIS. WAS WHY. SHE DIDN'T. TALK! TO MEN!

"Oh, it's dreamy is it?"

"Hey, look at the time. I gotta go."

Xeni squeezed her eyes closed at the sound of his rumbling laugh. His laugh was kind of dreamy too.

"You secure the license and I'll see what can be done about a pastor. Worst case scenario, I'll have my cousin ordained over the internet."

"Deal. I'll be in touch."

They said their goodbyes and a few minutes later, Xeni had their marriage license in hand.

"Give us a call if you have any questions," Deborah said.

"I actually do. I know this town is small, but Reverend Pummel can't be the only man of the cloth around. We need someone to perform the ceremony tomorrow. Do you know anyone who might be available on such short notice?" Xeni knew the answer would be no. Twenty-fours just wasn't enough time. Maybe an online certification was the way to go.

"I'll do it," Deborah said, all dry and casual like.

"You will?"

"If you do it after five-thirty, yeah."

"Okay, great. If we have to wait twenty-hours and that'll put us around four-thirty, another hour won't kill us."

"No if. Twenty-four hours or that marriage is void. Twenty-four hours. No less, not even by a minute."

"Okay," Xeni said, fully admonished. She didn't want to see what Deborah was like when she was losing at poker. "We can do five-thirty. We're doing it at Silas and Liz McInroy's hou—"

"I know where they live."

"Okay. We'll see you then."

"See you then."

Xeni tripled checked that she had all of their paperwork, then practically skipped back out to the car. She waited until she was behind the wheel before she texted Mason the good news.

Deborah's gonna do it!
We just have to get married after 5:30.

Mason responded right away with a gif of Rocky and Apollo Creed frolicking in the ocean. Xeni snorted and almost reconsidered his dinner invitation. Almost.

Fresh from the shower, Mason tossed his towel on his broken recliner and then stretched out on his bed, ass naked. He had to be up early the next morning, like every morning. Breakfast rush waited for no man. Usually after a long shower at the end of a long day, he was asleep before he hit the mattress, but now he was wide awake. And he only had one thing on his mind.

Well two things, but one person was the reason behind all of it.

He knew Xeni had a lot on her plate, things more demanding than his asshole of a father, but he wished she had come by for dinner. Like a fool, he kept listening for Silas's doorbell to ring while they all watched Palila make a mess of her peas and mashed potatoes. Xeni was smart and resourceful. If she changed her mind, she'd find her way over to their farm house.

But she didn't show. And why would she? Along with being smart and resourceful, she didn't seem like a bullshitter. If she said she was busy, she was busy. And if she has something to handle, something to do with her mother and Ms. Sable? Well that he could definitely believe. He should have offered to help her. He didn't know the ins and outs of Ms. Sable's private business, but he had been to her home dozens of times over the years, spent hours with at her piano.

He at least had a sense of her house and two pairs of hands were better than one.

He reached for his phone and pulled it off his charger. It wasn't late, but he wasn't sure what her sleep schedule was like, especially after the last few days. He decided to text her instead of calling her.

Me and my dreamy accent missed you at dinner, he typed. "Maybe a little much," he said to himself before he hit send anyway. It was the truth. Why shouldn't he tell her the truth? Something about her sparked something in him. A few women had expressed interest in him since he'd moved to New York, but for some reason he kept his distance. Now he was lying awake, trying to get to know a woman who had no interest in him, beyond a financial one.

He didn't take her comment about his accent to heart. He got a lot of comments about it. For the first year he was here, some customers would ask him to repeat some word or phrase for their amusement at least three times a week. One day he started to say no. It felt good, the simple refusal, but people still commented on the way he spoke and playfully mocked it from time to time. No one had ever called it dreamy, even if they were only joking.

He clicked around his apps aimlessly, then went back to their conversation.

Any luck finding what you were looking for?

Xeni replied.

Oh that accent. *drool emoji*
And not yet. I'll keep looking for it
after our super rocking wedding.
Are you excited? A hot wife and one hundred grand.
That's quite a deal.

Mason smiled at his phone and tried to think of a witty comeback. He failed and settled for a gif of that Jamie lad from Outlander telling some other Scotsman he was a lucky bastard. When Xeni responded with a crying laughing emoji, he knew he'd made the right choice.

Off to bed, but don't hesitate
to call me if you need anything.

I won't. Good night.

Night.

Mason set down his phone, feeling better that he'd gotten to talk to her one more time before he called it a night. He went to double check that the door to his studio apartment was locked before he turned the AC unit down to low, then shut off the light and climbed under his sheets. He stared up into the darkness, thinking of the small glimpse of Xeni's smile he'd caught earlier that morning. He knew that even if she stayed in town for a few weeks, he wouldn't see much more of her. That didn't stop him from wondering what it would take to make her smile that way again.

7

Xeni followed Liz's directions just past the public entrance to McInroy Farm and pulled down a long road paved with loose gravel. The two-story white farm-house with its gorgeous wraparound porch came into view and Xeni couldn't help but be a little charmed. The sun was still up and little white Christmas lights already glowed from the porch roof. It was quite the romantic setting. Definitely a perfect place to get married with nearly no notice.

As she pulled closer, she could hear the sound of barking. Sure enough, as she pulled up next to a red McInroy Farm pick-up truck parked out front, a black and white pit bull and some kind of cattle dog mix came bolting around the side of the house. The dogs stopped just short of the front of her car, barking and pacing.

Xeni loved dogs, but this wasn't how she wanted to die. While she was mentally casting the small boy who would play her son in this remake of *Cujo*, Liz stepped out on the porch and waved. A golden retriever and another dog with red fur pushed past her and stopped on the stairs.

Xeni cracked open the driver's side window. "Are they friendly?"

"Yes, just loud. Morty! Hank! Come here!" Loud and well trained apparently. Both dogs snapped to attention and ran back up the porch to join Liz. Xeni climbed out of the car and carefully made her way across the lawn, holding up the hem of her dress. The golden retriever ran down the porch and licked her hand.

"Hi buddy," Xeni cooed.

"That's Gala. The pit is Morty. Hank is the mutt and this is Honeycrisp." She watched as Liz scratched the red dog behind the ear. "She's my constant companion."

"Your familiar?"

Liz chuckled a little. "Exactly. You look amazing."

Xeni glanced down at the pink and blue flowers that covered the bright yellow dress. It went all the way to the floor. The loose short sleeves and deep open collar that showed off her ample cleavage were perfect for the summer that didn't want to end. She'd pulled her hair back in two rope twists and topped it off with the cute flower rhinestone crown she and Liz had found at Target. She felt light and a little sexy, if she was being honest.

"Thank you."

"Come on in." She followed Liz inside and only the red dog followed them. "You ready?" Liz asked as they walked through the large house.

"Yes. Just had a long day."

"Anything we can help with?"

"No, just family stuff. Word is going around that I'm getting more than my fair share of my aunt's inheritance. Got a few calls and texts from my cousins. I'll deal with it over the weekend."

Her cousin Rosia had left a voicemail, trying to give Xeni a heads up. Her Aunt Dianna had spread the rumor that Sable may have had more money than she was letting on. Her cousin Kellen had taken particular offense to that and vowed to reach out to Xeni to make sure he wasn't missing out on more cash. And sure enough, he did. Xeni had no problem sharing more money with her cousins, but she had bigger problems to deal with, like her mom.

Xeni still wanted answers, lots of answers, but today was supposed to be a good day for her and for Mason. She'd save the next inevitable screaming match with her mother for the weekend. For now, it was her damn wedding day.

When they stepped into the kitchen, Xeni saw the gorgeous wedding cake sitting on the counter and she forgot all about her fucked up family.

"Holy crap. This is beautiful." The two-tiered masterpiece looked rustic but elegant with "naked style" butter cream and an assortment of wildflowers. Xeni hadn't gotten around to pinning what she wanted for her real wedding, but this cake would definitely make the cut. She stopped herself before she ran her fingertips through the frosting.

"When you do what you love," Liz said.

"I can't wait to taste it. Mason here?"

"Yeah, he's out back with Palila and her puppy."

"More dogs?"

Liz rolled her eyes. "Silas lived out here alone for a while, so it made sense at first, but he just really likes dogs."

"I know you must be tired."

"Luckily he takes care of them, but it's a lot of fucking dogs. Come on." Xeni followed her out the back door and was struck breathless again when she glanced around the yard. They'd bought paper tablecloths and cute disposable flatware, but Xeni wasn't expecting floral centerpieces and candles and more twinkling lights. She also didn't expect the sight of Mason in full Scottish formal wear playing with a toddler and puppy to catch her so off guard. She grabbed the railing and pretended she was protecting the hem of her dress instead of stopping herself from falling down the stairs.

"Miss Palila, can you come inside and help mommy get ready?" Liz asked her daughter. The little girl held a fist full of something Xeni couldn't see to her chest.

"Can Dirt come?" Palila asked.

"No, Dirt can stay outside. Come on. Daddy will back soon. We gotta get ready."

"So Uncle Mason can get married."

"That's right. Come on."

"Here," she handed off whatever was in her hands to Mason, then shimmied past Xeni and made her way up the stairs.

"It's your lucky day, Dirt." Mason bent over and fed the golden retriever puppy a handful of treats before he dusted off his palms and turned Xeni's way.

"I didn't mean to interrupt." She walked across the grass, which was enough to send the little dog scurrying away. "No Dirt, come back."

"He's got a lot of work to do, that Dirt. I was trying to teach Palila a magic trick using the treats. Poor Dirt was sick of waiting for his reward."

"I take it Palila picked out that name."

Mason tapped the tip of his nose.

"Love it."

"You're a bit early. What brings you by the farm? You got plans here tonight?"

"I got a little antsy tearing my aunt's house apart looking

for that thing, so I decided to get ready. Then by the time I was ready, I realized how much time I still had and got antsy again waiting, so I just came over."

"Well, you weren't the only one who jumped the gun a little." Mason motioned all the way down to his shiny black shoes and up to the socks wrapped around his large calves.

"You look sharp."

"As do you. Thank you."

"Uh, so I know this isn't for real real just for play play, but I thought maybe we should have, like, one conversation about us before we tie the knot."

"Not a bad idea. Someone should know about the illegitimate children I have scattered about this hemisphere."

"Too soon, bro," Xeni responded automatically, even though part of her wasn't bothered by the innocent joke.

Mason's expression blanked out. "I'm sorry. That was out of line."

"It's fine. First things first. Let me see your hands."

Mason was clearly confused, but that didn't stop him from stepping closer and presenting Xeni with his upturned palms. She took his right hand in both of hers and turned it over. She looked closely at his neat and clean fingernails, and had to stop herself from running her fingers over his unexpectedly soft skin.

"Do they pass inspection?"

"Yeah… yes. Sorry, I have a thing with hands." That was an understatement. She had a downright hand fetish. This whole arrangement was strictly business, but that didn't stop her from imagining what it would be like to have Mason's hands on her body or between her legs. That wasn't going to happen though. Fingerbanging wasn't part of the deal. She turned his hand to the side and saw a line of puckered skin that stretched halfway up his pinkie.

"What's the scar from?"

"Waffle iron. Forty leaf peepers came through town and I was determined to get them all fed and out the door so they could stay on schedule. I paid the price."

"Honorable. I like it." She dropped his hand and then took a step back, putting her arms behind her back so she wouldn't be tempted to inspect any other part of him. She went on with her twenty questions. "Uh, what's your pet peeve?"

"Erm, let's see. Rude people. There's no need for it."

"Oh, hard same. Biggest mistake you've ever made?" she asked.

"Agreeing to get married the first time," Mason replied. A hint of red spread up his neck as he said the words, even though the kindness remained in his eyes.

"Okay, I know it's not my business—well, maybe it is. But you gotta tell me what happened there." Whatever it was had really hurt him.

"Tomorrow. You said we had tonight."

"Yeah, right, I did. But tomorrow. I really want to know."

"I'll tell you everything. What's your biggest mistake?"

"Trusting my family?" Xeni said with a mirthless laugh. Her heart thudded at the way he smiled in response. Obviously he wasn't in the same bind, but it was kind of nice having him on the inside of all of this bullshit with her. As unexpected as it was, she felt like she could draw a little strength from the fact that he knew just how betrayed she was feeling. She cleared her throat and tried again to be more honest.

"I'm not sure what regrets I have. I've made some

mistakes, but I tried to learn from them. When all of this is…
I want to make sure things are good with my step-dad. I was
kinda mean to him on the phone the other day, but I know
he was just doing what my mom asked him to do. But still,"
she said with a little shrug. "Okay, last thing. What's one
thing you absolutely want me to know before we do this? I
want you to know that I'm actually kind of glad we're doing
this. You're kinda sweet and a little funny. I'd be really pissed
if my aunt picked out a total asshole for me."

Mason's smile reappeared, wider and brighter than
before. "I'll do my best to never be an asshole."

"I'm stubborn too. Like, really stubborn, but I'm working
on it. Sort of. Also, I'm a witch." Xeni couldn't remember the
exact moment she'd embraced energy work and her relationship with the moon, but as she got older, both had grown
stronger. She didn't talk about it much, and definitely not
with strangers, but her close friends and her mom knew.
Aunt Sable had known too.

The letter her aunt had left her flashed through her mind.
If you ever feel lost, trust the moon.

Xeni shook off those words and focused back on her
groom-to-be as his eyebrows shot up. "A good witch, I hope.
I'm trying to get myself out of trouble. I don't need some
stubborn woman cursing me because I was late with her
supper."

"Good, and don't worry. You won't have time to cook for
me. I have to be out of here in, like, nine days. Sadly there
probably won't be time to put dinners with my husband on
the schedule."

"Well good. I've always said, 'when you do get married,
Mason, make sure you avoid your wife at all cost.' You're
doing the lion's share of the work for me and it's greatly

appreciated."

Xeni snorted. "Tell me your *thing*."

Mason straightened his back a bit and Xeni braced herself for the worst. *Whatever it is, let it be something punishable by a simple fine,* she thought to herself.

"I'm bisexual," Mason said. "In theory and in practice. I want to be more open with people about that so they know the real me. All of me."

"Thank you for sharing that with me. And you should know that's something we have in common."

"Really?"

"Yeah. Bisexual witch at your service."

"It's a shame you're not sticking around. We could get a van and go on husband and wife supernatural adventures."

"No, no. I don't fuck with ghosts. You start talking to them and then they want to be friends or they want to use you as a vessel. No one needs that."

"Is this a problem you've had before?"

"No, it's just common knowledge. You don't fuck with ghosts."

"I can't argue you that. I do have one question for you."

"Yeah, of course. Shoot."

"Are we kissing at the end of this? Am I laying one on your cheek? Perhaps a peck across the back of your hand."

"Uh…" Xeni leaned back and considered Mason for a moment. He did have some nice full lips. They seemed moisturized enough. Like he wasn't afraid of a plain stick of ChapStick lip balm. A little voice in her brain said it didn't matter.

The kiss wasn't necessary. All they had to do was agree to be husband and wife. A friendly handshake would probably be the best move. Too bad another louder, hornier-due-to-lack-of-physical-contact-with-a-man-for-almost-five-whole-years voice screamed KISS HIM! HELL, FUCK HIM! YOU LIKE HIS HANDS! Xeni swallowed as if that would stop her from blurting the words out.

"No, I think we should kiss," she said. Her voice was a little too high, but Mason didn't seem to notice.

"We'll kiss then."

"Okay then." Xeni suddenly felt hot all over, Which was just silly. Her light sundress was perfectly breezy. "Um, I—I'm gonna go powder my nose. I'll see you soon, at the end of the aisle."

Mason turned and pointed to a large oak tree beyond the porch. "I'll be right there waiting with our good friend Deborah."

"Can't wait." Xeni turned and casually walked back up the stairs into the house. She managed not to turn back to see if Mason was watching her. Why would she? She didn't care about Mason McInroy at all. Sure didn't. Not at all.

Deborah arrived at five-thirty on the dot. They were still waiting on Bess and Lucy Pummel to arrive and Maya was closing things up at the cannery, but Deborah had no time for their lolly-gagging.

"Let's get on with this and then you kids can party into the night. I can't stick around. No one goes to weddings for the vows anyway. They come for the booze."

Xeni wanted to tell her to give them fifteen more minutes, but had a feeling Deborah would leave if they didn't get on with it. They needed her to work her legally binding magic.

"We'll record it so my grandma and Maya can see what they missed," Maya's niece Sydney suggested. She'd popped up fresh from volleyball practice.

"Alright. I guess we should tell Mason we're ready," Xeni said to Liz.

Deborah chimed in before Liz could respond. "Tell him yourself. Come on, you look great. Let's go." She turned around and marched out of the back door and right down the back steps.

Suddenly, Xeni felt like calling on Deborah may have been a mistake.

"Right this way, I guess," Liz said, pointing toward the Deborah-shaped cloud of dust. Xeni grabbed her bouquet of wildflowers off the dining room table and followed Liz and Sydney. Mason was waiting right were he said he would be with Palila and Liz's husband, Silas. A few of the farm hands who'd stopped by to see if the rumors of the wedding were true were sitting at the tables, chatting, waiting for the festivities to begin. Mason straightened up as soon as he saw her. Xeni wasn't sure how she felt about skipping a ceremonial walk down the aisle, but at this point, getting rid of Deborah seemed like the best way to preserve whatever mood they'd intended for the night. She followed their cranky officiant right to her husband-to-be.

"This is a perfect spot. Wanna do it right here?" Deborah said.

"Uh..." Mason looked between them.

"We're getting married right now," Xeni replied. "Deborah has to be somewhere."

"Oh. Okay."

"Go stand next to the girl," Deborah said, flicking her hand in Xeni's direction. There was an awkward shuffle and just as everyone rearranged themselves, Lucy, Bess, Maya and a White woman Xeni didn't know came around the side of the house. Deborah ignored them and kicked things off.

"We are gathered here today—"

"Wait. You're starting?" Maya asked as she rushed over. Deborah didn't skip a beat and she was doing it from memory. There was no Bible in her hand, no slip of paper, no iPad.

"If anyone present can show why these two shouldn't be joined, speak now." There was some grumbling about what the fuck Deborah was doing, but no objections. She kept right on, bulldozing through appropriate phrases. Xeni responded at the right moments, repeated the words she needed to say, and the whole time she could feel her anger growing. Fuck Deborah. This was supposed to be her day. Their day. The next thing Xeni knew, she was pronouncing them husband and wife. "You two may now kiss," she concluded with no enthusiasm whatsoever.

A sudden wave of disappointment washed over Xeni. She should have expected this. She couldn't have a single moment of peace now that her aunt was gone. The mess she had left behind felt cursed. Or maybe the ancestors were punishing her for rushing into this without talking to her parents or trying to make peace with her mother. Maybe this what she got for going through with a wedding and not even giving her step-dad a chance to walk her down the aisle. Her confident impulsiveness had led to some amazing experiences, but every once in a while it bit her in the ass. She just wanted a blip of happiness, just a taste. Somehow the universe and Xeni's own stupid choices had managed to screw that up.

She registered Mason's hand brushing against her neck a

split second before he stepped into her space and then his lips were on hers. She leaned back, involuntarily. They'd agreed this kiss was going to happen, but she wasn't expecting his lips to be so soft and warm. He didn't pull away. He was waiting, waiting for Xeni to get with the program and join him.

Kiss him, that stubborn part of her ego urged her on. *Fuck Deborah and kiss the shit out of this man.*

She slid her hand up his large shoulder and kissed him back, soaking in his warmth as his other arm wrapped around her waist. She leaned into him further, stretching up on her tiptoes as her lips parted just enough for his tongue to brush against hers. Xeni swallowed a desperate groan, pressing closer and wishing the height difference between them wasn't so great, just for a moment. And then his firm hand scooped her up by her ass and hoisted her in the air until they were face to face. She broke away for a moment, scanning his pretty brown eyes that seemed to be searching for the same happiness, craving that moment of peace. Maybe the height difference wasn't so bad after all.

She pressed her lips against his again, until she heard Silas cough. When Mason finally set her down, Xeni could barely connect her head to her ass, but she could feel herself smiling. She opened her eyes and saw Mason gazing back at her, the same dazed look on his handsome face.

"How was that for a kiss?" he teased.

A joke about having had better died on her lips. Instead she just laughed and took Mason's hand. She turned to face their small wedding party, raising their joined fingers in the air.

"Friends, family and farm folk, I now present you with my husband," she said.

She was sure the responding cheers of celebration could be heard clear across the orchard.

8

Mason didn't know what to make of it, but he was having the time of his life. There had been dinner, a little dancing, some damn good cake, everything he and Xeni wanted from tonight. He'd never thought his own wedding could be something he wouldn't absolutely dread or live to regret.

He sat back in the sturdy folding chair, listening to Maya and Ginny tell another animated story. It was their ritual at least once a week. Sit down, grab a few beers and go on about the good and the absolute worst customer behavior. Diner patrons who sent back their food a record seven times, parents who couldn't be bothered to follow the rules of the petting zoo and the teenagers. Mary and Joseph, the teenagers, climbing the trees and trying to concuss each other with unripened apples. It was their release at the end of the long day and Maya and Ginny were the best storytellers of the bunch. This time though, they only had a fraction of Mason's attention. He was listening to Maya and Ginny, but his eyes were on Xeni.

They'd followed through with the terms and conditions of Ms. Sable's will. There were married now and tomorrow they would each be able to claim their portion of the inheritance. Finally, Mason would be through with his father. He'd dreamt about how relieved he would feel when that moment eventually came. Granted, with what he was bringing home from the cafe, he figured his father would actually be dead before he finished paying off his debt. But that sense of relief, that eventual freedom, had kept him going.

Right now, though… he was trying to focus on the moment. They only had a handful of hours before he stuffed himself back into Mr. Barber's stuffy office with its poorly placed furniture, where he'd signed off on the solution to all his problems. He wasn't going to waste that precious time worrying and he wasn't going to take his eyes off his bride.

Yes, for now she was absolutely his bride, especially after that bone-shaking kiss. He'd meant to keep it tame, A light little peck on the lips., When he saw the emotions on her face, the anger and disappointment, he'd wanted to bring her back to the moment.

He saw the effort she'd put into looking beautiful for the ceremony. For the first time, he'd allowed himself to really look at her body. The way the bright yellow fabric hugged her breasts and her wide hips, and how it did not do a damn thing to conceal her amazing ass. The braids in her hair and the flowers. He even noticed that she'd matched her makeup to the pinks and blues on her flowery dress.

And then Deborah stomped all over the joyful seconds they had tried to pull together. Mason had ironed his shirt, for Christ's sake, and there was this cranky woman nearly shouting instructions, forcing them to hurry up and move on. They only paused long enough to unspool the baker's twine Liz suggested they use as rings. He'd gently tied the string in a small bow around Xeni's finger and he couldn't miss the way her jaw tensed or the subtle flare of her nostrils.

She was upset and he suddenly felt protective over her, responsible for her. It wouldn't be good for him to fist fight an elderly ordained member of their community, but he could try and distract Xeni from the way Deborah was fucking up Xeni's vision for how this bizarre, yet special day was supposed to be.

When he'd felt her tongue against his, he'd figured it worked. And, at least for him, the effects of the kiss hadn't worn off. Maybe come midnight, he'd come back to himself and remember he was still the single guy working on his cousin's farm. But for now, they had this moment.

Mason watched Xeni as she opened the cooler and pulled out two beers. She was also caught up in Maya's story.

"I'm standing there, waiting for his mother to say something or do something then," Maya paused and glanced at her mother, Bess, who still laughing. Maya lowered her voice a bit. "Then this motherfucker goes 'okay honey we can touch, but be gentle.' She hands her two-year-old this heavy ass jar of lavender honey—"

"That I made from scratch. With my own blood, sweat and tears," Ginny added.

"Gross," Xeni replied. A burst of laughter sputtered out of Mason. She turned and winked at him as she popped the top on one of the beers. He couldn't help but smile back.

"Literally so much blood. So much sweat," Ginny said.

Maya went on. "There are no bodily fluids in any of our products. Anyway, so she hands this damn baby a very heavy, very full jar of honey and he doesn't just drop it. He looks at it and then smashes it on the floor. What part of 'please do not let your children touch the breakable jars of honey' don't you understand? So Ginny just looks at her and goes…"

"…that'll be seventeen fifty-nine."

"The woman looks between us and goes 'for honey?' When I tell you I've never been so happy to have a White wife."

"I walked over to the register and rang her up. I didn't even try to clean things up."

"So she pays and then—"

There was more to the story, but Mason wasn't listening. Xeni was coming right for him with a determined look in her eyes. He followed the movement of her curves in that amazing dress and straightened up just in time for her to take a seat on his lap.

"Is this okay?" she asked quietly.

"Absolutely, but hold on." Mason lifted Xeni just enough to shift his foot. He pulled her closer with a hand on her thick thigh.

That kiss.

Mason knew what was happening. Xeni was hurting and, thanks to her family, she couldn't even grieve properly because they wouldn't stop throwing obstacles in her way. He'd felt it in that kiss. They'd both found a way to turn some sort of release valve. Instead of tears, there was that kiss and if Mason was reading things correctly, Xeni was holding on to that feeling, leaning into it. But he wasn't stupid. It was only for tonight.

Then he nodded toward the beers in her hand.

"Is that for me?"

"Yes." She handed him an amber lager, then tipped her own bottle back and took a deep pull. He thought she might drain it in one go, but she came up for air and whispered in his ear. "But don't get used to this. I'm not that type of wife, bringing you cold drinks at the end of the day. Hugging all up on you," she said as she wiggled a little closer.

"What kind of wife are you?"

"Cold. Distant. Harsh. Demanding."

"I don't see it," Mason said as he took a sip of his fresh beer.

"Take it back, McInroy. I'm a cruel, cruel mistress."

"Sure thing, love."

Suddenly the music stopped and Silas cleared his throat, grabbing everyone's attention.

"Okay, get off my property. We have a farm to run tomorrow."

It wasn't that late, but Silas wasn't wrong. Mason had the lunch rush covered, but he still had to be up at dawn to open the cafe for breakfast.

"Let us help with cleanup," Xeni stood and chugged the rest of her beer, then started going around to the tables, grabbing the paper plates and plastic cups that were strewn around. The small party had made a bit of a mess.

"We got it," Silas replied. Mason knew that tone. His cousin had hit his peopling limit for the day and he just wanted to recharge in bed with his wife.

"At least let us help with the stuff raccoons will find of interest. More hands. It'll go much faster," Xeni insisted.

Silas shrugged in agreement and pulled the forty-gallon trash can he'd set out earlier closer to the tables. In no time, they had the whole yard cleaned up, with all the decorations, tables and chairs stashed neatly on the porch.

After they gathered up their stuff and said their thank yous and good nights, Mason walked Xeni to her car. They both seemed to have something they wanted to say. They waited by the Mercedes until they were finally alone, after the rest of the guests had walked or driven off into the night. Xeni pulled her keys out of her bag.

"Do you want a lift back?" she asked.

"I think I might walk. Take in the fresh air. Let the fact that I'm a married man really sink in."

"Hmm," Xeni said, looking in the direction of the farm. "Not a bad idea. Maybe I should walk with you."

Mason was about to ask what she planned to do with her car, when he realized what she was really saying.

"I'd love the company, but I have to warn you, my place isn't really set up for guests."

"Good thing I'm no regular guest then. I'm your wife."

"That you are."

"I'm going to be completely honest with you. I'm lonely," Xeni said.

"Another thing we have in common."

It was dark, but the lights from the porch were still shining and he could see from the look in her eyes that she was trying to figure him out.

"We're adults, right?" he asked, like he wasn't entirely sure.

"We are. I'm not saying I think we should engage in adult activities, I just—"

"Don't want to be alone."

"Bingo."

Mason didn't say a word and just held out his hand. As soon as her fingers intertwined with his, he led her across the apple orchards back to his one-room apartment above the cafe.

There was nothing wrong with what they were doing, Xeni told herself. Technically they were married, so it made sense for them to spend the night together. And she'd been completely honest with him when she said she was lonely. She was drained and, if she dug down to the next level self-awareness she'd been trying to hide from, there was still a sadness she couldn't really describe that was eating at her.

She knew if she went back to her aunt's house, she would finally cry. The night had taken such an unexpected turn. It had only been a day, but she immediately recognized the energy in Liz and that they were destined to be friends. Ginny and Maya were hilarious, and it was nice to have Bess and Mrs. Pummel there. Their auntie energy helped with the fact that her own parents had no idea the wedding had taken place. Sydney was great, sweet, funny and just happy to be involved.

And then there was Mason. He was so warm and easy to be around. The way Mason had kissed her, the way she fit so perfectly on his lap. She was on a high and that high only brought the bleak chasm that was so close to swallowing her whole into clearer focus. Xeni had given herself permission. She had one day and that day wasn't over yet. She was going to let herself enjoy the way she felt around Mason for a little longer.

Plus, she was stupid horny. She hadn't been touched by a man in so freaking long. And Mason's hands…

When they reached the cafe, Mason led her around back, then up a set of wooden stairs to the second floor. Mason opened the door and ushered her inside. The light on his bedside table was still on. Xeni looked around, shocked by how clean the place was. Most guys she knew who lived alone had given up the moment they left their mothers' homes. Clothes and crap everywhere, with floors that had never known the taste of a vacuum. Mason kept his little bachelor pad pretty neat. Her eyes roamed around the room, noticing a full wall with crates and crates of records centered around a complex stereo system.

There was a makeshift desk under the far window. Cases that Xeni thought held different wind instruments. Two guitars were on stands. She wondered if he played all of those instruments or if he just found comfort in having them around. She walked over and saw that the desktop was an old door. An old recliner looked like it had seen much better days and then there was the bed. A very large bed that probably wouldn't seem so large with Mason in it.

It had no bed frame, just a box spring and a Cal King mattress on the floor, but it was enough. Xeni noticed the way Mason had to tilt his head a bit to the side to avoid the ceiling. The space may have been nice, but it wasn't built for a man of his height.

"Sorry I don't have much in the way of furniture, but have a seat wherever you like. The bathroom's through there." Xeni looked off to the right and caught a glimpse of herself in the old mirror hanging over the sink.

Xeni walked over to his desk and pulled out his rolling chair. "I have another confession. Well two. I didn't bring anything to sleep in, but also I usually sleep naked. It's not a sexual thing. I just don't like having any kind of clothing on. I get itchy and then I get hot." Xeni shuddered at the thought. The best part of her day was her naked time. "But if you're not into it, maybe I can borrow a shirt of yours."

"You're asking me if I have an issue with a naked woman in my bed? I sleep naked too, and it's definitely a sex thing. But I can loan you something to wear. And I can put on some shorts. Since this isn't a sex thing," he said motioning between them.

"Well, I mean, it could be like a finger banging thing."

Mason turned and opened his closet and pulled out a McInroy Farm t-shirt. He set it on the bed. "I was going to step into the restroom, but what kind of husband would I be if I didn't offer it to my wife first?"

"Why thank you." Xeni crossed the small space, brushing past him as she stepped into the bathroom. She didn't take the t-shirt with her. After she turned on the lights and closed the door, she decided it was best not to give herself time to think. She loved her body and had no shame showing it off, so there were no issues there. And she knew exactly what could go wrong and she knew how to make sure those things didn't happen. She just wanted a little cuddling. Maybe another mind-blowing smooch and a two-finger tickle. Nothing else had to happen. Or maybe nothing would happen at all.

She was already wet though. Her body had sparked to life the moment their lips touched and her pussy had been aching since the first casual touch Mason had eased across her back. Sitting on his lap didn't help one bit. He was so built, so sturdy. She couldn't help but picture the kinds of acrobatic shit they could get up to. She hoped a little something happened or she knew she'd find herself in the bathroom in the middle of the night trying to ease the ache with her own hand.

She got undressed, shoving her clothes into her bag before she walked back into Mason's bedroom. He'd stepped out of his shoes and had unbuttoned his dress shirt, but he stopped in his tracks as soon as he saw her. Xeni tried it keep it nice and cool and casual. She set her bag down on the recliner, then looked toward the bed. "Do you have a side you usually sleep on?"

"Uh, I'm right up the middle."

"Okay. Well, bathroom's yours."

"Thank you." Mason coughed a few times, clearly trying to put his eyes back in his head before he excused himself to the bathroom. Xeni folded the t-shirt and put it back on the arm of the recliner. She found an outlet and plugged in her phone. She had a bunch of alerts, but a quick glance told her there were no emergencies. She'd get back to her life tomorrow.

Xeni climbed between Mason's comfortable sheets and waited.

He came out of the bathroom a few minutes later. She couldn't help but laugh at the way he shuffled into the room, taking small baby steps as he hunched over, covering his junk with both hands.

"What are you doing?" Xeni laughed even harder. Tears pricked the corners of her eyes.

"Not all of us have your confidence."

"Here." Xeni closed her eyes and covered her face with her hands. "This is your apartment. You shouldn't have to hide your shame."

"Thank you, but this is for the best. Trust me."

She could hear him moving around and then, finally, the right side of the bed dipped under his weight. Xeni was instantly surrounded by the warmth of him. Their legs brushed together under the sheets and another zing of excitement hit her right at the height of her slit. She moved her hands, then rolled over to face him.

"Sorry, I'm shy," he said.

"You're a lying ass liar, but that's okay. I thrust my naked-ness on you. You didn't deserve that."

"Did you have a nice time?" he asked. The kindness that Xeni didn't want to get used to returned to his voice.

"I did. I had a great time. This is going to sound horrible, but I really want you to kiss me again. I have so much shit on my mind and I don't want to think about any of it right now."

"I think we might have to discuss your sense of bad and good." Mason moved closer, rolling Xeni on to her back with ease. She wrapped her arms around his shoulders and just as their lips met, she felt it. His massive cock pressed against her hip. She pulled back, her eyes springing wide.

"Mason," she gasped.

"What?" he said, pretending to be confused.

She reached under the covers and wrapped her fingers around his sizable length. Her eyes narrowed as she glared at him. She fondled him, her hand stroking up and down, real-izing there was no way in science or in fiction that she was going to be able to wrap her hand around the thick girth. He laughed as her expression pinched further.

"You were ashamed of this."

"I never said I was ashamed. I was hard as a rock and trying not to scare the shit out of you."

"Clearly you've underestimated your wife."

9

"I don't have any condoms. I should have asked Silas if he had any stashed around."

Disappointment poked at Xeni's stomach. She realized then, as his hand engulfed her large breast, that she subconsciously had put sex on the table.

"It's okay. We can do other things."

"Other things like what?"

Xeni released his erection, reaching up to take the hand that covered her breast. She watched his face closely, noting the few freckles across his nose and the scar in his right eyebrow as she moved his hand down between her legs. She hadn't touched herself, but she knew she was shamelessly wet, her arousal already creeping toward her thighs.

She pressed his fingers over her core, parting the short soaked hairs that covered her slit.

Xeni knew how she liked it, knew how to make herself come in seconds and she could show him, but she wanted it to last. Pressing even harder, she rolled her hips and started moving their hands together in a torturously slow circle.

"Make me work for it," she said, trying to be a little bold and mysterious.

Mason shook his head a bit, his lips curving down in the universal expression of nah. "Maybe next time, love."

"Is that right?" Xeni groaned as his fingers moved closer to her slick entrance.

"It is." Mason let out a little grunt of his own as he shifted on the bed. "You see, you didn't ask me what kind of husband I really am."

Xeni almost fainted as he leaned in closer, his lips barely brushing hers. "What kind of husband are you?"

"Cruel. Impatient. Very demanding. If I want you to come, darling, you're gonna come."

"Oh my god, please stop talking. That accent is killing me."

He flashed a devilish smile as he slipped one finger inside her cunt.

"You don't like it when I talk dirty to you? You're lucky I can't remember a lick of Gaelic. You might not survive 'til morning."

She tilted her head back into the pillows, but Mason moved before their lips could touch. His eyes traveled over her face and she wondered if he could tell how desperate she was, if the way she was panting or the way her pussy was clenching on his finger was giving her away.

"Pull back the sheets," he said before he kissed her. Xeni heard him loud and clear, but she didn't move except to kiss him back. And she may have squirmed a bit, rolling her hips as his middle finger slowly pumped in and out of her. Her eyes blinked open when he pulled back. She looked at his lips as his tongue crept out like he was still trying to taste her.

He leaned down and pressed his lips to her ear. A pathetic shiver rippled over every inch of her skin.

"Move the sheets, love. I don't want to have to ask you again."

"I don't know who you're getting all buck with. I'll move the sheets when I'm good and ready," Xeni said as she pulled the covers off them both, exposing them to the cool air.

"Thank you. I didn't want to suffocate down there."

His gaze held hers as he slid to the floor and pulled her down the bed with a firm grip on her hips.

"I'm a bit out of practice, but if I'm remembering correctly, it should go a little something like this." Mason leaned down, broad shoulders pushing her thighs farther apart as he licked the length of her pussy. She watched as he turned his head a bit to the side and licked his way slowly back to her clit. A weak moan slipped from Xeni's mouth. Her eyes wanted to close, but needed to watch. She needed the sight of her juices all in his beard burned into her memory.

He pushed two fingers back into her cunt and set about gently sucking and licking her clit. She hadn't had her pussy ate in fourteen election cycles or so, and it had never been this good. As a matter of fact, her ex had been so bad at it she'd asked him to skip the act all together. Of course, his selfish ass didn't mind because it just meant more time with Xeni bouncing on his dick. But now Xeni couldn't even remember that bum's name. Mason McInroy knew exactly what he was doing. Xeni eased up on her elbow so she could get a better view of his fingers covered in her juices and the way his tongue was working overtime to lap them up. She realized then that his left hand was busy between his own legs.

"Are you stroking your dick?"

A wink was his only reply.

"Don't. Don't do that either. Don't you dare wink at me," she groaned. "Shit." Her eyes slammed closed again as a tiny orgasm rushed through her. She wanted more. So much more. She wanted him inside of her. She wanted to feel that thick cock punishing her pussy from the inside. She flopped back onto the bed, pinching her own nipples as her hips arched against the sheets.

"Fuck, Mason. Oh my—fuck." She came, harder, feeling herself squirt a little even though her body was fighting against it. She was done, completely wrecked. She scrambled to get away from him, trying to move up the bed, but he wouldn't let go. He gripped her thigh with his whole ass arm and kept up the punishing strokes with the two fingers buried deep inside her. She came again, so hard she was sure she blacked out for just a second.

"Have you had enough?" he grunted, making her pussy clench all over again.

"Yes," she whined. "Yes. I'm done."

She looked down as he dragged a trail of her wetness over her thighs with his fingers, then followed the damp streaks with open mouthed kisses and swipes of his tongue. Yeah, this asshole knew exactly what he was doing. Xeni was aching all over again by the time his lips hit her hips.

Finally he sat back, wiping his mouth with his forearm.

"I hate to end this perfect wedding night," he said. "But I have to be up at four-thirty."

"Wait. You didn't come," Xeni said. She usually made guys work for head, but she was ready to get to sucking.

"Yes, I did." Mason did something around his groin area, then held up what had been a fresh tube sock.

"You're nasty. Talented, but nasty."

"You have no idea." She watched him as he stood and walked into the bathroom, where he most likely tossed the sock into the hamper she'd seen in there. When he came back, he was walking upright and she got a glimpse of his semi-erect cock. Before she went back to L.A., she might have to take on the challenge of maximum-length Mason.

"It's a shame I have to leave soon," she said as he pulled the covers back over them.

"We better ask how soon you can divorce me, 'cause as long as you're my wife, I'll always come after you."

"Oh, is that right?"

"I licked it, so it's mine," he whispered in her ear right before he slapped her ass.

"Jesus," Xeni actually squealed. Before she could recover, he used his grip on her butt to pull her closer.

He kissed her on the mouth once more, then pressed his lips softly to her forehead. "Goodnight." He turned off the lights, plunging the room into darkness.

"Well, goodnight then," Xeni chuckled a little bit, but she didn't stop herself from settling into his arms. Fuck, he was warm. Mason fell asleep almost immediately. Xeni lay awake, listening to his low rhythmic breathing.

She knew he was just teasing about coming after her when she left town, but part of her almost wished it was true. For once in her life, it would be nice to be pursued. Even if she was already married to the guy.

"Dude. Did you get married last night?" Ernesto came back to the kitchen, tying his apron around his waist.

"That is correct. It was a beautiful evening." Mason shot his fry cook a smile, but didn't take his eyes off the griddle top. He had four breakfast combos in the works for table two.

"Congrats, man!"

"Thank you."

Mason figured he had twelve hours before news of his marriage to Xeni spread around the farm. Reggie and Tina, their orchard managers, had shown up to the wedding and Mason hadn't had time to swear them to secrecy before Deborah was rushing them through their vows. He was sure they'd tell a few people here and there, but they weren't the problem. The problem was Maya and Ginny.

They knew when to keep deadly secrets to themselves, but *he knew* a quickie wedding, even if just to keep himself out from under the financial thumb of his father, didn't fall under the criteria of top secret. As soon as the cannery opened, the news would spread across the farm, into town and probably throughout the county. They might even drop mention of it into the Farm newsletter.

"Really? That's awesome, but last I knew, you were on some quest for monkhood. Like, single as fuck. Who the fuck did you marry?"

Ernesto knew the handful of women who'd come knocking on Mason's door. He'd even tried to set Mason up with his step-sister after her divorce. But he also knew Mason's take on the whole idea of relationships. He had no room in his life for romantic attachments at the moment. He had no direction, no future, and if his father had been right about one thing, Mason needed to figure all that out before he dragged some poor woman along for the ride. He'd taken what some viewed to be a vow of celibacy and, no thanks to

Maya and Ginny, rumors spread. Mason had taken himself off the market, but now he had a wife.

"Ms. Everly's niece," he said.

"Really? The chick who came in here the other day with Maya's mom?"

"Very same." He plated the sides and eggs, and slid them under the warmer just as the timers on the waffle irons went off. Shelby, one of their two first-shift servers, swung by the counter just as they were ready. She grabbed the plates, but didn't seem to be in a hurry to get them to their intended destinations.

"So, you really are married?" she said. "This is wild. Do we get to meet her?"

"You already met her on Tuesday. She had lunch with Bess."

"Oh, I remember her. Gosh, she's seemed so cool, and her hair? I know, I'm White, but I wish I had hair like that."

"Your hair is plenty cool." Shelby was currently rocking a style that was blue at the roots, then changed from purple to pink. The customers complimented her on it all the time.

"I know, but my hair is so flat. I would kill for those curls. Plus, she was, like, super pretty. I can't believe you married her. Did you know her? Like, before?"

Mason nodded to the plates on her arm. "Those are looking for a home."

Shelby rolled her eyes, then effortlessly glided across the diner. She was back before Mason could get another batch of eggs going. "Well, did you?"

"No, I didn't, but Ms. Sable thought we'd be a good match and we decided why not."

"That's so… romantic," Shelby sighed and her whole body

sagged. When she spoke again, a familiar wobble returned to her voice. "I miss her."

"I miss her too, Shelbs."

"We should do something. Maybe ask Silas if we can get a little plaque for her table. It's so strange not seeing her every day."

"That's a good idea."

"So, are you guys gonna have a party or anything to celebrate? This is a big deal. You're married!" Shelby said.

"Probably not. Just gonna enjoy married life," he said with a smile. "You have some new friends at table four."

"Oh." Shelby glanced over her shoulder at the couple that joined the elder man who was almost finished his breakfast. She shook her head. "He said they weren't coming. Excuse me."

Mason laughed a bit, focusing back on his work. He knew he'd be explaining himself for months to come. He didn't mind people knowing, but he wasn't looking forward to the questions people were going to ask when she went back to California. A thirty-day marriage wasn't the worst thing to happen in their small town and it wouldn't be the worst thing to happen to Mason. So far, it was the opposite.

He and Xeni has agreed on a cordial, honest partnership and while he'd been attracted to her from the moment they'd met, he had no idea the night would end with her naked in his bed.

She wasn't the only one who had been struggling with complex feelings of loss and loneliness. For as long as she was in town, Mason was willing to admit that he would take whatever comfort she could give him.

"So, what's she like?"

"I'll ask her to come by Cozy's sometime if you guys stop

asking me questions." Mason usually met up with Ernesto and a few of the other guys in town at the bowling alley/bar now that Silas's weekends were spent with his family. He knew Xeni would reply to that request with an enthusiastic no, but Ernesto didn't need to know that.

"Done. I can't believe you're married. It's crazy."

The previous night and this morning flashed through his mind again.

He'd expected a little pushback when he woke Xeni up at four-fifteen so he could ask her for her keys. He'd wanted to let her sleep in as long as she could, but he didn't want her to have to walk clear across the farm by herself to get her car. She'd reached for her bag and dug for the keys while her eyes were still closed. Before Mason could leave, she'd called him back to the bed and pulled the covers down, exposing her breasts.

"To remember me by," she'd said, her voice raspy with sleep. Then she snuggled back into the covers like she hadn't just flashed him. Mason didn't know what to make of Xeni, but damn, he really liked the girl.

He fed two dozen more people before Tamara came in to take over. He ran upstairs to change and grab the relevant paperwork he needed, then headed out back to his SUV. He checked his phone as the air conditioning cranked up. Liz and Ginny had sent over a bunch of pictures and videos from the wedding, but his pulse jumped at the text alert from Xeni.

Hey hubby.
We moved the meeting to my aunt's house.
Same time, but don't rush.
Get here when you can.

"Shit," Mason said, dropping his phone in the cup holder. He was definitely going to be late.

When Mason arrived, he didn't see any other cars in the driveway. He usually came in the side door that led into the kitchen, but this time he walked to the front and rang the bell. When Xeni opened the door, he was stunned by how good she looked, even better than the night before. Her thick hair was up, piled on top of her head. She was wearing loose, flowy pants and a skin-tight t-shirt. Her breasts looked amazing.

"Hey, come on in. Ms. Jordan got stuck in traffic. You're the first one here."

Mason's eyebrow went up as he smirked. "So, we're alone."

"We are, but I'm not blowing you on the porch, so please come inside. It's hot as hell."

He laughed and followed her through the house to the large remodeled kitchen. Xeni had set out refreshments on the kitchen island. She turned toward him and leaned against the counter. He knew she could feel what he felt. Whatever had happened between them the night before, that energy, that pull, it was still there. Xeni cleared her throat and straightened her shoulders like she was trying not to notice it.

"I asked Mr. Barber if we could move things here so you'd have somewhere to sit. I can't believe he made you stand that whole time. That was so rude."

"Thank you."

"It's nothing. Just basic home training. You don't make your clients stand. Can I offer you something to drink? And I am offering as a hostess catering to guests, not as your wife."

Mason crossed the room and stopped just inside Xeni's

personal space. He didn't know what it was about her, but now that he'd had a taste of the way things could be, a taste of her, he didn't want to go back to being strangers.

Xeni gazed up at him, puffing out her chest. Her confidence was sexy as hell and far from a turn-off.

"Can I help you?" she rasped out.

"Did you enjoy yourself last night?" Mason asked.

Xeni scoffed, then walked backwards toward the fridge and grabbed the door handle like it would keep her from floating away. "No. No way. I'm not stroking your ego."

"This isn't about my ego. I genuinely want to know. If you had a shit time, please tell me. Critique me. I want notes."

"You want notes?"

"If you have notes. I want 'em."

"Ugh. I'd love to crush your spirit right now because there's nothing I love more than putting a man in his place, but I have no notes. You made a bitch greedy for more. Happy now?"

"Yes, I am."

"Uh huh." She opened the fridge and pulled out a pitcher filled with ice water and lemon slices. "Water?"

Mason moved closer, taking the pitcher out of her hand. He pulled her to him, cupping her beautiful cheeks in his hands. Her brown skin was practically glowing.

She rolled her eyes and groaned, but didn't stop herself from settling against his stomach. Her fingers lightly stroked his back.

"When you have to go, go," Mason said. "But while you're here…"

"Oh, we fucking, I know. Beeteedubs, it's tomorrow. You said you would tell me what's going on with this debt of yours tomorrow." Just then, the doorbell rang.

"I'll tell you everything tonight. Have dinner with me?"

Xeni was quiet for a moment, but she didn't step away. "I'll think about it, okay?"

"Okay." She let him kiss her on the lips, then went to answer the door.

10

Xeni was trying her best to play hostess, but even after Mr. Barber, Ms. Jordan and Bess were settled around her aunt's large kitchen table with the refreshments Xeni had prepared, she felt like her skin was trying to relocate to another country without the rest of her vital parts. All at once, she was anxious to get this process over with and dreading the reality of taking on her aunt's estate. Her brain couldn't process other stuff at the moment, like what had happened the night of her birth or little pesky facts, like who her real father was.

It didn't help that Mason was in the room. She tried to shove the time they'd spent together out of her mind, but that wasn't happening. She'd been thinking about him since she'd woken up alone in his bed, surrounded by his scent. Her stomach had tied in little knots when she realized he'd brought her car over from Liz's house. A trek across the farm would have been adequate penance for their wedding night booty call. Things had gotten a little out of hand and, unfortunately, Mason was now her bright spot. She could feel all types of ways about her mom, her aunts, the money, even the secrets she was keeping from her friends, but one thing was clear. She was desperately attracted to her new husband. The way he touched her, the way he made her feel? Xeni felt high from it and, if she knew herself, that feeling could only go wrong.

She waited until Mr. Barber was settled at the kitchen table before shoving the necessary paperwork in his face.

"Here's the marriage certificate." She'd stopped herself from cussing Deborah out when she stopped by the clerk's office to pick it up that morning.

"They threw together a fun party," Bess said, offering Xeni a genuine smile. It *was* a fun party. Didn't make the reality of the situation any less fucked up. She was legally married to a man she barely knew and she couldn't wait to get under him again.

"Why don't we get Mason squared away first?" Mr. Barber suggested. "Then let him get on with his day."

Mason looked over at Xeni, waiting for her to give the go ahead. "Yeah, of course. I think I'm going to have to set up the pull-out for Ms. Jordan anyway, if my stuff takes as long as I think it will. You get started."

Xeni wanted to get up and go pace in her aunt's garden, but she needed to stick around. This was part of Mason's truth. Part of Sable's plan. She sat quietly as Ms. Jordan recapped the details of his inheritance and Mr. Barber gave him various pieces of paperwork to sign.

"Can I have a portion of this transferred directly into another account?" he asked.

"Yes, if you have all the proper routing information," Ms. Jordan replied.

"I have it right here." Mason opened the folder he'd

brought with him and slid a bank transfer slip across the table. He'd already filled most of the information out.

Ms. Jordan looked everything over. "It's after business hours in Scotland right now, but I can initiate the transfer in the morning. It should go through Tuesday morning our time, at the latest."

"That'd be fine."

"Just confirming the amount," Ms. Barber turned the paper back to Mason and pointed to the amount with the tip of her pen.

"Yes, forty-seven thousand dollars, US."

"To Jameson McInroy."

"Correct."

"Okay, thank you. The remaining balance will be transferred to your account. Unless you have any more questions for us, you're all set."

"No more questions from me, but I have your information if anything comes up."

"You do."

"We don't have to discuss it today, Mr. Barber, but if you have time soon or can refer us to another attorney who might handle this, I'd like to sit down with you and Xeni and discuss post-nuptial terms," Mason said as he stood up from the kitchen table. "When we dissolve the marriage, I just want to make sure there's nothing legal that says she has to share any more of the estate with me."

"We can definitely do that."

"Excellent. Well, I'll be going." Xeni was still a bit in shock from his offer. Not that she thought Mason would try and take half of everything that wasn't even officially hers yet, but she didn't know him that well. Clearly, money made people do crazy things, and thanks to Aunt Sable's ridiculous terms, he was well within his rights to take Xeni to the cleaners when she eventually filed for divorce. She appreciated that he was doing what he could to protect her.

She cleared her throat when she realized she'd been gazing at him a moment too long. She stood and motioned toward the door. "Here, let me walk you out."

He gathered up his things, saying goodbye to the rest of Aunt Sable's legal dream team, then followed Xeni back through the house. When they stepped out onto the small porch, Mason turned to her, crowding her personal space again. She wanted to hate the overfamiliarity, the closeness, but she couldn't. Mason reached up and smoothed the pad of his thumb down the side of her neck. A shiver ran over her. "Do you want me to stay? I've heard I'm very good at offering emotional support."

"No, but thank you for asking. I feel like there's more bullshit that I'm not ready to hear and I just—I know me. It's better if I have a little while to process on my own."

Mason glanced at his watch. "Let me come back at six and make you dinner. I'll feed them too if they're still here. One less thing for you to worry about."

Xeni didn't want him to go to the trouble, but she knew it was foolish to turn down the offer. She had the massive, newly remodeled kitchen. He knew how to cook. Having him back for dinner was just good sense.

"Okay, I would appreciate that. Thank you. Oh, I don't know if I told you, but—"

"No meat, but seafood's acceptable. Liz told me."

"Right. I'll see you at six."

They both stood there for a moment, looking at each other. Mason didn't turn to get back in his truck and Xeni didn't hightail it back into the safety of the house. Not that she needed protecting from him. No, she needed to stop herself from letting this go on longer than it already had. They could talk. They could share a meal. She was definitely going to sleep with him, but this thing between them? It wasn't a pulsing heat. It was starting to feel like warmth, comfort, and she knew her emotions were too muddled to handle it like an adult. She forced her gaze away from his and took a step back.

"Six," she said.

"I'll see you then."

Xeni's head was spinning. She'd spent hours going over everything with Mr. Barber and Ms. Jordan. She was grateful to have Bess there to hold her hand. All Xeni could think over and over again was how her aunt could have possibly kept all of this from her family and why her family had kept so much information from Xeni. She wanted to know why her aunt had dumped it all in her lap. There were the two houses to deal with and the liquid assets—she double checked what that meant—her stocks and investments. What scared Xeni were the music publishing rights. Ms. Jordan gave her the information for a Martin Hooper who actually handled everything for her aunt. She'd call him in a few days, but she was terrified of what he would tell her.

Finally at five, Ms. Jordan called it quits. "I have to get back to the city, but call me if you need anything and Monday we can go over any questions you have."

"I will and I'll give you a call anyway after I meet with the realtor." Ms. Jordan had given her opinion on what the best move would be with her aunt's properties, but she didn't know much about either local market, so Xeni was handed off to the next expert. She thanked Mr. Barber and Ms. Jordan as they rushed off so Ms. Jordan could jump back into bumper-to-bumper traffic on her way back in Manhattan. Bess hung back.

"You're doing great," she said once they were alone.

Xeni sagged against the counter. "You think so?"

"This is overwhelming as hell and part of me wishes I could go back in time and talk some sense into Sister Sable, but we're here now."

"Yes, we are."

"Take it. All of it. Don't be afraid to embrace this blessing, even though it feels like too much right now."

"I will. Would you like to stay for dinner? Mason is coming back over to cook."

Bess smirked as she hoisted her bag over her shoulder. "Do you need a chaperone?"

"No. I just figured if Mason was already planning to cook, you could stay and enjoy the meal as a thank you."

"No, I have to get home and make sure I see Sydney's face before she tries to disappear with her friends for the weekend. Maybe another time."

"Okay." Xeni walked Miss Bess to the door and they said their goodbyes.

When she was gone, Xeni dug into her contacts and pulled up her Aunt Hazel's number. They weren't close, even though they should have been. Her grandmother had started having kids so early, still in her teens. She'd taken a break, then had four more kids. As a result, Xeni was actually older than her Aunt Hazel, the baby of the bunch. Xeni's mom had always treated her like a child and after a while it had put a strain on their relationship. It was a strange dynamic, but

Hazel had always been nice to Xeni, even when she wasn't getting along with her mom. It took Xeni a few tries to get the wording right, but eventually she finished drafting the text and sent it off to her aunt.

> *Hi Aunt Hazel.*
> *Sorry to bother you.*
> *I need to ask one of your sisters*
> *some questions about Aunt Sable.*
> *Who has the most information*
> *and is likely to give me the least push back?*

She responded right away.

Hi Baby.
You need to speak to your Aunt Alice.

> *Thank you.*

No problem.
Don't be afraid to call me if you
need anything else.

> *I will.*

Xeni thought about waiting, especially with Mason on his way over, but she wanted to at least try to get her Aunt Alice on the phone. The oldest of the Everly sisters, Alice was a retired backup vocalist, living in their grandmother's Victorian mansion. Even though there was a pretty good chance she was busy, Xeni risked the call anyway.

"Hello?"

"Aunt Alice? It's Xeni."

"Couldn't get a word in edgewise with your mother, so you decided to call me?"

Shock closed Xeni's throat before she could respond. "I—"

"It's fine. She called me all in a huff yesterday. So, you know?"

"I—I know that Aunt Sable is my real mother. Is there more?" *Please don't let there be more.*

"No, that's about the sum of it. Listen, your mother and Sable could never get it right. They were fighting since the day Sable was born and then, after Sable's titties came in, it was like they were at war with each other day and night."

"So, how did she end up giving up her baby to the person she hated the most?"

"Who said anything about hate? This is what you only children don't understand. You don't know what it's like to share your life with a sister. And you sure as hell don't know what it's like to share your life with seven of them. My momma had eight girls, Xendria. You can't understand what that bond was like. So yeah, we're at each other's throats sometimes, but there's nothing we wouldn't do for each other."

Xeni closed her eyes. Her mom and her Aunt Alice were very different people, but just like all of the Everly sisters, her Aunt Alice sure knew how to get worked up on a tangent.

"I just want to know what happened."

"Sable got pregnant. The label wanted her to go solo. They told her to get rid of the baby, of you, but she wouldn't. So, your mother agreed to take you."

"Okay, well, that sounds simple enough, but why not tell

me? Why spend years of their lives fighting? Why wait until now to drop this in my lap?"

"Well, it's hard to stop people from doing shit when they're dead," Alice said bluntly. "We all agreed not to tell you because we wanted you to have a normal life. The Everly Sisters was done. We all decided we were going our separate ways. Me, Janice and your mother were done with that side of show biz and none of us wanted you raised in it. Before you were born, we all sat down, your grandmother and Grandpa Sandy too. We all agreed. Sable would go on with her career and Joyce would give you a normal, stable childhood."

"So what changed? Why the fighting?"

"Sable did. Every few years, she'd come back and want to take you, but she had no plan. She wanted to pull you out of school. Move you around the world. There was a tentative plan to turn you into a child actor. She regretted her decision, which we all understood, but she wanted to throw your life into chaos to make up for it. Finally, your mom and your Aunt Janice put their foot down and said they'd take her to court on child neglect claims if she tried to fight for you."

"Jesus."

"Yeah, it was a little extreme, if you ask me, and I wasn't sure they actually had a leg to stand on since she was your real mother after all, but the threat was enough. Sable changed her tune and said she didn't want you anyway. She didn't mean it," Alice rushed to say. "She was trying to hurt your mother, but you know sometimes when things get heated and people say things they can't take back. Then she doubled down and went out and bought our publishing rights from our old label. If she still has them, I suppose they're yours now."

Xeni let her head drop. Her mother was going to fucking freak. That catalog had to be worth a lot of money and Xeni couldn't imagine the kinds of royalties their Christmas hit 'Love You Like Christmas Morning' alone was pulling in. It made a resurgence every damn year.

"How are you so calm about this?" Xeni asked.

"Your aunt kicked out a share of the royalties for a few of the tracks and the rest isn't my business. You were loved and you were safe. Your school was paid for, we got you into your first apartment. You have a great job now. I couldn't stop those two from going at each other, so I got out of the way. If I had thought, if *we* had thought, you were in danger, you know we would have stepped in."

"I know." Xeni's family was a fucking mess, but there was always a line. Yeah, she didn't have sisters, but that same bond still existed with her cousins. Even when they drifted, they always had each other's backs.

"I don't agree with things either of them did, but I do wish they had both shut up and just loved each other, because now Sable's gone and we're not getting her back." Xeni closed her eyes, feeling like a grade-A dick. Her family, they were all still grieving. She wanted answers, but maybe this could all wait.

"I'm sorry, Aunt Alice. I didn't mean to upset you."

"You didn't. You just have to remember our time is limited. It's silly to waste your time being angry at people you're supposed to love."

"You're right."

"I hate to leave you like this, but I have to go get my friend from the doctors."

"Of course. Thank you."

"You can call me anytime."

"I know. Thank you. Oh, Aunt Alice. One more thing. Did Aunt Sable ever tell you anything about my dad?"

"Oh, we all knew your dad. Orlando. He was a studio musician. Handsome devil. He died before Sable knew she was pregnant."

"What happened?"

"Fist fight at the airport, of all places. Other guy landed a hard punch the wrong way and your dad passed away."

Xeni let out another painful sigh before she thanked her aunt.

"Dante loves you like his own, Xeni. That's more than something."

"I know. Go pick up your friend. I'll talk to you when I get back."

"Come on by and see me. It's been a while since you've been over." They'd seen each other during her aunt's home-going, but she was right. Xeni hadn't been to Pasadena in ages.

"I promise I will."

Xeni ended the call then sent her mom a text.

> *Hey mommy. Just checking in.*
> *Everything's going fine.*
> *I'll call you and Daddy tomorrow. XP*

Okay. Thanks for texting
Love you, baby. XM

They needed to talk, but Xeni had a feeling she wouldn't be able to do it over the phone. She needed time to process and gather her own thoughts. Her Aunt Alice was right about how precious life was and how little time they had to spend it together, but that realization didn't make Xeni any less human.

She needed time to set some of the anger and the hurt aside. She felt like a pawn and a mistake. She thought back to the times she'd spent alone with Sable. The snide comments her aunt had made about her mother, how Xeni had chalked them up to Sable being the cool aunt with no man and no kids tying her down. So cool, there was no way her mom could understand her. How would have Xeni acted if she'd known the truth? Did it even matter now?

She sunk down in her chair, trying to force herself to cry. She needed the release, but the tears wouldn't come. Eventually she gave up, accepting the numbness that had come back to smother her like a pillow in the face. She picked up her phone again and went to her text conversation with Mason. She hoped his kindness could stretch a bit further with her.

I don't know if you're already close but could you grab some beer and some ice cream. I need to drown my sorrows in booze and sugar.

The little response bubbles popped up before her phone went dim.

Was looking for the perfect gif response.
Nothing was good enough.
But the answer is yes, love.

Thanks, dear.

Xeni put her phone down, leaned over and pressed her forehead against the wood of the table. She could hear her mother, feel her slapping her shoulder, telling her to get her face off that dirty tabletop, but her mother wasn't there to chide her. She closed her eyes and rolled her face back and forth, willing Mason to hurry up. She needed her husband.

11

The moment Xeni opened the door, Mason regretted leaving her. She still looked beautiful. She'd slipped on an oversized cardigan that somehow made her look even more comfortable and sexy, but the afternoon seemed to have aged her. There were bags under her eyes and there wasn't even a ghost of a smile when she let him in. He'd planned to cook for her and hoped she'd let him spend the night fucking her into next Christmas, but first he wanted to bring the light back to her eyes.

Mason lifted an eyebrow and shot her a smile.

"What, you weirdo? Are you coming in or not?"

"I am, but first, I have one question for you."

She rolled her eyes, then popped her hand on her hip. "Sure, but make it quick. You're gonna let the bugs in."

"Oh, right." Mason stepped inside and used his body to playfully nudge her out of the way.

"Hey!" she laughed.

"Sorry, madam. I just need to put my groceries down." He

felt her behind him, following him into the kitchen. He set the groceries on the counter and turned to her.

"You wanna see a magic trick?"

Xeni shot him a confused look. "I guess, but my standards for sleight of hand are pretty darn high. I'm not Palila. I expect to be wowed."

"First off, don't insult my niece that way. Her standards for everything in life are top shelf. Secondly, when have I not wowed you?"

"I can kick your ass out any time, you know."

"Okay. I'm gonna need a five dollar bill from a member of the audience."

"Jesus." Xeni grumbled, but that didn't stop her from going into her pocketbook and pulling out a crisp twenty. "Here. Don't rip it in half."

"No destruction of legal tender involved, I promise. Now watch, as I make this twenty dollar bill disappear." Mason made a big show of slowly folding the twenty in half and then in quarters. "One." He pushed his hands out in front of his chest making sure she could see the folded bill between his fingers. "Two and three." Mason tossed the bill behind him. Xeni eyes followed it as it bounced on the counter. Mason glanced over and saw it wedged behind a jar of sugar.

"Poof." Mason said, waving his now empty hands in the air. "Magic." It was his worst work by far, but he held the bright smile on his face as Xeni fought to suppress any kind of reaction. He knew he had her when her nostrils flared and her lips started quivering. She held out her hand.

"Give me my money back."

Mason grabbed the bill and gently unfolded it before placing it in her upturned palm.

"All my terrible jokes aside, if we can find a deck of cards around here, I can show you a pretty fun trick."

"All serious magicians should carry the tools of their trade with them."

"Well, I forgot to keep a fresh deck in my pocket, but I did happen to remember these." Mason reached into one of the grocery bags and pulled out a six-pack of beer. "And this," a pint of cinnamon swirl ice cream. "And these," a box of condoms.

"Thank you and good thinking."

"For our main course this evening, I'd like to offer the lady a seafood alfredo."

"Ooh, that sounds good," Xeni groaned.

"Excellent." Mason pulled his keychain bottle opener out of his pocket, cracked open one of the beers and handed it to her. "Please sit back and relax. This won't take too long."

"Don't mind if I do."

Xeni collapsed at the kitchen island with a sigh as he went to work. Miss Sable's kitchen was pretty well organized. She'd never let him cook for her before, opting to have him bring food from the cafe when he came over to jam.

"Would you prefer music or sparkling conversation while I prepare our meal?"

"How about you finally tell me what's going on with your whole situation and we put on a little background music?"

Mason thought for a moment, wondering if talking about his father while deveining shrimp was safe. He turned back to the counter, pulled up a streaming jazz station he'd been enjoying lately on his phone, then started unpacking the wrapped shrimp and scallops. He went to the sink and washed his hands before he grabbed what he needed from Ms. Sable's magnetic knife rack.

"Our story begins back in the Spring of 1986. A boy child came screaming into the world—"

"Dude." He turned and caught the are-you-fucking-serious look on Xeni's face. "Let's fast forward just a little."

"First year of uni, I started a band. Our drummer, Duncan, and I fell in love. My father found out. Threatened him enough that he was too scared to carry on with me. A year or so later, my father sets me up with one of his business associate's daughters. I go back to law school, so I can become my father's idea of a proper man." Mason paused for a moment to look for a pot for the pasta. A memory of Ms. Sable suddenly popped into his mind and he chuckled.

"What's so funny?" Xeni asked.

"Just thinking about how annoyed your aunt would be seeing me searching through her cabinets."

"Well, it was her bright idea for us to get married and to leave me this house. Some concessions from the afterlife will have to be made."

Mason glanced over his shoulder and looked at Xeni's beautiful face as she became fixated on the label of her beer. He ducked back into the cabinets and found the big pot he was looking for. He let the music fill the air while he filled the pot and set it on the stove. He found a skillet and set that to heat while he got the shrimp ready. Eventually Xeni spoke.

"I talked to my Aunt Alice today. And, ugh…" She tilted her head back and sucked in a deep breath, blinking a dozen or so times. "I can't cry right now."

"Why not? Nothing beats a good cry."

"Well for one, I don't like crying in front of people. Also, the levels of frustration I'm dealing with right now? If I start, I might not stop crying until New Years. I don't have time for that."

"As your husband, I want you to know that it's okay for you to cry in front of me."

Xeni let out a mirthless chuckle. "I appreciate that. I prefer to cry alone in my car or late at night in the dark. It's more dramatic that way. More cathartic."

Mason thought back to the last time he cried and he guessed she had a point. "Had a real good cry in an alley behind my favorite pub once. Wasn't cathartic exactly, but it had to be done. I didn't need anyone to witness that event."

"Finish your story and then maybe we'll find someplace quiet to sit back to back and we'll cry together."

"That sounds romantic. Anyway, Moira and I actually started to get pretty close. I thought she was a great girl. A few months before the wedding, we were talking and I told her about the band and I mentioned Duncan. I maybe put a little too much emotion behind his name, because she had follow-up questions. I thought I could trust her, since we were about to get married. So, I told her we'd been serious, but he was an ex. We all have exes. He'd moved on. I'd moved on."

"Right. This sounds like normal ex stuff. Minus your father threatening him."

"Exactly. She asked me if I was gay. I said no, I'm bisexual. I gave her the basic definition of what that meant to me. She seemed to accept that and I thought that was the end."

"But it wasn't."

"She was a no show on our wedding day."

"Oh, okay. Also holy shit."

"Two hundred guests packed into St. Sebastian's and she's not there. She told her father she just couldn't. There's a conversation between our fathers and somehow it's reported that I've told Moira I am gay and that it's a secret I asked her

125

to keep to herself. I never asked her to keep anything to herself. I thought I was just letting my wife-to-be get to know me better."

"Jesus. Right, go on."

"Everyone's upset because you know my being gay is akin to me being a serial killer. And the wedding's been cancelled, so people are even more upset. A couple of days go by, I finally talk to her and she tells me she never said that. She just isn't secure enough to be with a man who might want to sleep with men again in the future. *I* thought I would be spending my future sleeping with *her*. But I guess I was confused about how monogamy and marriage go hand in hand. I don't know."

"Ah. Yeah, a lot of people struggle with bisexuality as a concept and they also struggle with the fact that bisexuality and commitment can work together just fine. It's annoying. I came out to my parents because I didn't want them to be shocked if I popped up with a person who wasn't a cis dude. They handled it well, but I don't think my mom fully gets it. But this isn't about me. Please continue."

"No, you talk about yourself too. Open forum. Free exchange of ideas here."

"No, I want to hear the rest. So, she makes it clear that she just can't hang and your wedding day was probably the worst day to share this information. Then what?"

"I didn't really have time to be upset or hurt or whatever because her father takes back his offer to hire me at his firm and apparently I've botched some investment deal he had with my father that would have secured funds to keep a small bit of family land and restore the even smaller castle that sits on it."

"Wow. Shit."

"Wow shit would be right. We—" Mason stopped himself from going on. He wasn't proud of what happened next. "Things were said and then things got physical. I'll spare you those details, but in the end, my mum thought it would be better if I came to the States for a while. Put a whole ocean between me and my father, and give us both a chance to calm down."

"And how long ago was that?"

"Seven years."

"So what exactly is your dad charging you for? I'm guessing that money was sent directly to him."

"Law school and the wedding. Moira's father wanted his money back."

"Ouch."

"With interest."

"And I'm sure—or I hope—Silas is letting you live rent free, but I doubt he can pay you eighty-five dollars an hour. Question, though. You said you had dual citizenship. You're a White dude and you're clearly smart and talented. Why didn't you look for something that paid more the cafe? Not that I'm knocking that gig. It seems like you guys are having a blast over there. It just, you know…"

Mason had asked himself that question many times and lately he was less and less impressed with his own logic. At first, he'd convinced himself he was sticking around for Silas. After his falling out with Scott, Silas had spent years building up the farm, living in that huge house all alone. But after Liz moved in and it was clear that each was exactly what the other needed, Mason wasn't sure what he was doing anymore.

He'd used Palila's birth as an excuse for a while. Of course, he wanted to help out with the new baby, but between Ms. Bess, Maya, Ginny, Sydney, and Liz's sister and friends from the city, there was practically a line around the corner of volunteers asking to look after the adorable child. Now he knew that the longer it took for him to pay back his father, the longer he could put off going back home.

"I was dragging my feet," he admitted. "Your aunt knew and I suppose that's why she gave me the money. She didn't want me to spend my life fighting with my father. Or maybe she didn't want me to spend my life hiding from him."

"Are you going to quit now and go back home?"

"Another good question from the Mrs." Mason set the cooked shrimp and scallops aside and started on the sauce.

"It's okay if you don't want to go back. You can say that. This is a safe space. A circle of sharing, if you will."

Mason didn't want to be an asshole and say all the terrible things that had run through his head over the years out loud. Still, one thing was true. While he missed his mom, he didn't miss his father and he wasn't sure he ever wanted to see him again. Mason was who he was. Yeah, he wasn't his father's ideal version of what a McInroy man could be, but he was a hard worker and a loyal friend. He'd been there for Silas and Liz through their ups and downs. He knew what he had to do to get back in his father's good graces, to restore the peace in his family and it would only cost him his soul.

"I've considered not going back." He looked over at Xeni to gauge her reaction. She just shrugged and took a sip of her beer.

"Understandable. If your father hadn't ruined things between you and Duncan, where do you think you'd be now?"

"Finishing up a sold-out North American tour. Duncan and I would have broken up seven or eight times and I'd be dating our new bassist to make him jealous." Mason was joking about the last part.

"What instrument did you play in the band?" Xeni asked.

"You're looking at lead vocals and any wind instrument we could fit my old truck, but mostly bagpipes. You've never heard real funk until you've heard funk on the bagpipes."

"Really?" Xeni laughed.

"Look up Reggie Harkness on your cellular device there." Mason added more salt to his sauce and, just as he was about to taste it, heard the opening chords to Reggie and The Blaze's "Bagpipe Blues, On the Bay" drown out the light jazz coming from his phone.

"Oh my god," Xeni laughed as she paused the video. "I know this guy. I think he dated one of my aunts."

"According to Ms. Sable, he dated at least three of your aunts. He's the only reason I took up bagpipes. Dear old dad wanted me to carry on the tradition. I hated going to lessons, but when my instructor realized I didn't give a shit about tradition, he played Reggie's first LP for me. I was hooked after that." Hearing the Blaze's first album had been transformative for Mason. He knew then he could make any kind of music with any instrument. He could be unstoppable.

"That's amazing."

"They asked me to play the national anthem over at the high school for one of the football games. Your aunt came up to me at the cafe the next day and asked me if I'd heard of the Blaze. That was the start of our beautiful friendship."

"The musical accompaniment at her service makes a little more sense now."

"I promise, that was one hundred percent her idea."

"I believe you." Mason looked over as Xeni let out another heavy sigh. Almost as quickly, her expression changed and she cocked her head to the side. Her eyes narrowed and her tongue darted out, wetting her bottom lip. Mason couldn't help but think about what it would feel like to have that tongue wrapped up in other places.

"Are you checking out my ass again? I saw you at the clerk's office," he said.

"Yes and no. My friend told me she fell for her husband because he was a good cook. I mean, he's tatted to the nines and hot as hell and great with her kids, but I'm starting to get what she means about the cooking thing."

"I'm sure it's nice to have a man who can keep you fed."

"That and it's kinda hot watching you work. You've been talking to me this whole time and whipping up a meal I've been too lazy to make like it's nothing."

"Well, it's a very easy recipe. I can show you anytime you like."

"That's fine. I like the view from here."

"You're not flirting with me, are you now?"

"If you couldn't tell, I barely have an internal filter, especially when it comes to you. I'm not flirting. I'm just incapable of not telling you what I find attractive about you. It's embarrassing as hell, so if you could please stop pointing it out, I'd appreciate it."

"I'll consider it. It's kinda cute when your voice gets all high that way."

"It does not." She pressed her hand against her cheek, crossed the kitchen and grabbed another beer. Mason liked teasing her, but he knew he had to give her a break. He checked his pasta, then searched for a colander.

"And what about you?" he said to her. "What dreams are you putting off to the side?"

"What makes you think I'm not living my dreams?"

"You tell me. What's it like teaching the wee ones? I did magic tricks for two of Palila's little friends and I thought they were going to eat me alive."

"Oh, the kids are easy. I don't know. They're... they're easy, but the work? It's not as fulfilling as I'd hoped it would be."

"How so?"

"Well, I knew I was going to aim for a private school. Higher salaries, better resources. I work with two of my best friends. It's a great school. Not too many problems from the administration. The parents are okay. But, like, these kids do not need me. They have everything. Money, access, privilege. A few times, I've thought about moving over to a school where I can really mentor students who need it, but I'm not sure I want to be a teacher for the rest of my life. Wow, I have never said that out loud to anyone."

"What do you want to be when you finally grow up?"

"I'm not sure."

"Well, come Monday, when all the paperwork is filed, you won't have to do it for the money anymore."

"God," Xeni said, making a noise like a strangled gasp. Mason looked over to see a sort of wide-eyed terror spreading over her face. "I didn't even think of that."

"Of what?"

"The actual money being *mine*. I was so stressed out about my mom and my aunt and my aunt mom and all this other shit. I didn't *think* about the actual money and what it would mean for me. What is wrong with me?"

"You're under a lot of stress and you just lost someone very close to you. It's not like you won the lottery or got luck at the slots."

"Do you play piano?" she asked, abruptly changing the subject.

"I do."

"Will you play something for me after dinner?"

"What movie are we roleplaying? Pretty Woman or Twilight?"

"Actually, another one of my favorites. The Oscar award-winning hit You're Sleeping Alone Tonight, Chump."

"Available now on Blu-ray and Redbox."

"Yup."

12

"Here's a question for you."

Xeni heard what Mason had said but she was distracted by the amazing aroma coming from the pasta he'd just set down in front of her. She leaned in close, inhaling the creamy, lemony scent of the Alfredo sauce.

"Mmm, I already know I'm gonna destroy this. It smells so good."

"That would be quite the compliment." He set down his own plate and a glass of white wine, then took a seat beside her at the island. Or tried to, anyway. His legs didn't quite fit under the marble ledge.

"High enough, but not deep enough. Story of my life."

Xeni laughed. "Come on. Let's move to the table."

They gathered up their meal and moved to the large dining table across the room. Xeni made herself comfortable as Mason took the seat beside her again. She looked around at the four other open chairs.

"You can sit across from me, you know. More elbow room."

"Then I won't be able to grope you under the table while you eat," Mason replied, all casual like as he grabbed the pepper.

Xeni froze, her whole body lighting up like a matchstick. Her nipples tightened as if they were begging to be touched first. Somehow, though, she managed to play it cool. "If you could at least let me eat half before we move to the groping portion of the evening. I'm starving."

Mason lifted his wine glass. "I'll try my best. To us figuring out what the hell to do next."

"Cheers to that."

"Please enjoy."

Xeni picked up her fork and piled it high with a healthy serving of pasta and a fat shrimp. Everything was perfectly cooked and the sauce melted on her tongue. "Oh my god," she groaned. "So good."

She glanced over at Mason as he took his own forkful. They ate in companionable silence for a few minutes, then Mason turned in his chair to face her.

"Back to the question I was going to ask you."

Xeni nodded for him to go on. She was too busy stuffing her face to give a verbal response.

"You know my whole story, but how are you single?"

Xeni swallowed as she shook her head. "No, no, no. I know why you're not with Duncan and I know why you're not with Moira. But you said you've been here for seven years. That's plenty of time to get over a broken heart, start over and fall in love with a sexy farm hand. Why are you single?"

"I asked you first."

"That's petty and immature, but fine. If you must know. I Practical Magic'd myself."

"You what?"

"You ever seen Practical Magic?"

"Can't say that I have?"

"Well, you done fucked up because I'm going to make you watch it. Anyway, I won't spoil the plot for you, but one of the women does a spell, kind of outlining what she wants in the perfect man. She thinks it'll stop her from falling in love, but of course she meets the perfect man. Except in my case it's working too well."

"So, you mean to tell me that you did a spell to stop yourself from falling in love."

"Nooooot exactly." Xeni didn't know when, but somehow she'd turned herself into a cliche. She'd been so upset by the way things had ended with Patrick, that she'd allowed so many bad things to happen in their relationship. Yes, in retrospect, she knew it wasn't her fault. Patrick was just a trash-ass human and it was better that they'd went their separate ways. That didn't change the fact that it took her years to get back to herself and a few years more to realize she was worthy of what she needed. But Mason didn't need to know all that.

"At the time, I was being thorough in what I wanted. I'd just gotten out of a bad relationship and I was very focused on avoiding some of the mistakes I made in my youth. I made a very specific list, communed with the ocean and lit a few candles. I wasn't going to settle. I got so busy not settling that fifty years went by and here I am married to you."

"Yeah, I don't think your spell actually worked. I'm everything a woman could ever want."

"I see myself ending up like half of my aunts, living in a big house alone with several birds I've taught to shit-talk the mailman. Once a week, a handyman named Daryl—Daryl's a widower—comes over to blow my back out. We see each other at church or at the store and act friendly, but secretly we both know what's really going on."

"And when are you supposed to meet Daryl? Or is he someone you already know?" Mason asked.

"Don't know him yet, but I've imagined that I meet him around 2055 if climate change doesn't kill us all first."

"You've really thought this through."

Xeni lifted her shoulder in a little shrug. "I just know what I want. But you!"

"What about me?"

"No one said you needed to full on settle down, but have you dated at all since you got here?"

"I've been busy. Also, there's this movie called Practical Magic—"

Xeni reached over and squeezed his knee. "Not funny."

"Wrong. Hilarious."

"You still haven't answered my question." Xeni took the last bite of her pasta and strongly considered going back for seconds, but there was a difference between carbo loading for sex with a Scotsman and giving yourself the pasta sweats. There would be room for seconds later. She sat back and waited for Mason to cough up an explanation. "I refuse to believe none of the eligible folks in this small town have tried to climb all this."

"Maybe I don't want to be climbed. Maybe I want to be romanced. Maybe I want to be courted properly. Maybe I want to feel like a prince. Maybe I don't want to be a Daryl. Ever thought of that?"

"So, now might be the wrong time to tell you to hurry and finish eating so we can clean up and stretch? 'Cause, honey…" Xeni's eyes widened as she looked him up and down and she made a big show of dragging her tongue along her upper lip. "I'm kidding. Do you want more, though?"

"No, I think I'm good."

"You cooked, so I'll clean. More wine?"

"Please."

Xeni went and grabbed the bottle off the counter and, after she topped off his glass, found some containers for the leftover pasta. Whoever he eventually found his happily ever after with was gonna be a lucky person. Boy knew how to cook.

She started running the water to rinse the dishes when she felt him step behind her. She slipped the pot into the sink, doing her best to ignore the way he was just barely touching her, but still towered over her all at once.

"Would you like my help?"

"No. I—I think I can handle things here. Um... grab that box of rubbers and meet me in the living room in four minutes." Without a word, Mason took the box of condoms off the counter and disappeared into the other room. Xeni threw all the dishes in the sink and quickly splashed them with dish soap and a light sprinkling of water before she ran down the hall to the guest room. She quickly stripped out of her clothes and grabbed a washcloth. She'd showered that morning, but a thirty-second birdie bath, as her mom liked to call them, wouldn't hurt anyone. She washed up and quickly re-lotioned her whole body before she threw on her long navy striped cardigan again. It was far from a sexy piece of lingerie, but it would do just fine.

When she walked back into the living room, she found Mason sitting at the piano bench. He'd spread out a nice array of comfortable looking blankets on the carpet in front of the coffee table.

"I thought you'd be naked," Xeni said.

"You know I'm shy."

"Mmmhmm."

"Come here." Mason held out his hand. Usually Xeni didn't like to be told what to do, but she found herself walking right to him. He lightly took her fingers when she was within arm's reach and pulled her closer so she was standing between his legs. Slowly he parted the halves of her draping sweater, exposing her body to his heated gaze. Xeni held her breath as his large hands cupped her waist.

His thumbs moved upward in light circles, tracing the skin just under her breasts, then up higher until the rough pads of his fingers slid over her sensitive nipples. Her pussy clenched on itself, just aching to be filled. She wasn't in a rush, but damn did she want him to get on with it. She felt like she was going to explode.

"Tell me what you like," he said before he leaned in close. He found her constellation tattoo, the delicate lines she had etched up her sternum. Closer. Xeni's eyes slid shut as his lips pressed against her skin. She reached up and dug her fingers into his thick, loose curls.

"What, like, porn-wise?"

"No," Mason laughed, looking up at her. "How do you like to be fucked? What turns you on?"

"You seemed to have figured that out already. I told you I have no notes."

"All that tells me is that I got lucky, but there's a whole lot more to life than me going down on you. Tell me what you like. Tell me what you want. Tell me what you're gonna have Daryl do to you in the year 2057."

"No, that doesn't count. Daryl and I are doing it from the back over the kitchen counter every time. Daryl is about function and convenience. I don't think you want that for our marriage."

Mason pressed another kiss right between her tits. "So, tell me. What you do want?"

Now. Her stupid fucking body would choose now to conjure up some water works. Xeni swallowed and blinked the tears back. It didn't work. Xeni quickly turned away and pressed the heels of her hands against her eyes.

"Hey, hey hey," Mason said quickly as he gathered her into his arms. "Come here, love. What's wrong?"

That didn't help at all, his tender affection. A trembling sob ripped through her body and it took everything Xeni had to swallow it down. The sudden pain in her chest came out as a harsh sigh instead of the scream that was threatening to crack her in half.

"I am not crying about my bad sex life right now."

"It would be fine if you were."

Okay, maybe she was crying about her sex life a little. She had plenty of annoying problems, just like anyone else, but for some awful reason her brain decided this was what it wanted to dredge up. Not the feelings about her parents. Not the crushing fact that she would never even get a chance to speak to her birth father. Not the haunting realization that she was unhappy with her job and had no clue if she was brave enough to walk away from it or if that was even a sensible option.

There was plenty for her to be upset about. But no, she was in Mason's arms, soaking the comforting embrace of a man she barely knew because she hadn't had sex in ages while she was too busy guarding her heart. And no, it didn't make a lick of sense that she was so willing to sleep with

Mason. She just wanted him and that annoying logical voice in the back of her head could just shut up about it.

Xeni blew out a breath and tried to speak. "I'm amazing, you know. I have great friends. A great family. They're nuts, but I know they love me. I'm cute as hell. I am so good at my job. I shouldn't quake in the face of honesty and intimacy. It shouldn't be so hard for me to find someone to love me."

Xeni knew she was being ridiculous. She wasn't surprised when Mason's broad chest shook with laughter.

"Yeah, ha ha. Laugh at the gorgeous woman with amazing breasts who can't find love."

"That's not why I'm laughing."

"Why then? Huh?"

"Let's just say that's another thing we have in common."

"Oh yeah?"

"Xeni, look at me." Xeni looked up at the mountain of a man looking back at her. "Do you see this face? Do you see these rugged good looks? You ran your fingers through this hair. I deep condition once a week. You see the results. You said it yourself. It makes no sense. Why would a *god* such as myself be all alone in the world?"

"Okay. You've made your point. No one can have it *all*."

"Come sit." Mason sat back down on the piano bench and pulled Xeni onto his lap. She tucked her sweater tightly around her chest and gave in to the urge to rest her head against his shoulder. He wrapped his arms around her and then they were quiet. Xeni knew she could fill the silence. She had the jokes, the slick banter, but in that moment she didn't want to be on and she was glad that Mason didn't seem like he was about to push her.

"Who knows you best? Like, who knows who you really are?" she asked him.

"That's a good question. Now? I would say Silas and mostly because he doesn't care. It's easy to be yourself around someone who isn't going to judge you. And Liz. And Ms. Sable."

Xeni squeezed her eyes closed again. Her family knew her, the real her, but she knew she'd hid parts of herself from other people. She always tried to be her most honest and authentic self, but fear sometimes kept her from really being open. And that was it. That said it all. The reason her aunt had come up with this crazy scheme and she had to pay someone in a bind to marry Xeni. She had to bribe Xeni with literal millions in property and other assets just to force her to consider what a partnership with someone like Mason could be like. But this wasn't real and in twenty-seven days and some odd hours it would be over.

"I don't know what I want," Xeni finally admitted to Mason and herself. "I've never trusted anyone enough to find out."

"Hmm, another thing we have in common." That didn't ease the ache in Xeni's chest at all. She was starting to like Mason. She could see herself really caring about him. He deserved love. He deserved all the things he wanted and needed, but hadn't been given the room to discover yet.

Xeni eased off his lap and paced over to the fireplace and back. "I need water. You want some water?"

"I'm fine, thank you. Xeni, we don't have to—"

"Oh, but I want to. Unless you don't want to. I don't know what a naked woman crying in your lap does to your mood. Is that your thing?"

"No," Mason said as he smiled a bit and shook his head.

"Well, we don't have to if you don't want to."

He nodded toward the kitchen. "Why don't you get your water and then we'll see how we're both feeling."

"Okay." Xeni went into the kitchen. She grabbed a glass of water and looked down at the piece of baker's twine still tied around her finger. It was a little damp from her birdie bath. She'd noticed earlier that Mason had taken his off. He'd been preparing food all day, so that didn't surprise her. Still, it was a stark reminder, proof of just how ridiculous this whole situation was. None of it was real and if it wasn't real, then Xeni didn't have to be afraid of getting hurt. There was no risk and, really, no limits. Well, there were some limits. Xeni had her hard nos. But just like their quickie wedding, she and Mason could make this night whatever they wanted it to be.

She found him still there on the piano bench, waiting for her to pull it together. Xeni couldn't read the expression on his face, but she could feel the energy in the room. He wasn't bothered at all.

She nodded toward his hand. "See you ditched the string."

"Still have it, though. Don't worry, love. Just took it off during my shift. It's sitting nice and safe on my desk back in the apartment."

She didn't expect that to reinflate her cold dead heart, but it did. "Oh."

"How are you feeling?"

"Better. Thank you for asking." She let out a deep breath and made the decision to put her feelings away. "So, I think I know what I want tonight, but I need you to be cool about it."

"Cool's my middle name."

"Also, you have to keep everything that happened here tonight to yourself. The streets can't know I'm this soft."

"I promise your reputation is intact."

"I want you to make love to me. Like, painfully slow. Early nineties R&B video, silk shirts in the rain slow. With lots of kissing. Are you okay with that?" Xeni didn't know if Boyz II Men or Silk videos had made it over to Scotland, but it was worth a try.

Mason crossed the room and met her in the doorway. He had to duck his head to keep from bumping against the millwork. He crowded her against the jamb, then pressed his lips to hers. Just as his tongue swept pass her lips in a lazy, sweet motion, his hands came around her waist and he lifted her. Xeni couldn't get her legs all the way around him, but it didn't matter. He had her firmly in his grip as he carried her over to the pile of blankets. He set her down and Xeni did her best to be patient as he shucked off his clothes and rolled the condom on his impressive erection.

He climbed over her and picked up right where he left off, kissing her deeply on the mouth. Xeni could tell he was trying to be careful with her, bracing his hands on either side of her. He was being considerate, but Xeni wanted to feel him. All of him. She wanted to feel his weight and his warmth, so she slid her arms around his shoulders and pulled him closer. She opened her legs and reached between them, giving his cock a few strokes until he pressed himself inside her. Xeni broke the kiss, arching in the blankets as he stretched her pussy inch by inch. She was so wet, had been all night even through her tears, and finally, he was where she really needed him.

He did exactly what she asked, fucking her slowly, softly, his thick erection working her from the inside. Xeni soaked it up, basking in every sensation. The way his lips moved over hers, down to her neck, lightly tracing her nipples before sucking them both to painful peaks, until she was crying out. The orgasm that hit her wasn't enough. She came, hard, but it didn't satisfy the ache. She only wanted more. Mason was right behind her, letting out a groan that let her know he felt the same way. They'd only taken the edge off. They'd have to do it again and maybe a dozen more times, just to make sure they got it right.

He carefully rolled to his knees beside her and when he came back from disposing the condom, he lay down beside her and pulled her closer.

"I have notes this time."

"Oh yeah?" He perched up on his shoulder, concern creasing his forehead. She reached up and tried to smooth the worry out with her finger.

"Next time we do it at the piano."

"Only if you promise me that you and Daryl are never together near a musical instrument."

Xeni rolled on her back, laughing at the ceiling. "I can't make any promises."

13

X eni was exhausted, but all the unanswered questions in her head and the daunting to-do list, which included what she came all the way to New York for, made it impossible for her to shut her brain off.

She rolled over and looked at Mason, who was snoring softly beside her on the living room floor. They probably should have moved their sexcapades to a bed, but he seemed so peaceful that she didn't want to wake him. She found her cardigan piled up next to Mason's discarded jeans and slipped it on, then went to find her phone. She grabbed it off the kitchen table and slid open the back door to the screened-in porch. She'd learned pretty quickly that Kinderack had a mosquito problem the likes of which Los Angeles had never seen. Nothing sounded better than a midnight stroll through her aunt's garden, but she didn't want her legs to get all chewed up.

Another thing she had to add to the list: figure out if her aunt had any help keeping up the immaculate back yard.

She took a seat in one of the rocking chairs and pulled up

her LetsChat app. Another Friday night and the girls were all chatting about their plans. They were all boo'd up with the exception of Xeni and Meegan. If she were home, she and Meegan would be on their way out to find some acceptable amounts of trouble. Maybe Shae would ditch her man, Aidan, and join them. Or Keira would invite them all over to her house if her husband was out on the road seeing to some pyrotechnics business. From the look of things, Sarah, Meegan and Joanna were headed to the movies. She switched over to her text conversation with Sloan. It was time she told somebody in her life what was going on.

> *A little bit of personal news.*
> *I may have gotten married yesterday.*
> *Cutie pie of a Scotsman named Mason*

She pulled up her favorite picture of her and Mason during the ceremony. She was in his arms a few feet off the ground and they were kissing. It was Pinterest worthy, like one of those photos that came with the frame. She stared at it for a while after she hit send, then went back to her camera roll and looked at all the photos Liz and her friends had forwarded that night. She'd saved them all to her phone so they would be safely stored in one handy place.

Clicking over to the last photo, Xeni turned her phone to the side and looked at the picture Liz had taken of her sitting on Mason's lap. Suddenly her phone started ringing in her hand. It was Sloan. Xeni hit ACCEPT.

"What in the whole world is going on?"

"Hi." Xeni almost teared up again. It was so good to hear Sloan's familiar voice.

"Are you okay? Have you been kidnapped? Did a cult get

you? Do you need reinforcements? I'll send Rafe. He's amazing at organizing and lifting heavy boxes, but he can also spring you from a cult. He can have a man to man with this… Mason? That's his name, right? Rafe wants to know if you're okay."

"I'm fine. Honestly, the whole new husband thing is the least crazy part of all of this. Do you have a few minutes?"

"Of course. Hold on." Xeni could hear a muffled "Here, babe," before Sloan returned. "Sorry, just had to hand off my baby," Sloan groaned. "Okay. Tell me literally everything." And Xeni did. Well, mostly everything. She told Sloan about the inheritance and the hoops they had to jump through to get it. She kept the truth about her birth to herself. She couldn't talk about that until she fully wrapped her mind around it. She definitely didn't want to talk about it until she and her mom had at least one calm conversation, but in the meantime, there was Mason.

"So, you're like married married. It's all legal and everything."

"Yeah."

"What's he like?"

"Tall. Very tall. Burly. He's like the definition of burly. He looks like he just walked out of the woods and onto a farm."

"Cute enough to make you pop a titty out?"

Xeni laughed, remembering all the conversations she and Sloan had had when she'd first started seeing Rafe. Their stakes had been a bit higher since Sloan was Rafe's boss at the time. She'd hired him as a live-in nanny to take care of her twins, but once they realized how attracted they were to each other, things had changed. Sloan had been wary because dating the nanny was a red-flag recipe for disaster. Luckily, things worked out just fine. Great even, and there was a new infant son to prove it. But before they'd said their own vows and decided to go half on a baby, there had been many nights when Sloan and Xeni had been up texting and talking about what Sloan should do about the new man in her life. Now it looked like it was Sloan's time to return the favor, even if there was no real relationship to speak of.

"He is very cute, very handsome. I don't mind looking at him at all."

"Do you like him?" Sloan asked. "I mean, you two look pretty cozy in those pictures. That doesn't look like a shotgun wedding between two strangers who can't stand each other."

"Well, there was never a point at which we couldn't stand each other. There hasn't been time, but you got the strangers part right. He's... I'm trying to think of the right word. He's easy to be around. You know me."

"I do," Sloan laughed. "I know how careful you are, but you didn't answer my question. Do you like him?"

"I like him as well as I can, since I barely know him," she said cautiously, like he wasn't just inside of her a couple hours ago. "He seems like a good guy. He's kind. Very considerate. He can cook. I know that'll score him some major Sloan points. He plays the bagpipes."

"He sounds like a well-rounded young man," Sloan teased.

Xeni was quiet for a second. She realized then that she actually wanted Sloan to meet him. She wanted all of her friends to meet him. "I mean, yeah, I like him. And I may have done more than let him touch my butt."

"Aww, Xeni," Sloan cooed. "Is the dry spell broken?"

"It is."

"How does it feel?"

"Good. I mean, I embarrassed the shit out of myself by

crying on him during foreplay, but we managed to pull it together."

"And it was good?"

Xeni instantly felt her cheeks and her thighs warm all over again. "Yes. It was very good. Ten out of ten, would fuck again."

"Yay," Sloan giggled. "I'm so happy for you. And you said you were gonna give Miss Havisham a run for her money."

"Hey, there's still time. He might break my heart and then I'll go mad and convince your girls to go out and destroy a few men, just for a taste of justice. Anyway, none of that matters. It's over in thirty days."

"What if you don't want it to be over in thirty days?"

"Things are a little more complicated than that."

"What do you think he wants?"

"To sample more of this sweet, sweet ass," Xeni replied.

"Well obviously, but I have a hard time believing he's not half in love with you already. Do you have any more pictures of him? I can't really see his face too well."

"Yeah, hold on." Xeni sent Sloan the picture of them with clasped hands high in the air, husband and wife.

"Girl," Sloan said.

"What?"

"Are you sure you just met this guy? You two look so happy."

"I mean, we were having fun, but that was mostly chaotic energy manifesting itself as joy."

"Uh huh, sure. So, when do I get to meet him?"

"Never?"

"Nah. No way. You're not hiding a whole ass husband from me."

"No, I'm hiding a whole ass husband from everyone. You're the first person I've told," Xeni confessed.

"Wait. You haven't told your parents? You haven't told your mom?"

"Nope."

"You know Joyce is going to flip out, right?" Sloan laughed. She'd hung out with Xeni's mom a handful of times and heard dozens of stories of her day-to-day antics. She knew the headache Xeni was in for if and when she found out that Xeni tied the knot without even so much as a phone call. *If* being the key word. She knew she should tell her parents. She should have told them as soon as it happened, but then she'd have to tell them everything and that wasn't an option at the moment.

Besides, Xeni was owed her own secrets for a while. Thirty years should about cover it.

"She's going to flip out, but I'm going to worry about that when I get home."

"That's true. How's the packing going?"

"It's not. My mom wanted me to look for something for her. I moved some stuff around, but I haven't actually moved anything yet. Had to get married for the money first." Just then, Xeni heard Mason moving around inside the house. She stayed put, though. He was probably looking for the bathroom.

"Don't say that. He's in love with you. Pictures like that don't lie." Xeni knew Sloan was only kinda joking. Sloan was a hopeless romantic, an optimistic dreamer, whereas Xeni was a realist. Who believed in witchcraft? It didn't have to make a lick of sense to be the truth.

"He is definitely not in love with me and even if he were, it wouldn't change anything. This isn't a romcom. If anything, it's some sort of sick joke at my expense. You understand that after I dig through all my favorite aunt's possessions and decide what to do with her houses, I then have to fly back to L.A. and explain to my family why this woman left me a literal fortune?"

"Well, at least you have money to hire someone to come help you pack."

"That is true." Xeni heard the porch door open. She looked over as a shirtless, sleepy Mason stepped outside, rubbing his eyes. "Sloan, hold on one sec. Hey."

"Everything alright?"

"Yeah, just talking to my friend. I'm bragging about suddenly having a husband."

"Don't tell her how good looking I am. I don't want to make her jealous."

"Too late. She's seen photos."

Mason sighed and hung his head. "I don't know if I can handle two women at once, love."

"I'll be in in a sec."

"Okay. Take all the time you need. I'm going to see about that ice cream."

Mason slipped back inside and Xeni was glad no one else was around to witness the dopey grin on her face.

"Hey, sorry."

"Was that him?!" Sloan practically screeched.

"Yeah."

"That accent. I thought the Southie thing Rafe has going was hot. Phew."

"You just had a baby. Please relax."

"Sorry," Sloan laughed.

"I should go. You get back to your man and said baby."

"Okay. Call me anytime. It's just me and the boys this

weekend. Addison and Avery are at Disneyland with Monica and Joe."

"I will. Enjoy your kinda quiet house."

"Oh, we already are." That was code for "we just finished fucking and we're gonna fuck again." They said their good-byes, then Xeni stood to go inside. She looked out at the night sky. It was clear, no moon.

She found Mason in the kitchen where he held out a spoonful of cinnamon swirl for her to taste. After they finished half the pint, she took him to the room she'd dubbed guest room B where she'd already made herself comfortable. While she wrapped her hair, he climbed under the covers of the queen sized bed that barely provided enough room for his large frame. When she joined him, he curved his body around her, tucking his knees in tight behind her legs. It was a perfectly tight squeeze and in that position they both fit on the bed just fine.

An odd but welcome sense of clarity had come over Xeni some time during the night. She'd slept like shit 'cause, while cramming into the bed was romantic as hell, Mason actually needed all the room he could get. Xeni ended up sleeping half on top of him and woke up with the worst pain in her lower back, but as she made her way to the bathroom, she realized some of the numbness that had been weighing her down had finally lifted. She didn't have it all sorted out. For that day, though, she had a plan.

She showered and when she came back to the guest room, still wrapped in her towel, Mason was awake, sitting on the edge of the bed.

"Ooooh, Christ, I slept like the dead."

"That makes one of us," Xeni said, smiling a bit.

"We need to move our sleepovers to a bigger bed."

"Agreed. Do you have plans for today?"

"I told Silas I'd watch Princess P tonight, but my day's clear until then. What's on your schedule?"

"I'm going to start packing up this house. Like, actually do it. Even if I don't sell it, I want to get all my aunt's things packed up. I'll junk stuff that needs junking and ship stuff I want or think my mom or my aunts might want back to L.A.." Just saying it out loud made her feel better. She had a plan.

"Happy to lend a hand if you like."

"I would like, thank you. And then maybe if you want, I can come watch Palila with you."

Mason sat up straight and Xeni watched as a little smile tilted up the corner of his mustache.

"What? I don't have to come if you don't want me to."

"Of course I do. I'm just pleased and a little bit shocked by your request. It's not every day my wife asks if she can spend more time with me."

"I think we need to get this out of the way. I like you. I like you a lot. I like your energy and I like your big ass hands. Maybe after we get divorced, I might fly back out here and ask you on a date. Maybe."

Mason came across the room and Xeni suddenly remembered how naked she was under the towel. Mason pulled her into his arms, but instead of kissing her, he leaned over and pressed his lips to her neck. She let out a noise like a frightened peacock when the kiss turned into a tickling raspberry. She squealed, trying to get away from him, but he just held her closer, blowing bursts of air up and down her shoulder until she was doubling over from laughter.

He let her go and set his expression to neutral, like his own face wasn't bright red from their playful struggle.

"You have boxes?" he asked, running his fingers through his hair.

"No, I need boxes."

"You get dressed. I'll run back to my place and change. I'll grab us breakfast and coffee, and you head over to Home Depot and get the boxes. It's right near the Target."

Xeni remembered seeing the big home improvement store on her way to meet Liz. For some reason, though, she didn't think this plan of attack was the best use of their time.

"Or we could just go together. Seems silly to take two cars," Xeni said. So chill. So cool. Not clingy at all. She had no business interacting with other humans.

"Okay, new plan. I find my pants. You put on shoes. No need for pants, Just wear that towel. We swing by my place so I can shower and change, and then we get our day started."

"Let's do it." Xeni started for her suitcase, but Mason's fingers lightly touching her forearm stopped her in her tracks. She looked up at him just as he swept her up in his arms and kissed her senseless. She didn't realize he actually lifted off the floor until her toes touched back down on the hardwood. Another light brush of his lips against hers and then he released her from his grasp.

"Good morning," Mason said quietly before leaving her alone in the guest room with a molten heat building between her legs.

She was still trembling a bit when she climbed in the passenger seat of his oversized SUV. She hadn't planned on spending the whole day soaking wet, but if he kept kissing her like that, she didn't have much of a choice.

"So, last night," Mason said as they pulled back on to the main road. Her aunt really lived in the middle of fucking nowhere. They passed a large wooded area and then an open field before the crumbling stone wall that surrounded her closest neighbor's property. It was the shit horror movies were made of. Xeni shook off the thought of herself running through the woods, trying to get help, and turned to Mason.

"Which part? A lot happened last night." Like how I cried on you just as you started having fun with my tits, she almost added.

"You're looking for more trust and freedom with your intimacy."

"Yes," she said, letting out a reluctant breath. She usually confessed her feelings on her own terms, like blurting them out randomly, but she felt like she could talk to Mason. Damn this whole vulnerability thing. "I—with my ex, there was sex, but I always felt like I was having sex with myself."

"Elaborate please."

"I don't know if he was bad, so much as he was just uninformed. Or lazy—actually no. He was bad." Xeni thought of the times she'd tried to explain to Patrick what her body wanted and how he would just ignore her and do whatever he could to get off. "I've had a couple flings here and there, but that became too much work and then I just didn't feel like going through with emotionless hook ups."

"And with Daryl, things will be more routine."

Xeni laughed, "Exactly. I don't know what I want or like beyond the standard because I've never been with anyone that I feel like I could explore those things with. I want to feel comfortable enough to try some real freaky shit with a partner or just spend all day laying around, making out. I want to actually enjoy myself and not feel like sex is something I'm *supposed* to do."

"That sounds more than reasonable to me."

"What about you?"

"When I look forward to the future, I think of my neighbor Darlene. She's a widow, who's vowed never to remarry. I've been married once, of course, to a beautiful woman from California, but after she left me, I couldn't bear to love again," Mason said.

"Mmmhmm."

"Darlene and I strike a deal. We meet every Tuesday and take turns doing each other up the bum."

"I like that. Peak equality." Xeni watched the side of Mason's face. She waited for at least a trace of a smile to appear, but when it didn't after a few seconds, she realized she wasn't the only person in the car who hadn't exactly been sexually satisfied over the years.

"Listen, I've never pegged a guy before, but if you're willing to teach, I'm willing to learn."

Mason was quiet for a few more seconds before he said, "I don't think they have what we need at Home Depot."

Xeni pulled out her phone and went to a website that might have equipment that was more Mason's speed.

14

By the time Xeni ordered everything they needed, she was very much into the idea of pegging Mason. He made a simple "good morning" sensual as fuck. She was sure he could handle giving her a few pointers. The more she thought about it, the more the idea turned her on. When they pulled into Mason's parking space behind the cafe, she couldn't help but wonder how much packing they would actually get done.

All of it, the responsible part of her brain said. Right. Adult now. Have reward sex later. They hopped out of his car, then Mason nodded toward the wooden steps that led up to his apartment.

"Do you want to come up or hang out down here while I get ready?" he asked.

"I'll wait down here," Xeni replied. Her voice did that weird squeaky thing. Being in close range of a naked Mason wasn't the best idea at the moment. He definitely noticed, but he just smirked a bit instead of giving her a hard time.

"The cannery is open. You should say hi to Maya and Ginny. Try some of the samples."

"Oh, good idea." She could ply her mom with regional honeys and jams while she explained that, even though she had gotten married without telling her parents, they still weren't even for a lifetime of secrets. Mason gave her hand a little squeeze, then bounded up the stairs, two at a time. Xeni walked around to the front entrance and noticed the red dog and the pit bull that were napping under a nearby tree. She remembered what Liz had said about the dogs following her everywhere. She was probably inside.

The bell above the door rang out when she stepped into the cannery.

"Welcome," she heard a voice call out. She stepped around a rack of postcards and spotted Ginny behind the cash register. "Oh, it's you." Ginny leaned against the counter and flashed her a knowing smile. "Xeni, hello."

"Oh god. Here we go."

"Babe!" Ginny yelled. "Get out here." A big swinging door behind the counter flew open and out popped Maya sporting a green McInroy Farm apron.

"What—oh, hello."

Xeni rolled her eyes. "Go ahead."

"Did you happen to bring our sweet Mason home this morning?" Maya asked.

"I did. He's upstairs right now."

"You know, when he told me you guys were getting fake married for real, I thought it was just a legal formality and then yesterday I saw a certain someone had never left the property."

"I was too tipsy to drive." Which was a complete lie. She'd spent most of the night drinking the lemon-berry punch Liz had bought for the reception. The two beers she'd had over the course of the night weren't enough to get her close to tipsy, but they didn't need to know that.

"Mmmhmm," Maya went on. "And then imagine my surprise when I called our darling Mason to see if you guys wanted to join us for game night and his response was a measly. 'Can't Come. Busy'." The air quotes she used really added to the drama of it all.

"I don't know what you're talking about," Xeni replied. She made her denial all the more convincing with a casual shrug of her shoulder. "I needed some work done over at my aunt's house. You know, light plumbing, some electrical. He offered to help." All night.

"Yeah, I bet he was over there checking the pipes," Maya said under her breath.

"I'm just saying, if you two are going to be sleeping together, you can at least give us the juicy details. We might both be super gay, but we're here for the gossip," Ginny said.

"Seriously. It's all been very platonic. Very boring."

"Whatever, Xeni. Just admit you are participating in ho behavior. I'm not judging. I'm here for it," Maya said. She leaned over the counter and held up her hand to give her a high five. Xeni rolled her eyes, but slapped her palm anyway.

"Is it ho behavior if we're married?" she asked.

"I knew it!" Ginny said. "They're doing it."

Xeni looked up as the door to the kitchen pushed open again. Liz backed in, carrying a plate of biscuits. "Okay, I'm done. This kid keeps kick—oh. Hello, Xeni." She set down the pastries and shot Xeni the same knowing smile.

"Come on. Let me have it," Xeni replied.

"Oh no. If you've been here for more than four seconds I know these two have already tried to climb all up in your business. I mean, we all want to know if you and Mason are sleeping together. Aside from that, how are you?"

"I'm okay. Better, thank you." She felt a bit of relief just saying the words out loud. There were still all kinds of emotions shoved below the surface, but she was starting to feel more like herself. "We're gonna start packing up the house today."

"If you need help hauling boxes tomorrow, let me know," Liz said. "Silas can come over and help. He's good at the heavy lifting."

"I'll let you guys know, thanks. I actually wanted to grab some jam and honey for my mom."

"Oh please, step over to our tasting bar," Ginny said as she motioned to the end of the counter with a flourish. They'd arranged a rather large assortment of items to taste. Xeni didn't know where to start.

"Try the lavender honey," Ginny suggested. "Or the Family Jam. Those are our best sellers." She uncapped a cute little jar, then swirled a little wooden tasting stick in the thick dark red jam and handed it to Xeni. It was like a berry explosion on her tongue.

"Oh man, that's good."

"And try this." Ginny moved further down the bar and dipped a fresh stick in one of the dozens of jars of honey.

The lavender flavor was downright sensual. "Jesus. Is everyone in this place a culinary master?"

Suddenly the air in the cannery grew still. Xeni took a step back as Liz, Ginny and Maya all converged on the edge of the counter.

"Did Mason cook for you?" Liz asked slowly.

"Yes…"

Maya threw her hands in the air and turned to face the wall. "Wow."

"What? Did he poison me?"

"Mason doesn't just cook for anyone," Liz replied.

"More like Mason hates cooking with the fire of ten thousand suns," Ginny said.

Maya pointed toward the wall the cannery shared with the cafe. "If he isn't cooking in that kitchen, he's not cooking," she said, mocking his accent. Xeni tried not to snort and failed.

"Maybe one of you should have married him first."

"Shit, if I knew he was cooking, I would have asked him to join our throuple," Maya said. "But, for real. He hates cooking. A lot."

"So, why is he running the cafe?"

The bell over the cannery door rang out and in walked Mason. He smiled at Xeni and then immediately his expression dropped.

"Have they convinced you to join their coven?" he asked.

"No, but the fact that you cooked for me seems to be a big deal."

"What did he make?" Maya asked.

"A delightful seafood alfredo," Mason said, glaring back at her.

"Wow, Mason. Wow," Ginny said. "I am, like, seriously wounded."

"None of you have the right to question what goes on in my marriage."

"Oh, good lord," Liz groaned. "We've created a monster."

"So, when are you making your move here official, Xeni? If he's letting you taste the goods, this is forever shit right here," Maya said, motioning between them.

"I didn't say a word about tasting any of your goods," she made very clear to Mason before she turned back to the mischievous expression on Maya's face. "And no, as much as I'd love for this to be the location for a full on mid-life crisis, I have to get back to L.A.."

"That's a shame. I was hoping you could slip us some leftovers."

"I don't know what's happening here, but I don't want to be in the middle of it," Xeni laughed nervously.

"Nothing is happening here. Silas pays me to cook in the cafe. He pays these two to run the cannery and—" he stopped himself before he got to Liz.

"And he what?" Liz said, putting her hands on her pregnant belly.

"Anyway. Are you ready to go?" Mason asked Xeni before he got himself into some real trouble.

"Yeah. Can I come back later for the honey and some jam? I want to take more time to look around."

"Of course," Ginny said. "We're open seven days a week."

"Okay, great. I'll make sure to stock up before I go."

"The Mrs. is going join me tonight to look after Princess P, if that's okay," Mason asked Liz.

"Oh, sure. She'll love that."

"Wait," Ginny asked. "What happened to your rings?"

"Saints, woman! Xeni can we please go?" Mason pleaded.

"Sure. Bye ladies." Xeni grabbed Mason's hand and pulled him to safety outside the cannery.

"Do I want to know what that was all about?" Xeni asked when they got in the car.

"They just like to give me a hard go because I never cook for them. I spend most of my life behind a stove. I'm not gonna do it for fun or for free," Mason said as they pulled out of the farm. "But for you, love, I'd do anything."

Xeni wasn't sure how to take this bit of information. She was flattered, but she didn't want Mason to cook for her if it was something he hated.

"You don't have to cook for me anymore. I can cook for myself and I'm sure there's some interesting local restaurants I can try out while I'm here."

"Whatever you like."

"Are you okay?" She thought everything was all jokes back in the cannery, but a cloud seemed to have settled over Mason.

"Just an email from home."

"Oh."

"It'll be fine. I just need a few minutes. Thank you for asking if I'm alright."

"You're welcome. Take all the time you need." Xeni settled into the quiet and watched the scenery as they drove back into town.

When they reached Dunkin' Donuts, Mason felt like he'd done enough sulking. He knew his mum meant well, but her periodic requests that he try to make things right with his father were never welcome. She knew better than anyone the way his father treated him. He understood that she wanted peace between them, but now, especially after he was able to unburden himself to Xeni, he knew he didn't want to go back to what was waiting for him in Edinburgh. He deserved better.

He put his car in park and took a moment to choose his

next words wisely. Xeni was being very patient with him and he didn't want his mood to ruin their day.

He looked over and she was looking back at him, her fingertips worrying her bottom lip. Mason held out his hand, palm up. Xeni looked down, considering his offering.

"You want another twenty?" she teased, but that didn't stop her from lacing her free hand with his. He lifted it to his lips and pressed a kiss to the back of her palm. "I told my friend Sloan about you last night."

"How'd that go?"

"Good. She thinks ya cute." She flashed him an adorable smile and he wondered what the fine would be if they were arrested for getting down in front of a Dunkin' Donuts at ten in the morning. "I think I have to tell my other friends soon. That's a hell of a secret to drop on just one person in the clique. All of your friends know and you see how badly they're behaving."

"I'll take it as a compliment if you want to brag to your friends about me."

"I'll consider it. You cool off a little?"

"I did. Being around you makes it easy."

"Flatterer."

"Do you want to get real rings?" he asked, surprising himself a little.

"Oh, I—"

"Think about it while we get some breakfast."

"Okay." They went inside and grabbed their coffee and breakfast sandwiches, then headed over to the Home Depot to grab as many boxes as Mason could shove in the trunk. When they got back to Ms. Sable's house, Xeni announced her plan of attack.

"I'm thinking about the most important rooms to a

prospective buyer, so the master bedroom, the kitchen, the bathrooms and then I want to just see what of her personal items, like personal personal stuff, is just laying around the house."

The place was very clean, but even Mason noticed notes for doctors appointments Ms. Sable had posted on the fridge. "We'll go room to room together?"

"Yeah."

"Great. Let's do it."

"One more thing."

"Sure," Mason said.

"We had a real wedding. We had a real wedding night. If you know what I'm saying. Ahehehe."

"I do," Mason chuckled.

"Why not get real wedding rings? A little something to remember this all by."

"Do you know your ring size?" he asked.

"No. Do you?"

"Size huge. Monday after I finish at the cafe, would you like to join me down at Ghent St. Jewelers? We'll get sized up."

"Love it. There's one more thing I need from you," Xeni said.

"What's that?"

"A kiss."

Mason set down the flattened boxes and scooped Xeni up. The moment their lips touched, he realized just how much anger and tension he was still holding onto, because as she wrapped her arms tighter around his shoulders, the stress, the pain that was trying to resurface, drained away.

Asking Mason for help was the smart thing to do. For one, there was just too much stuff, at least fifteen years' worth of accumulated crap. They worked all day, only taking a quick break to finish off the leftover Alfredo for lunch. Around five, they decided to call it quits. Together they were able to pack up the master bedroom, clear all of her aunt's personal items out of the bathrooms and start on the office.

Xeni gave herself permission to feel how she was going to feel. Laying her aunt to rest twice was hard, but that was before she knew the truth. She'd never been saying goodbye to her aunt. She had said goodbye to her mother. She wasn't angry anymore. All she could feel was a heavy sadness. It felt like it was pressing down on her forehead, causing all her muscles to tense. The physical act of folding Sable's clothes, sorting through her little knickknacks, at times felt like more than she could handle.

A small plastic bag with two Christmas ornaments made out of yarn. Mardi Gras beads. Six pairs of readers. An unopened pack of Dr. Scholl's gel inserts. Cotton swabs. Programs for the eight a.m. prayer service at St. Michael's. A canister of Chock Full O' Nuts coffee, now brimming with loose change.

Xeni could only think of all the moments she'd missed. She'd had her own moments with her mom and Dante. Good moments. But as she and Mason moved through the house, she wished her mom had let her spend more time with Sable. She understood—well, she was trying to understand—the complicated decision Sable had made to give her up and the choice her mom made in fighting to keep her, but that didn't stop her from asking the what ifs over and over in her head. After lunch, she decided to focus on packing, on the items themselves. She gave herself permission to keep as many of

Sable's things as she wanted for herself. So far, her own personal box contained two photo albums, an amazing silk shawl and a button that said Spinsters for Obama.

Mason was the perfect partner to help her take on this painful endeavor. He let her work in silence when she clearly had no emotional energy for words. He offered to change their working music to something more upbeat and bizarre when the nineties hits station they were streaming took Xeni back to a particular time and place in her memory that she didn't want to visit at the moment.

He sat with her on the bedroom floor when she broke down again, seemingly out of nowhere. It was a little jade figurine of a rabbit that set her off. Where had Sable gotten it? Was it a gift? Were rabbits her favorite animal? Mason draped an arm around her as the tears silently fell and in that moment, Xeni realized she had to forgive her mother and maybe go one step further and make the effort to get to know her. She knew next to nothing about her birth father and Sable had been a mythical being in her eyes. Now they were both gone. Xeni didn't want to look back and wonder simple things about her mom or Dante.

When they finished for the day, they stacked all the full boxes in the dining room. The progress they'd made brought on a sense of morbid satisfaction. She would get through this.

15

Another shower was in order after all the moving and lifting. Mason went back to his place to change and their plan was to meet up and head over to Liz and Silas's house, but when she got out of the shower there was a text from her new husband.

Babysitting services no longer needed.
Silas asked for a night in.
Still want to see me?

He added a gif of a little kid with his fingers crossed, begging please.

Yes, I still want to see you.
Can I also request a night in?
With sexy times of course.
I'm too tired to people.

Xeni really liked Mason's friends, but she'd used up all her smiles that morning chatting with the girls. She knew that if they went out, they'd likely run into more people Mason knew and she just didn't have the energy for more introductions or explanations.

We can absolutely stay in.
Your place or mine?

A few hours wasn't enough time to have one of the guest room beds replaced and even though Sable had a pretty big bed in her master bedroom, it would take more than new sheets for Xeni to feel comfortable having sex up there. Especially the kind of freaky sex she hoped she and Mason would get into. There was only one option that would guarantee maximum comfort.

Your place.

7pm. Dress for a night outdoors.
I'll take care of the mosquitoes.

Xeni sent back the best fist pump gif she could find.

At seven on the dot, she pulled into a parking space behind the cannery. The farm was closed, but she could still see a few people buzzing around closing up the place for the night. Just as she hopped out of the drivers' seat, Mason came around the side of the cafe.

"Evening, love."

"Hello." Xeni went with the feeling that was carrying her feet forward and walked right into his arms. It shouldn't have been so easy, so natural for her to kiss him on sight, but she couldn't help herself. She stood up on her tiptoes and pressed her lips to his. His lips were so soft and warm, so welcoming, she wondered for a moment if they could skip dinner and get right to the fucking.

Of course her stomach chose that exact moment to let out the craziest growl.

"A wee famished, are we?" Mason laughed.

"I'm starving."

"Well, follow me right this way." He took her hand and led her out to the cafe's patio. All the tables and most of the chairs were stacked neatly to the side. In the center of the patio, there were two tables and two chairs. One table was set for two with a large citronella candle at the center. The other table was filled with what had to be no less than twenty Chinese takeout containers. There were also a few buckets of ice loaded down with beer, champagne and bottled water. Mason had thought of everything.

"Well, this is romantic as fuck," she smiled up at her date for the evening and gave his hand a light squeeze.

"I jumped the hedge a bit and put in the order without asking what you wanted. Then I panicked and basically ordered everything on their menu. Whatever you don't want, I'll eat."

"Sounds good."

"You might not remember, but Emma Chen, one of the truant teens who showed up to the memorial?"

"Yeah," Xeni laughed. Sable really had an interesting assortment of friends.

"Well, this is from her mom's restaurant downtown, Szechuan Garden."

"Shit, maybe we should have gone there to dine in tonight. If she was friends with Sable, I want to at least say hello."

"Monday. It's across from the jewelers."

"Perfect. Let's do it."

"Please have a seat." Mason pulled out one of the patio chairs for her.

"Thank you."

"And what will the lady be drinking this evening?"

"That champagne looks good. Let's go with that."

"I think I'll join you."

Xeni shook her head and smiled at Mason's over-the-top behavior. She didn't hate it one bit. He pulled his seat closer to her so their legs were touching under the table, then lifted his glass.

"A toast if you will."

"I'm always down for a toast."

"To my wife—"

"You like saying that, don't you?"

"I only get to say it for twenty-six and a half more days. I'm running it into the ground."

"Fair enough. To me," Xeni said, raising her glass.

"To you and the strength and the vulnerability you've showed me the last few days. Just met and you're already making me want to be a better man."

"Okay, you're gonna make me cry again."

"No! Don't cry. Just drink." Mason rushed to clink their glasses together, then tossed back the champagne. Xeni took a smaller sip, appreciating his enthusiasm.

"So, tell me more about you?" he asked as he handed her the shrimp fried rice.

"Let's see. I'm cute and an amazing dresser, but you already know that. What else do you want to know?"

"What do you do with your free time when you're not involved in an elaborate marriage plot?"

"I mean, I'm always involved in an elaborate marriage plot. You're my fourth husband this month."

"That must be exhausting."

"No, I don't know. I hang out with my friends. I spend time with my folks. See my cousins when I can. I'm kinda boring. I watch a lot of T.V.. I'm quite the crafter, actually."

"Are you now?"

"I am. A little crochet, a little bit of cross-stitch, some knitting when I have the patience for it. One summer, my mom made me and my friends pick an activity so we wouldn't just be roaming the streets of L.A. and I picked this crafting camp down at our church. I really got into it. Here." Xeni pulled up her phone and showed Mason the picture of the blanket she'd made for baby Rowan. "I made this for my friend Sloan's baby."

Mason took her phone so he could examine the picture more closely. "That's excellent work."

"Thank you. Yeah, I just kinda craft and chill. I wish there was more to tell you, but that's it."

"You have any good T.V. recommendations? I've been stuck in a bit of a documentary rut."

"Oh, uh... I mean, I mostly watch reality shows. It's easy to zone out and tune back in when the drama kicks up."

"Okay," Mason chuckled. 'What are you watching?"

"Waiting patiently for a new season of the Great British Baking Show."

"You and Liz both. She is obsessed with that show and the French version."

"The French version is amazing. Let's see. My friends and I get together every Monday to watch a different reality dating show. Have you seen *A Match Made in Paradise?*"

"Only a few episodes, but I know it's very popular back home."

"We're watching the Australian version now while we wait for the American version of *Prince Charming* to come back."

"So you have a whole system?"

Xeni picked up her phone and pulled up a picture of her with Joanna, Shae, Keira, Meegan, Sarah, Erica and Sloan piled on Keira's sectional. Keira's husband, Daniel, had taken the photo and immediately escaped to a quieter part of the house.

"Here. Me and the girls."

"I have a hard time believing this group doesn't get up to its fair share of trouble."

"No. We are all pretty boring. Well, Sloan," she pointed to her pint-sized friend sitting on Meegan's lap, "she's a freaking heart surgeon. And Shae," she pointed to the sweet-faced, plus-sized beauty to her right, "she owns the best cupcake spot in the city. I should put her in touch with Liz, see if she's willing to share that apple cake recipe."

"Not a bad idea."

"Otherwise, I'm gonna have to ask Liz to ship cake to me like once a month. Or twice."

"She'd be happy to."

"Anyway. Sarah and Meegan teach with me at Whippoorwill. Erica's an adjunct professor at Cal State Dominguez Hills and Keira's a personal trainer." She pulled up another picture of the whole gang at Sloan and Rafe's wedding.

"I'm picturing a scenario where you're all secretly spies with your own areas of expertise."

"That would be fun and maybe a little bit porny. Actually,

Keira and her husband run a BDSM club and Meegan's a member."

"Really?"

"But, that's not me," Xeni laughed. "I already told you I'm just really hot, well dressed and boring. I go to work and I craft. And watch crappy television."

"I go to work and play music," Mason replied. "I don't think we're required to do more than keep ourselves employed and have one law-abiding hobby. So, tell me about this club."

"I barely know anything about it. There are rules. I'm guessing levels of nudity. Why? You want to go?"

"No. I've just had an erection since you arrived and I'm trying to make matters worse."

Xeni almost choked on her spring roll. She took a sip of champagne and did her best to clear her throat. "You want me to make you harder? While we eat?"

"Uncomfortably so," he said. Xeni knew he was just teasing, but she wanted to be sure. She looked over her shoulder to see if they had an audience. There was still one young man cleaning the cafe, but he was so intent on his work that Xeni figured they were in the clear. She wiped her hand with her napkin, then slid her fingers across his broad thigh. A tingling heat spread out of her own skin as his thigh muscles jumped at the contact. She moved her hand higher until she brushed against the thick bulge pressing against the seam of his khaki shorts.

Mason licked his lips and set down his fork. He looked over at her as he sat back and spread his legs further apart. Xeni rubbed a little higher, searching for the head of his cock through the fabric. When she found it, she teased the tip with a little pressure from her thumb.

"That's quite the big problem you have there."

"Mmmhmm."

"What are you thinking about right now?" Xeni asked.

"Would you like the romantic version or the truth?"

Xeni swallowed and tried, but failed, to compose herself. Her pussy throbbed just considering the dirty words he had waiting for her. "The truth."

"I'm thinking about coming on those gorgeous tits of yours. You're the only woman I've ever met that makes t-shirts looks sinful."

Xeni glanced down at her breasts that were now aching to be touched. She wanted Mason's mouth on her nipples. She wanted his rough palms caressing them.

"What else?"

"Finish your dinner and I'll show you."

Xeni withdrew her hand and did her best to focus back on the delicious food in front of her, but after nearly five minutes of silence, she was ready to tear off her own clothes. She watched Mason carefully, every feature of his face, the way he appeared to be restraining himself from shoving handfuls of food in his mouth so they could move this party up to his apartment. There was so much she wanted to do with him, so much that she wanted to do *to* him, but mostly she wanted to see what other tricks he had up his sleeves. All the shocking things he could do to make her wet in ways she'd never been wet before.

When she could say she was honestly full, she set down her fork and sat back. "That was lovely. Thank you. Take your time."

"No." Xeni snorted as Mason stood and started packing up the remaining food. It only made sense for her to lend a hand. They had the patio cleaned up in record time.

"I just need to tell Jimmy we're done out here."

"Okay." She grabbed the box with the leftover beverage bottles and followed him into the kitchen in the back of the cafe. They tucked everything into the corner of the large walk-in fridge. Then she took his hand and let him lead her back out to the main dining area where Jimmy was mopping the floor.

"We're all set out there."

"That was quick," the kid said. He straightened and rested his arm on the top of the mop handle. "Is this the wife?"

"Yes. Xeni, Jimmy Poulos. Jimmy, this is my wife, Xeni. We haven't had time to discuss last names."

"Nice to meet you, Jimmy," Xeni called over her shoulder as Mason pulled her back toward the exit. "Rude much," she laughed as he shooed her up the stairs.

"You want to go back and hang out with Jimmy?"

"No, I don't." She rushed up the steps with Mason on her heels, grateful to find the door already unlocked. They stumbled inside and both started to undress before Mason closed the door all the way. Xeni noticed that he'd tidied up. Not that his place was a sty before, but it seemed more in order. He'd also changed his sheets and made his bed. Not that any of that mattered. She was horny enough to have sex on the carpet that must have been installed sometime in the late eighties. Almost.

Xeni pulled off her shirt as Mason toed out of his sneakers. She undid her bra as he discarded his shorts and boxers in one go, and just as she was about to shimmy out of her leggings, he was completely nude, moving across the room toward her. He turned her around, pulled her against his chest and shoved his hand down the front of her leggings, over her underwear. Her nipples hardened even more as he pinched a puckered tip with his other hand.

"Fuck. Mason," she cried out as his fingers cupped her whole sex. She was still soaking wet, her panties drenched from her arousal, and the motion of his fingers moving up and down made her pussy weep with pleasure. He latched onto the sensitive skin of her neck, sucking and biting as she squirmed in his grasp.

"Inside," she begged. "Inside my underwear. Move your hand."

"Like this?" he asked, pushing her underwear to the side. Xeni sighed at the merciful contact, the feeling of his calloused fingers spreading her labia and her juices, making an even bigger mess. "Or more like this?" He pressed one finger and then another inside her aching cunt and Xeni thought she might pass out.

"Yes," she managed to whimper. "Just like that. Fuck."

Xeni rode his fingers, rocking her hips, soaking up the sensation of his strong hand in the front and his hot thick cock pressing against her back. When she felt the rising pulse of her orgasm threatening to overtake her, she grabbed his wrist and begged him to stop. He froze, then released her. She stepped out of his grasp and backed toward his desk, peeling off her damp leggings and underwear as she went.

"Can I taste you first?" he asked.

"Yes," she moaned.

Mason came over to the desk and dropped to his knees. Even on the floor, his head came up to the middle of her chest. He took a moment to worship her breasts the way she'd been wanting him to all night. Taking them both in his hands, he drew his tongue over her hard nipples, suckling each tip until she was gripping his hair, begging for mercy.

When they had more time, when she wasn't so desperate, she'd ask him to spend all night licking and sucking her tits. Another time.

His hands went to her waist as if to steady them both before he went down on all fours. He looked up at her before he reached out and stroked her leg. Xeni's eyes popped wide at the erotic sight. She'd never had a man prone before her like that. She threaded her fingers through his dark brown curls and tilted his chin up to her throbbing pussy. He pressed closer, pushing his tongue inside her. Xeni sagged back on the desk, doing her best to support herself with her other hand. She was going to come right in his mouth. There was no stopping her this time. He reached up and pinched her clit lightly between his fingers and that was all it took. That and the searching motion of his thick tongue inside her.

Xeni came hard, soaking his parted lips and his mustache.

Her orgasm was still echoing over her skin when he stood and encouraged her to turn around. She did what he wanted, bracing herself with her palm flat on the wood surface. It felt like years had passed in the time it took him to get the condom on when he finally stepped behind her and bent her over with a gentle palm sliding down her back. He cupped her ass and massaged her cheeks apart before he was at her pussy opening, slowly pressing himself inside. Xeni pushed back, taking him all at once. Her mouth fell open at the sound of the throaty groan that echoed over her shoulder.

She pressed her forehead to the cool surface before she turned her head to the side.

"Does that feel good, baby?" she asked. And for the first time, possibly ever, she realized what it meant to want to own a man. To have him craving you in ways neither of you understood.

"You know it does," Mason replied as he pulled out inch by inch before easing back in. Xeni clenched her muscles around him, driving them both crazy as he slid in and out again. "It feels so, so good," he moaned.

They found a perfect rhythm with her meeting his every thrust. She had to wonder if he knew how amazing his cock was. She came again, imagining what it would be like to wrap her lips around it. She wasn't close to done. She wanted to fuck him at least two more times before they called it a night. She wanted to sit on his face again, and the kissing? She wanted so much more of that. But first, she squeezed his thigh, asking him to stop again. He heard her through his own pounding lust and gave her the room she needed to climb off the desk and turn around.

Xeni went to her knees and took the thick length of him in her mouth. She didn't love the flavor of the latex, but it was mixed with her own musk, which spurred her on to take as many inches of him as she could and she wrapped her fingers around the rest. Later, she thought as he leaned forward and gripped the edge of the desk, filling the condom, later she would definitely let him come in her mouth and all over her tits.

"One second, love."

"Oh, sorry." Xeni moved so Mason could adjust his arm. He settled again and pulled her back against his chest. After she'd sucked his life force out through his cock, they'd collapsed on his bed in a naked heap. After they stopped kissing and paused long enough for a quick water break and so Xeni could twist back her hair and pull it back in the silk scarf she slept in, Xeni asked if they could watch *A Match Made In Paradise: Australia*. She'd missed Monday's episode and Mason understood what she wasn't saying. She missed watching the show with her friends. He saw the way her eyes lit up and how she smiled when she showed him the pictures of her girl crew. If she needed a taste of home and friendship, who was he to get in the way? He handed over his laptop and watched her do some illegal shit so they could watch the Australian-based reality competition.

"Okay. What's the point of this show?" Mason asked. Currently, seven couples comprised of sunburned twentysomethings were running around a villa in Fiji trying to take care of a bunch of screaming baby dolls.

"You just have to find love and, basically, the most popular couple wins a hundred thousand dollars."

"You mean I could have gone on a T.V. show instead of marrying you?"

"Har har, shut up."

Mason tried to figure out who was paired with who, but gave up trying and just observed in silence for a few minutes.

"What's your stance on kids?" He probably shouldn't have asked. The answer didn't matter much, as far as their non-existent future was concerned, but it just came out of his mouth.

Xeni sighed and shuffled on to her back. Mason kept his arm draped over her waist. She kept her eyes on the screen. "Not for me, I don't think."

"Another thing we have in common."

She turned and looked at him. "Really?" Her voice sounded hopeful, like that information changed something for her.

"I love kids, don't get me wrong, but after Palila was born, I seriously consider getting a vasectomy."

"Real eye opener, huh?"

"I think the older I get, the less important it seems to me. I'm not hung up on carrying on a family name, which, *I know*, blasphemy, but you have to raise a person. Seems like a lot of pressure."

"I was pregnant before, twice."

"Wait, can we pause this? I want to hear you and the fake babies screaming is a lot to compete with."

"Yeah, sorry." Xeni laughed before she rolled over and

paused the show. Some guy on the screen was in the midst of tossing his fake baby a good twenty feet in the air. "Better?"

"Much. I can actually hear you." Mason couldn't resist pressing a soft kiss to her forehead. Xeni sighed and inched closer.

"So, yeah. I'm sure it's got to be some sort of reproductive abuse when your partner refuses to wear condoms whether you're on the pill or not. Anyway, I miscarried the first time before I figured out what I wanted to do and then terminated the second time."

"Neither sounds fun," Mason replied, gently caressing her forearm. Xeni smiled a little before she looked back up at him.

"I was grown or whatever. It was my senior year of college and I was afraid to tell my mom, but I felt like I had to tell someone, so I told Sable."

"How did she take it?"

"Great. Like always. She was the *cool* aunt. She flew out to L.A. and took me to the clinic and we had a little staycation at her hotel until I felt better."

Mason watched the emotions playing over her face. He wondered what that must have been like for her, the fear, the stress. What must be going through her mind now, knowing that her birth mother had been with her in that moment all along. He thought about everything he'd been though in his early twenties, what it would have been like to have any family members to rely on.

Xeni reached down and toyed with his knuckles before she spoke again. "After she left, I felt—I felt strange. I didn't regret it or anything, but I felt stupid. Like I knew better than to get pregnant in the first place, especially when I knew I wasn't ready."

"Doesn't sound like you got pregnant alone."

"Sure didn't," Xeni said with a mirthless laugh. "But yeah. There was this period of time where my brain couldn't really process it 'cause my ex didn't want to talk about it and no one else really talks about it. Like, way later, I found out a few of my friends had also had abortions, but we still only just kind of acknowledged it. We didn't talk about it. So, I became weirdly obsessed with pregnancy and childbirth."

"Trying to understand it all better?"

"Yes, I think that was it. I think I wanted actually know what would happen if I decided to have a baby 'cause no one really talks about that either. After I watched, like, four hundred home births on YouTube, I was fascinated by childbirth and kinda realized it wasn't for me, but it also kinda made me want to be a doula."

"Oh yeah?"

"Yeah. I wanted to help pregnant people with everything surrounding childbirth. Pregnant people and new parents need more support."

"You never thought of doing that instead of teaching?"

"Well, I can't now. I'm an heiress. I have to spend time designing and constructing my money bin."

"Ahh, Scrooge McDuck. A true Scotsman among ducks."

Xeni looked at him for a moment, her eyes narrowing. "Your energy really fucks me up."

"I'm sorry?"

"It's so easy to talk to you. And it's not just how you react. It's being close to you. Your energy really, like, soothes me."

"I'm glad to be of soothing service," Mason said before he leaned down and kissed Xeni on her beautiful lips. In a little more than a week, she'd be out of his life and they'd serve out the rest of their marriage requirement with three thousand miles between them. As she rolled toward him and slid her tongue against his, he wondered if the distance would be enough to help him forget that he was falling in love with her.

———

"I don't want to sweat anymore!" Xeni cried out. They were almost done packing up Sable's things, but there was no air conditioning in the office. Mason had found a box fan to help with the situation and they'd opened the back door and windows to get a cross breeze, but it barely put a dent in the stifling heat of that particular room.

"Let's take a break," he said. "Come."

"Ugh," Xeni whined as she followed him into the kitchen. It was much cooler in there. Too bad they'd already put away all of Sable's personal things from that part of the house and that Sable hadn't sprung for central AC. They both grabbed something to drink and while Xeni was going back for a refill, Mason wandered into the living room. Xeni followed and watched him as he sat down at the piano.

"You never played for me the other night."

"Well," he effortlessly tapped out a short tune on the keyboard. "Let's remedy that right now."

Xeni leaned against the wall as he started to play in earnest. The slow, sweet melody sounded familiar, but Xeni couldn't place it. She came from an intensely musical family and while she could carry a tune, she couldn't imagine having such skill on so many different instruments. As she watched him, his large frame so perfectly at ease behind the baby grand, her traitorous brain couldn't help but wonder what it would be like to come home to this every day. To have a man by her side every day to play her beautiful love songs.

When he finished, he turned around on the bench and looked back at her, his expression blank. "You know what this thing needs?" He tapped the edge of the piano.

"What's that?" For some reason, Xeni's tear ducts picked that exact moment to rev things up. Luckily she was able to use pure willpower to hold them back.

"A tip jar. That was amazing."

Xeni laughed and one stupid tear escaped. She was able to dash it away before Mason saw it roll down her cheek. "You're right. It was phenomenal. What song was that?"

Mason crossed the room and put his arm around her shoulders. They were both still so hot and sticky, but she didn't mind the close contact. Not from him. "It's a classic called 'My Romance.' Originally recorded in 1935? I think. My mom loves the James Taylor version. I prefer Doris Day's."

"Never heard it, but I like the way it sounds on the piano."

"You should give it a listen sometime. I think you might like it. Come on. Let's get back to it."

They walked back into the oppressive heat of the office and continued their torturous work. Xeni considered doing a little research to see if there as a quality spa anywhere in ole Kinderack country. She'd need a massage and some full body exfoliation when they were done.

"Books?" Mason asked. He'd been busy packing away all the little collectables Sable had on her shelves.

"Let's just leave those. Makes the house look lived in if we decide to sell it."

"We?"

"I can't handle all this by myself. My mom is a lot, but

when she listens, she does listen. I want to talk to her and my step-dad before I make any huge decisions. Besides, one of my eight hundred cousins might want to stay here. Anyway, it doesn't seem right to just up and sell the place without talking to my family first."

"Reducing the opportunity for another family feud sounds like a great idea. The record plaques?" He nodded toward the opposite wall. Sable's singles "All Yours Now" and "Lover Boy" went gold and platinum respectively in the early eighties.

"Gonna ship those home, but leave them up for now. I need to get, like, a metric ton of bubble wrap from the store tomorrow."

"Great."

Xeni watched Mason for a moment as he opened a small chest of drawers near the window. He pulled out a handful of office supplies and added them to the random items box. She realized then that this was gonna take a lot longer if she spent the afternoon staring at him. She opened the second drawer of Sable's desk and started looking through a stack of electric bills. On each one, Sable had handwritten the date it had been paid. Xeni shook her head, thinking about how her ridiculously rich aunt had gone to her grave resisting the ease of autopay. Those were going in the shred pile.

"Uhhh, love?" Mason suddenly said.

"Yes, dear." Xeni looked up and saw he was holding one of the blue tins of Royal Dansk cookies. "What's up?"

Mason crossed the room and handed her the tin. It was filled with jewelry. She looked up at him, her mouth hanging open. "You fucking kidding me?"

He shrugged. "Better than under her mattress?"

"She is so lucky she was never robbed." Xeni carried the

tin back into the kitchen, carefully set out each piece on the kitchen island and photographed them. Then she sent the pictures to her mom.

Is this what you were looking for?

She used it as an excuse to stand in the cool kitchen and chug more water. Finally her mom responded.

Yes!

Okay great.
I'll figure out how to get them home.

Thank you, baby.
Your aunts will be thrilled.

"All good?" Mason asked as he went over to the kitchen sink and started washing his hands.

"Yes. I'm handing these off to my mom. She and her sisters can fight over them."

Mason toweled off, then glanced at his watch. "I hate to leave you like this, but I have a standing engagement."

"You seeing another bitch behind my back? Sorry, that was aggressive."

"No, love. I would never." He leaned over the kitchen island and pressed his lips to hers. "Every Sunday at sunset, I play bagpipes at the farm. It's become an unofficial tradition. The farm will be closing, but some people stop by or park on the side of the road and just listen."

"Can I come?" Xeni didn't want to miss this.

"Me, miss a chance to show off in front of you? Again? Never."

"Great. Um, I desperately need to bathe. Can I meet you over there?"

"You know what? I'll text Liz. You should go over to their place. I've been told it sounds 'hauntingly beautiful' from their porch. Liz's words."

"Yeah, if she's okay with that. Sure."

Mason leaned over and kissed Xeni on the cheek before he backed out the door.

An hour later, just as the sun was starting to go down, Xeni pulled up in front of Silas and Liz's house. It was quite the scene. Liz sitting on the porch swing in the company of three of the dogs while Silas and Palila were playing in the grass with the rest. A couple of the dogs barked, but this time they managed to restrain themselves from ambushing her car. Xeni hopped out and instantly realized she hadn't brought anything for Liz. She made a mental note to make up for it before she left town.

"Just in time for the show," Liz said from the porch.

"Hi Xeni," Silas said in his flat monotone way, which she was getting used to. "Say hi to Miss Xeni, Palila."

"Hi Xeni," Palila said before shoving her thumb in her mouth.

"Hello to you both. Thanks for having me over." Xeni climbed the porch stairs and gave Liz a hug. "Sorry I'm the worst guest. Show up last minute empty handed. I should have brought you some non-adult beverages or something."

"Oh, don't worry about it. Come sit. Honeycrisp, move." The dog blocking Xeni's way just rolled on its side and not out of the way. Xeni careful stepped over it and took a seat next to Liz.

"I can't get over this view." The yard seemed to stretch on and on, and beyond the grass, the orchards began. She could see the top of the main barn way off in the distance and she knew that just a few hundred yards beyond that was the cannery and the cafe.

"I fell in love with Silas here," Liz said, gently rubbing her pregnant belly. Xeni looked over at her rugged ass husband.

"Don't blame you one bit."

"I wasn't sure if I wanted to kill him or keep fucking him, but one night we were sitting here and Mason started playing and it all kinda made sense."

"It's not gonna work on me."

"What?" Liz laughed.

"You're not gonna trick me into falling for all this. Your beautiful farm life with a hot buff husband and two-point-five kids and seventeen dogs. Not me, bitch."

Liz laughed even harder. "Girl, I was just taking a walk down memory lane."

"Mmmhmm." Just then, the first notes floated through the air. Xeni could have sworn they were a smooth half mile away, but she could hear the music perfectly. No wonder he suggested she join Liz. After a few seconds, she realized he was playing the same song he'd played for her on the piano. 'My Romance.'

"Oh, he's switching it up a bit tonight?" Liz said.

"Oh yeah?"

"He usually plays hymns, patriotic jams. Ends with Amazing Grace. This is a bit different."

"He played it for me earlier today." Xeni didn't mean for her voice to have such a dreamy touch to it.

"How are things going for you and him? I know it's only been a few days, but you've been spending a lot of time together."

"Good, I guess. This will definitely be a story for my journal or an attention grabbing thread on Twitter."

"And that's all?"

"That's all."

Xeni was grateful that Liz let the conversation die then. In the morning, she'd be back to dealing with complicated family affairs. For now, she just wanted to enjoy the moment. The song came to an end, but not two breaths later he started up another tune. It took Xeni a moment, then she recognized the early seventies love song by Cornelius Brothers & Sister Rose.

"Wow, he's really laying it on thick tonight," Liz teased before she started singing along quietly. "It's too late to turn back now…" Xeni knew the words too. She recited them in her head, reminding herself they meant nothing. Mason wasn't falling in love with her. She wasn't falling in love with him. They were just your average married couple who were growing closer and closer, feeling more and more comfortable opening up to each other. They also couldn't keep their hands off each other, which also meant nothing. Before it ended, her phone started going off in her bag. It was her mom's ringtone.

"That's my mom. I should get that."

"Go ahead."

Xeni pulled out her phone. "Mommy, hold on one sec." She stepped over the dog and made her way back down the porch steps. "Hi," she said when she made her way around the side of the house.

"What is that sound? It's awful"

"Uh. Actually—" For some reason her mom's comment set her on edge, made her feel defensive of Mason and his craft. A voice in the back of Xeni's head told her to shut the fuck up right now, but her poor judgement kept her mouth right on moving. "I have to tell you something and I know you're going to be hot pissed, but I promise I got it under control."

"What did you do? You're not pregnant are you?"

"No, mom. What you're hearing? It's bagpipes. It's my husband actually. He plays the bagpipes."

"What do you mean, your husband?"

"I got married."

"Sable put you up to this, didn't she? She said she was gonna find you a man and look—"

"Mommy, no," Xeni lied. "It just kind of happened. His name is Mason, he works at a farm cafe in the next town over."

"Dante, come in here. Your daughter is on my phone saying she got married to some man who plays the bagpipes?"

"What now?" she heard her dad grumble in the background.

"She got married."

She heard the ambient noise that let her know her mom had put her on speaker. "I thought you went out there to take care of the house," her step-dad said.

"I know it sounds crazy. It was crazy, but he's pretty great."

"This isn't funny, Xendria," her mother said. "I know you're upset with me, but this isn't how—"

"No, mommy. Mommy! None of this happened because I was upset with you. Was it a rushed, spur of the moment thing? Yes, but you have to trust me, okay? He's a good egg."

"Put this good egg on the phone, then."

"I can't. He's halfway across the farm."

"Well, when he's done serenading the sheep or whatever, you go find him and you put his ass on this phone. She got married," her mom grumbled.

"I'll explain everything when I get home."

"Is he coming with you?"

You fool!, her better sense screamed. "We haven't worked all that out yet."

"Oh, so you got married and you don't know if your husband is going to come back to L.A. with you?"

"Mommy. Please. Just trust me."

"Mmm," she grunted.

"You called," Xeni said, scrambling to change the subject. "You needed something?"

"I was just trying to figure out when you were coming home."

"Soon. Next Sunday at the latest." One week. She had one week. "I'll let you know exactly when."

"Okay. We'll get you from the airport."

"Thank you."

"You really got married?"

"Yes."

"Hmm," her mother's grunt was filled with disappointment. "What's he look like?"

"I'll send you pictures."

"I still don't believe you."

"Let me go. I'll call you tomorrow."

"No, you won't. You'll call me back as soon as Matthew's little concert is over."

"Mason, mom."

"Mason. Fine. And he's a musician, too? Lord. I know your aunt's involved in this somehow."

"I'll call you back."

"Fine." Her mom hung up on her. Xeni let out a deep breath and realized she had maybe fifteen minutes to prepare Mason for the most uncomfortable conversation he might have in his whole life.

"Everything okay?" Liz asked when she came back up the porch.

"Yeah. I fucked up and told my parents about me and Mason."

"Eeeyow. How did they take it?"

"As well as any Black mama who realized they missed their only daughter's wedding. She's definitely going to kill me when I get home."

"I met Silas's mom via Facetime and she thought I was using him to get back at his brother."

"Well then."

"But we get along great now!" Liz laughed.

Xeni closed her eyes and tried to focus on the music instead of the colossal mistake she'd just made.

M ason knew he was playing with fire. Doing a whole set of what could only be described as "Please notice that I'm in love with you" ballads was a gamble. He wondered if Xeni had even noticed. He could handle the sting of obliviousness better than flat-out rejection, not that he could escape rejection if it came his way. As he crossed the orchard, he realized he needed to tell her the truth. He was falling for her. Was it full blown love? No, that would be ridiculous, since it had only been a few days.

But in those few days, she'd revealed so much of herself to him. They were in a unique spot and, because of it, he'd seen her at what he imagined was her lowest, coping with unimaginable confusion and pain, and still he didn't want to be anywhere but by her side. He knew he was taking a chance, but there was no point in romantic gestures if he didn't have the words to back them up. He'd tell Xeni how he felt and hopefully she felt the same.

He could see her way off in the distance as he came through the trees, sitting alone on Silas's porch. Well, alone with Hank and Morty. She stood and met him halfway across the yard. Hank joined her, just to see if Mason had something fun in his hands. Mason had planned to tell her how he felt as soon as he laid eyes on her, but when she stopped herself from stepping into his arms, he realized two things were off: her mood and how quickly he'd come to expect affection she didn't owe him. Mason swallowed and immediately told himself it was time to pull back.

"Hello," he said, trying to keep his tone neutral.

"Hi."

Something wasn't right. "Is something the matter?"

"Um. I fucked up."

"How bad?"

"I told my mom we got married." Xeni winced.

"Ah…"

"And she wants to talk to you. My step-dad will probably want to talk to you too. Like, right now."

"I—okay."

"I am so sorry."

Mason took a deep breath and scrubbed his hand across his face. "Okay. How did this happen?"

"She called and she could hear the bagpipes and, I don't know… I panicked. No, I didn't panic. I just said it. Everything has felt awful and this," she motioned between them, "this felt like something good. Temporary, but good."

"I think it is good, but I also thought we weren't telling our parents." They had established pretty clearly that their situational vows were between the two of them, those dwelling in the happy bubble around Kinderack County and its governing authorities, and one of Xeni's friends back home. Telling their parents meant complications upon complications.

195

"I know. I—I don't know. I just know her. If I don't call her, she's gonna keep calling and then she's gonna try and track you down, and if that doesn't work, she's gonna show up. "

There was something else she wasn't saying, but she seemed so tense that he knew pressuring her for a reasonable explanation would only make her more upset.

"Okay. Well, let's call her."

Xeni pulled out her phone, slid her fingers across the screen a few times then handed him the phone. He glanced at the words MAMA EVERLY CALLING...

"What's her name?

"Joyce. She's fine with just Joyce. Again, I cannot stress how sorry I am."

Mason reached out and gave her shoulder a light squeeze, then shot her a little smile. "It's not okay, but we'll get through this."

"Your little husband done with his concert yet?" her mother suddenly said into the phone.

"Ms. Joyce? Hello. It's Mason."

"Oh! So, you do exist? Mason, do you and my daughter want to tell me who the hell you are and why you two decided to get married without giving her family a call?"

Mason glanced over at Xeni and realized there was no painless way out of this. "Let me apologize for that, but I will also admit that Xeni and I both agreed to keep this information from our parents."

"Sounds like a lousy idea, Mason. So, what now? Do you have a job? Where do you live? That's an interesting accent there. Where are you from exactly? Are you *White*?"

"I am White."

"Oh god," Xeni groaned quietly.

"I am also a citizen. My mother's from Cleveland and my father's a Scot. This was not a green card marriage, but I do think we owe you an explanation."

"I would say so. Go ahead. Explain yourself." Mason braced himself to have two members of the Everly family upset with him at once, but he didn't see any other way to handle it . He reached out and took Xeni's hand. She cupped the back of his palm with her other hand, holding on to him like he was the only thing grounding her to safety.

"I have my reasons for keeping things from my parents and I'll happily explain them to you, but I think Xeni was trying to keep you from having another reason to be upset with her Aunt Sable. Your sister left Xeni and me both a sum of money. She left Xeni a much larger sum than she left me, of course, but it was stipulated in her will that we needed to get married in order for either of us to claim our portion."

Joyce grumbled something unintelligible, before she went on. "So, my sister told you two that you had to get married and you just went ahead and did it. I don't see how that stopped my daughter from picking up the phone."

"No, that doesn't excuse our behavior, but I have a feeling Xeni didn't want to give you another reason to be upset with Ms. Sable, especially now. We only have to stay married for thirty days. We've already been transferred the funds. I know telling my parents would cause other issues."

"Well, I don't know what kind of people your parents are Mason, but that's not how we do things in my house. So, you got your money and this is over in thirty days?"

"Yes, ma'am," Mason said. He didn't like the way his chest was starting to hurt.

"I hope the money was worth it."

Mason glanced down at Xeni and took in the worry

playing across her face. "All in, I think Xeni received around twenty-three million dollars in assets—"

"Twenty-three what?!"

"Million. For marrying me. And I don't and won't see a dime of that. It's all hers. I know we went about this the wrong way, but Ms. Sable meant a lot to me and if marrying your daughter meant she could claim her inheritance, I couldn't see how I could say no. I apologize for how we went about it."

"Well—well I think I can understand. That's a lot of money."

"Would you like to talk to your daughter?"

"I—in a minute. You said you won't see a dime of that. What did you get?"

"Ms. Sable left me some money to cover my student loan debt and a bit of money I owed my father. I'm very grateful for it."

"I bet. So, I won't be meeting you then, since is this only temporary?"

"I'd be happy to meet you, if you like," Mason said carefully. The pain in his chest was now joined by a pulsing on the side of his head. His brain was doing all it could to punish him via hindsight. He and Xeni had really fucked up.

"Put my daughter on the phone."

"Yes, ma'am." Mason handed Xeni her phone. "She wants to speak with you."

Xeni pressed her cell up to her ear, then turned and started walking through the grass. Mason went and sat on the steps, his head still throbbing. He knew they both needed the money. Xeni's family probably needed what he knew she would end up sharing with them. Still, they'd been so focused on what they thought they had to do, they didn't stop long enough to think about how they did it. He didn't want to beat himself up for not considering how Xeni's parents would react because he never thought they'd find out. He never thought she'd tell them. He never thought he'd be considering a single 'what if' beyond the thirty days.

"Mommy, I know, but you have to listen to me. Do not tell your sisters about this. Do not tell Anton or Rosia. I want to get you and Daddy squared away first and there's still so much I have to sort out," he heard her say. Suddenly his brain forced him to tune out. What the fuck had he been thinking, on the brink of asking Xeni to think about a real future where she saw the two of them together? He heard her say a tense goodbye to her mother. He looked up as she made her way back through the grass, Hank tight by her side. She was so beautiful, Mason almost reconsidered doing the right thing by letting her walk away. Another deep breath forced its way out of his lungs.

"Thinking about moving up that divorce?" she said with a humorless laugh.

"What did she say?"

"Basically told me I was selfish. Then she told me how much I'd hurt her." Xeni tilted her head back, like she was trying to keep her tears inside her eyes. "But she doesn't seem to be upset with you, so thank you for that."

"I think the truth was the way to go."

"Hmm," was her reply and Mason knew this part of the conversation was over. He'd lost her to the inner workings of her own mind.

"Did you eat?" he asked.

"Not yet. Liz ordered pizza. It's uh—there's plenty inside. I'm not really hungry."

"I might grab a slice or two, but I have to turn in early.

Four-thirty start tomorrow." Regret washed over him as he watched Xeni's expression completely flatten out. He knew she was hearing the unsaid words. Tonight wasn't a good night for them to be together. Tonight wasn't a good night for *them*. Mason wanted to take it back, tell her she was welcome to stay over at his place and sleep in his bed, but he couldn't.

The last few days had finally caught up with him in a wave of exhaustion and clarity. They weren't a couple and even though they'd found layers of comfort in each other, his conversation with her mother had made one thing abundantly clear that they needed to take a more than a few steps back and remember why they'd gotten married in the first place. It had nothing to do with love, no matter what he was feeling.

"Yeah, okay. Um, yeah..." Xeni squeezed by him and grabbed her bag off the porch swing. She hurried back down the stairs, stumbling in the grass as she turned to him. He reached out to catch her, but she stepped out of reach.

"You okay?"

"Yeah, thanks. Sandal just got caught. Can you please tell Silas and Liz I'm very sorry, but I have to go?"

"Of course."

"Thanks."

Before Mason could hug or kiss her, or even shake her hand, she took off, practically sprinting for her car.

Tabitha Chever handed Xeni her card with a smile. She hadn't expected Sable's realtor to be a whole twenty-five years old, but a few minutes after the young White girl with jet black hair showed up, Xeni understood why Sable had decided to work with her. Tabitha knew her shit. She'd come prepared with a thorough list of questions for Xeni and a list of people who could help her with the minor repairs the house still needed. They walked through every room and thankfully Tabitha didn't do too much reminiscing about her own relationship with Sable.

She kept things nice and professional and by the time they'd circled back to the kitchen, Xeni felt better equipped to make an informed decision. They could get a decent little chunk for the house, but now that her financial situation was slightly different, that decent chunk wasn't the first thing on her mind.

"Again, take your time. You have plenty on your plate. Even if you decide to rent it out, I can help you out with that."

"Sounds great. Yeah, I just need to speak to my folks and my mom might want to come out and see the place first."

"Exactly. It's a big decision."

It was just one of the two real estate decisions Xeni had to make. She still had to think about Sable's place on Martha's Vineyard. She walked Tabitha back through the house to the front door and shook her hand one more time.

"You'll hear from me soon, no matter what."

"Great," Tabitha replied as she slipped her bag over her shoulder. "Oh, you have a package."

Xeni looked at the medium-sized box that definitely had her name on the address label. Her confusion only lasted a few seconds. It was the sex toys she and Mason had ordered. She plastered on a smile and glanced back at Tabitha.

"Oh, thanks."

"See ya!"

Xeni scooped up the box and waved at Tabitha as she backed down the driveway. Back inside, she found a knife and sliced open the taped seal. There was a harness, two different dildos, a butt plug, more condoms, two different kinds of lube and a six-pack of Fleet Enema. There was also a huge bag of Skittles. That had nothing to do with their previously scheduled sex acts, Xeni had just been craving candy. It was one hell of a starter kit and Xeni was pretty sure they would never get a chance to use it.

After she'd fled the scene of her epic and incredibly selfish blunder, Xeni had laid awake in the guest room and tried to pinpoint the last time she'd felt this foolish. When more than one instance came to mind and the twisting pain in her chest became too much, she knew she had two choices. Really lean into the humiliation, knowing that she'd disappointed her parents and put her temporary husband in a terrible position, or try to make things right.

She wasn't surprised that Mason had nicely told her he needed a night off from her and her family bullshit. She didn't blame him one bit. A week ago, he'd had no idea who she was and now her mother was probably assembling her old lady crew so they could roll up on him. He had his own problems to deal with and Xeni had opened her big mouth and piled on.

Liz had texted later that night to see if she was okay and that just made Xeni feel even worse. She'd barged into these people's lives and was making herself out to be a special kind of pain in the ass.

She put everything back in the box but the Skittles, then taped it back up. She could at least give the stuff to Mason as a parting gift. He could find someone else that didn't drive up his blood pressure to share it with.

As soon as that thought crossed her mind, the idea of Mason doing the intensely intimate stuff they'd discussed with someone else, her heart sank to her stomach. Her whole life was a mess, but she couldn't deny that she had developed some real feelings for Mason.

She crossed the kitchen and grabbed her phone off its charger, then sent Mason a text.

> *Our DIY porn kit arrived.*
> *I can leave it at the top of your steps.*

Just about to text you.
Mr. Barber has a simple post nuptial agreement
for us to review.
Want to meet me at his office in an hour?

Xeni chewed the inside of her lip as she considered how to reply. She wasn't sure she was ready to see Mason, but maybe this was a good way for them to say goodbye, stop this thing in its tracks for good.

> *I'll be there.*

Mason replied with a gif of SpongeBob doing a little jig. She'd miss their back and forths.

An hour later, Xeni pulled into a parking space across the street from Mr. Barber's office. Mason was waiting out front, leaning against the brick facade. He looked up as she hopped out and offered her the hint of a smile. She grabbed the box out of the passenger seat and crossed the street.

"Hey," she said. It took every ounce of her being to make herself sound normal. She barely pulled it off. Mason considered her for a moment, then sighed. Xeni braced herself for the most bizarre break-up in history. How do you get dumped by your husband when you weren't even in a relationship to begin with? Mason reached out and lightly caressed her cheek with his thumb, and fuck if her whole body didn't react. She was gonna miss those simple touches.

"You never told me what you thought of my piping skills last night."

"Oh, you want more notes?" Xeni teased.

"I always want notes."

"I thought maybe you were trying to tell me something, but you know what happens when you're busy projecting."

"Meaning?"

"Nothing." Xeni pushed down the lump in her throat. "Should we go in?"

"Hold on. I have something I want to say."

Xeni swallowed again. She was not going to fucking cry. He wasn't even her boyfriend. She needed to get a grip.

"Usually you follow up a serenade with some kind of verbal declaration, but the conversation I had with your mom caught me a little off guard," Mason said.

"I know. I pride myself on typically having my shit together, but last night I—I didn't realize how pissed I am with her still. It's really confusing when you feel betrayed by your own parents. I mean, you know."

"I do."

"I wanted to hurt her. That's the petty ass truth. She kept something huge from me and since I can't have it out with Sable, I decided that throwing low blows at my mom was the way to go. But I fucked up and dragged you into it. Not my finest moment. I'm sorry."

"I accept your apology. And I apologize for not saying this last night, though I did try to say it through song. We don't have to stay married at the end of this legally binding month, but I do have feelings for you, Xeni. I don't know how we'd make it work with you in Los Angeles and me serving high-quality meals at a reasonable price three thousand miles away, but I didn't want you to go away without knowing how I feel."

Xeni wanted to respond with something cute and clever, but she couldn't. Her heart had exploded and she'd died from a combination of relief and happiness.

"If that's too much for you in such a short period of time, I understand."

"There's another thing you should know about me. When I know, *I know*. Time doesn't really factor in. I told you I'm a witch."

"And what are your witchy senses telling you?"

"That I've got it for you pretty bad."

18

It took all of fifteen minutes to sign the post-nuptial agreement that Mr. Barber had prepared for them, including the time it took for Mr. Barber to answer their questions.

"Glad we took care of that," Xeni said when they stepped back outside.

"I'll have to concoct another elaborate scheme to rob you blind. Here, do you want to put that in my car?" Mason asked, reaching for the box. She happily handed it off to him.

"I was hoping I could keep walking around with a box full of dicks. Uh, do you still want to use all that fun stuff with me?" She knew they'd come to a truce and even slapped a declaration of like on top of it. Even so, she wanted to know if he still wanted her in all the ways she wanted him.

"I didn't regret getting a full night's sleep—"

"At least one of us got some rest."

"It wasn't by choice, love. I was staring at my phone, trying to decide whether or not to text you, and the next thing I knew, my alarm was going off. I needed that sleep, but I regret not coming to you. I don't want to think about going back to not having you in my arms."

"You're trying to make me fall in love with you. It's not gonna work, McInroy."

"Mmmhmm. Does that mean you don't want to join me at the jewelry store?" He nodded over Xeni's shoulder. She turned and looked down the street at the wooden sign for Ghent Street Jewelers.

"No. I mean, I wanna go."

"I had a feeling that might be the case. Let me just set this in my car."

Xeni followed him back to his SUV, then took his hand as they continued their short walk down the street.

When they walked into the jewelry store, they were greeted by a gray-haired White woman in a petal-collared blouse and short-sleeved sweater.

"Welcome! How are you folks doing today?" Xeni was shocked by her thick Southern accent.

"My wife and I are looking for some wedding bands. I'm sure I need to be sized for one."

"Oh, I love that accent," she said matter of factly, before she leaned closer to the counter. "I'm from out of town too, if you couldn't tell."

"Me three," Xeni laughed.

"What brings you here to Ghent?"

"Family. The both of us, separately. I mean we both came here for different family reasons, but we met here."

"I'm here for family too. My mama's from here, but she moved down to Atlanta to open another location and never looked back. But now I'm back and I feel like I'm just the person to help you. Julie-Pam Christie."

"I'm Xeni and this is my husband, Mason. We—"

"Oh, I heard about you two! Little, arranged kinda shotgun thing?"

"Um, sort of," Xeni laughed. Julie-Pam's bright mood was pretty infectious. "Who told you?"

"Mrs. Chen over at the Chinese restaurant. I've been eating lunch there every day and she's been catching me up on the goings on in town. She was wondering if you two would stop by and here you are."

"Julie-Pam, how long would we have to wait for my ring to come?" Mason asked. Xeni knew what he was thinking. They both hoped she at least got to see the ring on his finger before she left town on Sunday night.

"No time at all. My daddy is a big man like you, so I told my aunt it's a good idea just to keep a few larger rings in stock. Our customers come in all shapes and sizes. Give me one sec."

Julie-Pam disappeared into the back with a little extra spring in her step.

"We should have invited her to our wedding," Mason said quietly.

"She would have been a much better guest than Deborah," Xeni said.

"I have to agree with you there."

"Okay. Here. We. Go. I have these two. Simple, tasteful. And this one." Xeni watched Mason as he skipped right over the plain, but elegant white and yellow gold bands. He picked up the third option and examined it closely.

"What's this one made of?"

"The outside is titanium and the inside is lined with wood from an old whisky barrel. Not Scotch, but close."

"Oh babe," Xeni said as Mason's eyes lit up. He slid it on

to his thick ring finger and she was positive he was this close to a spontaneous orgasm. "Do you like it?"

"I've wondered what my purpose in life was and it turns out I was born to wear this ring."

"We'll let you wear that out of the store," Julie-Pam chuckled, before she turned to Xeni. "Now let's get you squared away. Are we just doing a band for you or—"

"Okay, yeah. I think I'm a little overwhelmed." For a small-town jewelry store, their bridal section was huge. She knew what she liked, but the truth was Xeni had never owned any fancy jewelry. Her parents had given her a charm bracelet for her sixteenth birthday, but the rest of her stuff was from Target or the racks near the check out at Old Navy. She'd never picked out grown folks jewelry before.

Xeni glanced up at Mason as his fingers caressed the back of her neck. "If you want a diamond, I'll get you a diamond. I came into a little money recently."

"Pssht. You know I want a diamond."

"How about this?" Julie-Pam reached into the case and pulled out a gorgeous diamond engagement ring with a matching band. "I think this matches your style and your energy."

"What do you know about my energy, Julie-Pam?" Xeni teased, before looking closer at the rings. "Damn, she's right."

"That's a cushion cut with diamond halo and they are calling that pretty band a Marquise and Dot. Both are set in white gold. Gorgeous, isn't it?"

"May I?" Xeni asked before snatching up both rings.

"Of course."

"Ah, allow me." Mason gently picked up the rings and took Xeni's hand. She saw the look in his eyes. She knew he was about to say some sweet as hell shit that would make her knees melt, but she was still a fragile mess and now was not the time. She pointed at him with her free hand and fixed him with a hard stare.

"I swear if you make me cry in front of our new friend Julie-Pam…"

Then this asshole got down on one knee. He didn't say a word, just slid the rings onto her finger. They were a tiny bit loose, but Xeni didn't care. Mason stood, brushing his lips against her cheek, before he whispered in her ear.

"I cannot wait until you fuck me in the ass later."

The sputtering snort that came out of Xeni was inhuman. Mason winked at her and turned back to Julie-Pam. "Is debit, okay?"

As Mason ushered Xeni through the entrance to Szechuan Garden, they almost walked right into Deborah. The cranky town clerk took a step back and gave them both a stern look.

"Glad to see this lasted the weekend," she said.

"Thank you again for officiating," Mason replied. Xeni shouldn't have been shocked by his politeness. He was kind to everyone, but as Deborah muttered her "you're welcome" and excused herself, Xeni realized something else. She'd share it with Mason when she felt Deborah was at least one hundred yards out of earshot.

"Welcome! Dining in or taking out, Mr. McInroy?" A young Asian woman said from behind the bar.

"In. Thanks, Rosemary. Xeni, this is Mei's other daughter. Rosemary, this is my wife."

"It's nice to meet you. Your aunt was one of my favorites. We miss her a lot."

"Thank you."

"Right this way." Rosemary led them through the half-full restaurant. It was some of the best take-out Xeni had had since she got to town. No surprise the place was live and bumping before five p.m.. Rosemary left them with their menus and went right back to grab their drinks.

When they were alone, Xeni said, "Deborah's a witch too."

"You think?"

"Yeah. She's pissed about something and it's bleeding into everything. Today's the equinox, so it makes sense. Her power is probably the strongest in the dead of winter. Getting a permit from her in late January must be a nightmare."

"You have to tell me more about this," Mason said.

"That's all I know. It's just a feeling. A feeling you have to trust, believe and embrace. Deborah knows her power and she just uses it to scare people away. Makes sense she was friends with Sable."

"Are all the women in your family witches?"

"All women are witches, period. Like I said, it just matters if you embrace it. If you believe."

"What about Julie-Pam?" he laughed.

"Oh, she's the kind of witch that accidentally makes wonderful things happen." Xeni looked up from her menu. "I know what—what?"

Mason was staring at her was a dreamy look in his eyes. He shook his head and opened his own menu. "Nothing."

A few minutes later, Rosemary was back with their waters and an older woman who could have been her twin, save the two wrinkles she'd acquired and a blunt bob hair cut.

"You didn't invite me to the wedding," she announced, playfully slapping Mason on the shoulder.

"Mei this is—"

"You're Sable's daughter, Xeni."

"I am. She told you?"

"Of course she told me. Sable was my best friend, but not that good of a friend if she didn't leave a note telling you to invite me to the wedding. I'm glad to see our plan worked."

"What plan?" Xeni laughed.

"The plan to find you a husband. See? Mason is a perfect choice."

"So far so good."

"Dinner's on the house. My wedding gift to you. In return, you have to name your first child after me."

Xeni glanced at Mason. "Not sure there are going to be any children."

"Oh. Then our plan failed. Eat and I'll come join you."

"I feel like the universe is trying to help me correct the last few days," Xeni said as Mei walked back into the kitchen.

———

Three hours later, they left the restaurant. They'd taken their time eating and talking, and in between customers, Mei came out to chat with them. Finally she'd told Rosemary she was taking a break to spend time with the newlyweds. She pulled up a chair and started telling Xeni all kinds of stories about Ms. Sable. For a moment, Mason was worried that hearing more, or anything, about this person who she still had such a complex relationship with, even in death, might make Xeni upset, but it seemed to do the opposite.

More than once, they both doubled over laughing,

hearing about the elaborate pranks Sable, Bess, Mei and Lucy had pulled on Reverend Pummel. Or the time they'd rigged the county fair's pie-eating contest so Mei could win. Bribing the one and only Deborah for midnight access to the park during Bess's son's final days.

Mason knew Sable and her crew were often up to no good, but he'd never realized they were a small criminal enterprise in the making.

As the sun went down and the evening stretched on, Mason focused less on Mei's stories and more on the beautiful woman sitting across from him. He'd seen the happiness in her face when he'd gotten down on one knee earlier that afternoon, but Mei had brought the light back to her eyes. He couldn't imagine how badly she needed this. A real break from the lies and secrets, a reminder of how amazing of a person Sable Everly could be. The good things mattered, maybe even more than the bad.

They finally said their goodbyes and carried their leftovers back out to Xeni's car. "I'm in love with Mei," she said.

"She's got character to go around. She comes to the cafe maybe once a year and tells me how bad my cooking is. It's how we bond."

"I'm—I'm glad my aunt... Sable. I'm glad she had good friends. I always wondered what it was like for her to be so far away from her sisters, have that many strained relationships, but clearly she had it figured it out."

"The family you create is sometimes just as important as the one you're born into."

"So true." Xeni paused. "So, where we doing this?"

"Doing what?"

Xeni held up her hands and slid her finger into the tight

hole she'd made with her index finger and thumb. "You know what. I want to get in that butt."

"You know, I made a list too," Mason said. "A list with all the things I want in a woman and the phrase 'wants to get in my butt' is number four."

"Listen, don't blame me. Blame Mei. Blame my aunt. They knew we'd be perfect together. So, your place or mine?"

"Mine. Bigger bed and the rest of my furniture is cheap. It's okay if we break it."

"Oh, okay, it's gonna be that kind of party. I'm perpetually horny around you, but say something really nasty to hold me over until we get over there."

Mason was glad it was dark and the streets of downtown were basically empty. Only Mei's place and the pub at the end of the block were still open. He stepped closer, caging Xeni in against the side of her car. The sound of her breath pushing out of her lips made him instantly hard. He leaned down and kissed her, tasting the apple candy she'd eaten on the way out. When he pulled back, he watched the dazed look on her face as he slipped a hand between her legs. She'd complained about not packing more nice outfits, but he'd do anything to see her in these tight stretchy pants every day.

She was so hot and he imagined that if he kept teasing her, moving his fingers up and down, it wouldn't take long for him to find out just how wet she was through the fabric of her clothes. He drew his tongue over her bottom lip before he kissed his way across her cheek.

"I'm going to make you forget all about Daryl," he whispered in her ear. She let out a sexy little whimper as he gave her pussy a light squeeze and then a pat. "Go on. I'll see you in a few minutes."

He waited until she buckled in behind the wheel before

he walked to his own car. If they weren't gearing up for a long sweaty night, he'd consider taking care of himself right then and there. Instead, he started for home, doing his best to mind the speed limits and stop signs.

The moment they stepped into his apartment, Xeni started taking off her clothes. Mason set down the box of fun.

"Can we talk a minute?" he asked. He was hard as a rock and he wanted nothing more than for them to get down to the business at hand, but they needed to have a real conversation first. Xeni stopped before she pulled off her pants and came back toward him. Mason pulled her into his arms, soaking up the heat of her soft body as she pressed herself against him. She looked up, resting her chin on his chest. "Yes, dear. What do you need?"

"While I appreciate your enthusiasm when it comes to getting naked in front of me, I need to know you want to do this. This is something I've missed, but I want you to be comfortable."

"Oh, I wanna do it. I wanna do it a whole lot. Just tell me what to do because I want you to actually enjoy it."

"I will give you notes if I have them. I'm gonna step into the bathroom for a bit. Give me a shout if you need anything."

"I will."

"Excellent," He gave her a quick kiss, then let her go so he could grab the things he needed from the box. "I'll just be a sec. Or fifteen minutes. Stay horny."

"I will," Xeni laughed. "Mason?"

"Yeah, love."

"I think you're super cute."

Mason literally bit his tongue to keep the words from flying out of his fool mouth. "If I could only match your beauty," he managed to say, instead of the four not so little words that would have ruined their whole night.

In the restroom, he prepped himself with one of the disposable enemas, then after he cleaned up, took a few minutes to stretch. He didn't want to embarrass himself by pulling something. When he came out of the bathroom, hard and definitely ready to go, he almost let the bold declaration fly. Xeni was standing in the middle of his bedroom, completely naked except for the strap-on harness and the neon purple dildo they'd ordered for it. She had her phone in one hand and the butt plug in the other.

"Hi. Just doing a little research. Do we need this?" she asked, wiggling the butt plug.

"I have plans for that later. Come here."

"In a sec. *I* just want to say something before I get all up in this. When I get nervous, I get silly, but I don't want you to think I'm being silly *at* you. I'm going to try my best not to make any jokes, but if I do, it's because I'm nervous. I want this to be good for you."

"Who says I don't want you to be silly?"

"I—okay. You got me there. Let me just go wash my hands and we'll do this." While she ducked into the bathroom, Mason made himself comfortable on the bed, idly stroking himself while he waited. Finally she stepped into the room. Mason stood off the bed and met her by the bathroom door. They didn't have to jump right to the main event, but he was tired of waiting. He wanted to hold her. Wanted her body against his. Mason leaned down and kissed her.

"You like to tell me how amazing you are, but I hope you believe it," he said against her lips.

"Sometimes I need a little reassurance."

"I'll see what I can do. Here, grab the lube and let's get that slicked up."

"'Kay," she replied, her voice a little unsure. Mason watched as she opened the seal on the water-based lube and smeared a generous amount all over the silicone cock she wore. Fuck, it was a sight to behold.

"You have no idea how sexy you look right now."

"Yeah?" she said, a little smile touching the corners of her lips.

"Definitely, yeah. All good?"

"Yeah." She handed him the bottle.

"You hold on to that." He pulled her close again and started to massage some of the tension out of her shoulders and neck. She sighed and leaned into him. Mason wasn't sure how he was going to watch her leave when the time came. "Now, I'm much bigger than you, so we'll try a few positions. And that cock's curved, so you won't have to do a lot of work to find my prostate. Let me know if you're uncomfortable or if anything hurts."

"And you tell me. Honestly, I don't know how you top all the time. The performance anxiety is maddening," she said dramatically.

Mason pressed a kiss to her forehead. "Harness the power of the moon, love. What is she telling you?"

"Oh, you're gonna use my own craft against me?"

"Like you said, embrace it."

"The moon is telling me that this is about to be the best sex of your life."

"That's the spirit. Lie down on the bed, gorgeous moon goddess. On your back."

Xeni made her way over to the mattress and made herself

comfortable. Mason followed, going to his knees on the floor. He spread her legs, marveling at the way the straps of the harness wrapped around her gorgeous brown thighs. He wanted nothing more than for her to fuck him until he shot his load, but first he needed a taste.

She was soaking wet, her juices coating her labia. Mason spread her lips with his tongue, sucking her clit into his mouth as his nose bumped the base of the harness.

"Babe, stop," she moaned, even though she tugged him closer with her fingers in his hair. The slight sting from the pulling went straight to his cock. He wanted to ask if she was sure, wanted to know what he could do to continue to worship her slick cunt, but he knew she didn't want to wait any longer. Later, he told himself. Later, he'd eat her pussy until she couldn't stand any longer.

Mason crawled over her, straddling her slender waist. His gaze roamed over her face and down to her hard nipples, then back up to her searching brown eyes as he reached between his legs and lined the silicone cock up with his asshole. He lost himself in the moment, easing himself down on the hard length, but it was Xeni's soft hands stroking over his thighs that brought him back. It was her in this moment, she was giving this to him. No questions asked. He almost slipped up and said the words again.

19

It took a few moments, but Mason was able to find a good rhythm, fucking himself on the purple cock. A few strokes later, Xeni caught on. He held still, giving her the time she needed to adjust her legs, the room she needed for more leverage, and then she was back with him. He could feel her hips rising to meet his ass, feel every bit of effort as she tried to hit the perfect spot just inside of him.

The view in front of him was just as good, made him just as hard as the fucking itself. He bent over her, bracing his hands beside her shoulders, careful to keep his weight off her chest. His swollen cock slid back and forth just under the soft skin of her breasts. He moved faster, rocking back and forth, filling his ass over and over. Xeni urged him on, a hand stroking up his broad chest, curving around the side of his neck and back down again. He looked at the hand on his thigh as the light from the bathroom caught the diamonds on her ring. His eyes slid closed on their own as he worked the inches in and out, and in and out again.

"Mason." He looked down at his wife as she repeated his

name on a breathless moan. "Do you want me to stroke it?" Her fingertips on his leg were already lightly brushing his dick as he moved on her cock. The silicone tip pressed hard against his prostate as his muscles clenched. He was about to come.

"You can touch me anywhere you want, love. Anywhere," he groaned. "You holding up?"

"Yeah. This actually feels real good. It's—it's pushing down on my clit. I—fuck. I could come just from watching you. Can you come on my tits from there?" she asked. "I want you to."

"Xeni, fuck. My god." Mason reached down and pushed her tits together. He teased her hard, dark nipples with his thumbs, pinched them between his large fingers. Precum leaked out of the tip of his erection at the sound of her moaning. She pushed her head back into the sheets. He knew she would say something about how they'd done a great job of messing up her thick curls, but in the moment it didn't matter. He just wanted to remember this, every second of it, so he could keep it close to his heart when she was thousands of miles away.

Cum shot out of Mason cock, coating the bottom of her brown tits. Mason thought he was gonna pass out as another thick stream followed and then another, some of it coating her nipples. The last time he'd come that hard had been a few days before when Xeni had taken him into his mouth. He paused for a minute or two, trying to breathe and blink his eyes back into focus. Xeni continued her caressing, running her hands over every inch she could reach.

Finally he climbed off of her and managed to stumble to his feet, his hard cock still pulsing between his legs. "Don't move," he told her. He should have been more specific. She didn't move from the bed, but her legs fell open and her fingers went right to her pussy, gleaming with her thick juices. Mason found the plug. He quickly went to rinse it off, then came back into the room. He grabbed the lube off the edge of the bed, then hauled Xeni into his arms. It took a lot of restraint not to beat his chest like a pumped-up caveman as she squealed with delight. He sat down in his desk chair and pulled her lush thighs across his lap, letting out a shudder as she nuzzled closer to him and started sucking on his neck.

"I thought we were going to do it doggy style," she said in between strokes of her tongue. "But I liked it much better that way. I liked watching you."

"So did I, love. So did I." Mason uncapped the lube and spread a healthy amount on the butt plug.

"What are we going to do with that?"

"I was going to have some fun filling you up." He tipped her back, but Xeni flinched, like she thought she was going to fall. "Lean back. Don't worry, I've got you." He tried again, bracing his arm in a firm caging motion behind her back. This time she went with it, let him hold her weight as he maneuvered between her legs. He found the tight bud of her asshole, already wet from her slick cunt juices, and gently nudged it with his finger. "Just relax for me. Okay?"

She let out a shaky breath, then gave him a little nod. "Okay." Mason watched her face very closely for any signs of discomfort as he pushed the toy in all the way. She let out another breath as he turned it a fraction, then she settled against him even more.

"You want to take this off?" He grabbed the base of the purple cock she was wearing and gave it a shake. Xeni let out another gasp, shaking her head.

"Leave it on."

"I just want you to be comfortable."

"I am," Xeni said, before she reached up and pulled him down to her. She kissed him like that was what she'd been wanting all night, deep and rough. Mason kissed her back, sucking her tongue into his mouth while he made himself busy between her legs. He teased her clit, stroking and lightly pinching the sensitive bud as she started to squirm in his arms. Then he pushed one finger inside her swollen cunt and then another.

"You said you liked my fingers," he breathed against her lips. He didn't get a chance to finish his thought before she kissed him again. He would just have to show her. Mason used his forearm to hitch up her thigh so he could have better access to her amazing body. Then he added more lube, covering his own fingers, her swollen labia and her dripping entrance. He took his time, slowly sliding one finger then two, fucking her hot cunt nice and deep. She whimpered in his arms he added as another finger another, three now pumping in and out. He fucked her this way for a while, watch the way she arched in his grasp, moaning his name now and again.

He leaned down and lightly took her bottom lip between his teeth, giving her a little bite. She moaned then, kissing him deeper.

"Do you want more?" he asked when he pulled back and bit. He stretched her more, nudging her with his pinky.

"Mhhmm," she moaned, nodding frantically. He added his pinky, and then his his thumb. There was a moment's pause. Mason wanted to give her time to adjust to the girth of his hand. She's stretched so beautifully for him, the lube and her juices easing the way. The only sounds in the room were the hum of the AC and their mingling breath. He moved his hand, just barely, but that was enough to spur his gorgeous partner on. She ground down on his clenched fist with her hips, her muscles tensing around him. He watched the not-so-subtle swirl of her pelvis a bit more before he started moving his hand in earnest.

That was all it took to make her cry out, her face tucked tight against his neck.

"How does that feel?" Mason asked. More like begged. He wanted to know that he was taking care of her in all the ways he could.

"Good. Oh my god. It—it feels good." Mason kept on with the motion, moving his wrist in slow but deep thrusts. "You can go—you can go faster."

"You sure, love?"

"Yes," she panted, grabbing his forearm to show him that she was ready to do it for him if he didn't get on with it. "Yeah, fuck. Just. That. Yeah, that."

Mason watched her closely, looked for any hint of pain or discomfort, but she held on to his wrist, encouraging him to fuck her harder. He did what she asked, followed through on her sensual demands, until he felt her clenching down on him.

"Oh, babe," she cried out as she soaked his wrist. He held on to her as her body tensed and trembled, then a few minutes later, he very slowly removed his hand.

Mason carried Xeni across the room and laid her down on the bed, and carefully removed the strap-on and butt plug. He took both into the bathroom and then returned with a wet washcloth to clean her off. She was still breathing heavy, her eyes slammed shut as he wiped his cum off her tits and her cum off her thighs.

"You want me to wrap your hair?" It may have been a foolish question, but he'd do it if she asked.

A burst of laughter sputtered out of her as she opened her eyes. "Quick learner, but no. Thank you. I forgot my bonnet at home anyway."

Mason would have offered to keep a spare at his place if they weren't running out of time.

It took some more maneuvering, but eventually they were both under the covers. Mason held still while Xeni made herself comfortable, then wrapped his arms around her. He listened to her breathing as she lightly toyed with his chest hair.

"You want to know what I want to be in my next life?" she suddenly said into the dark.

"What's that, my moon goddess?"

"A sex witch."

It was after midnight when Xeni realized what she would do with her newly acquired wealth. First she was going to get a bigger apartment. A house even, with high ceilings. Then she was going to get a huge bed with a sturdy frame and some kind of sex chair. Yeah, a sex chair. She realized she liked doing sex things in chairs. And then she'd invite Mason out to Los Angeles for what she now saw as mandatory bi-monthly dick appointments. The marriage wasn't meant to last, but she'd be a fool to give up the sex. With him, it was just too good.

She should have been exhausted. The man had played her like a sock puppet, made her come harder than she'd ever come before. Instead of that peaceful, dreamless sleep that came with so-powerful-it-reset-your-nervous-system sex, she'd had a filthy dream about her and Mason fucking in a field of flowers. The orgasm she'd had in her sleep woke her up. She rolled over and looked at her husband sleeping beside her, both arms up above his head. She left him there, snoring softly, and crawled out of bed to use the restroom. When she came back, he was awake looking at his phone.

"Good?" he asked.

"Yeah."

She put one knee on the bed and leaned over him. She lightly brushed her lips across his a few times, soaking up the soft warmth that she felt when she was around him. Then she glanced down and saw it, his erection tenting the sheets. She nodded toward his lap.

"Permission to come aboard?" she joked. Kinda. She knew he had to be up for the breakfast shift, but she figured it wouldn't hurt to double check. Who knows? He might be up for another round. "If that's something you're into. I know you're tired."

"Last night was a mistake. I'll never be too tired for you again. I'll embrace the sweet death of sleep deprivation if it means I can spend just one more moment joined with you."

"Okay. Relax, Romeo."

Mason chuckled and pointed across the room. "I think there are prophylactics there in the recliner."

Xeni grabbed some protection from the fresh box and came back over to the bed. She felt Mason's eyes on her as she slid under the covers and slipped the condom over his hard length. She didn't waste any time climbing over his hips so she could take a seat on his waiting erection. She watched his face as his eyes snapped shut. Her aching pussy welcomed him while she ran her fingers over his chest and down to his soft stomach. She took him easily, inch by inch until he was seated to the root. Rocking forward, she met him halfway as he leaned up so she could brush her lips against his.

So many things flooded her mind. How good it felt to be with him like this. How she knew this was more than just an arrangement, more than just a chemistry fluke. She knew in her heart that the spell she'd done had worked. She just never expected her perfect guy to be Mason McInroy.

———

"Okay, okay. I know your break is almost over, but finish your story." Xeni turned off the light to the garage and walked back into the house. She'd knocked a lot off her to-do list, including scheduling an upgrade to the house's security system for that Friday. Thursday, Mason was taking off so he could join her for a quick trip to Martha's Vineyard. She needed to see the other house before she went back to California.

The call from Meegan was a welcome distraction. She caught her up on the gossip from the weekend, including some more messy mess she'd gotten herself into, but somehow they'd gotten off track and started talking about the contestants from *A Match Made in Paradise*. The youths in the villa were always of interest to her, but she wanted to hear more about Meegan's drama.

"Oh sorry. Anyway, yeah. So, I told him if we talked about it, it would have to be after hours, off campus. I can't believe I fucked one of my student's fathers."

"It was an accident. And the kid has only been your student for, like, a week. You didn't know."

"I should screen next. Do you have any kindergarten-aged children, sir? Ma'am? Are you thinking public or private? Do live on the west side? If so, is it going to be an issue if I ask you to tie me up one night and then never call you again?"

"Do you think he's going to get weird about it?"

"No, but I just—I don't know. I feel like this is my life now. I can't find a *boyfriend* boyfriend and I can't find someone to just fool around with without some weird connection to some other part of my life popping up. L.A. is too fucking small."

"No, the kink community in L.A. is too small. Go vanilla, girlfriend. Find you a nice boring man who only likes missionary."

"But I'll die," Meegan said dramatically, before she burst out laughing. Xeni smiled and shook her head, happy she was finally back to feeling like she could have normal conversations with her friends. Well, normal for Meegan.

"I'm sorry I'm not there to laugh at you in person."

"Me too," Meegan sighed. "So, you'll be back in action on Monday?"

"Yes. I get in late Sunday night. I'll sleep as hard as I can and then I'll meet you bright and early for our coffee and bitch session before I make these toddlers wish they were keeping that sub forever," Xeni growled, completely joking. She was one of the softest teachers at Whippoorwill and the kids loved her. "Just a lot going on here still. I'll tell you guys all at once in person when I get back. Way too much to type and way too much to explain to six people six different times."

"I can't wait. We miss you!"

"I miss you too."

"Oh. There's the bell. Let me go get these little babies from recess. Text me later if you can."

"I will."

"Buh-byeeee."

"Bye."

She ended her call with Meegan. Xeni was glad to hear her voice and now she was anxious to get

home and see her friends again, but she'd learned her lesson, dropping that bomb on her mom. She wanted to tell her friends everything, but she wanted to do it in person. She wanted to explain how things had gone from zero to sixty with Mason. And she wanted them to know that even though it was sudden and unexpected and they had no fucking clue what they were doing or how they were going to make things work, she was falling in love with him. Falling. Just falling. One hundred percent not there, but she was definitely packing for a long trip to In Love.

She thumbed around her phone and went back to see what the most recent text alert was all about it. It was from her mom.

Can you help Audra with her college applications?

Usually Xeni would have been annoyed. It was barely the middle of September, so her cousin had plenty of time to get her college applications in order. And while Xeni didn't know how she specifically was the person for this job, she knew her mom's thought process. Xeni worked in education, therefore she knew every other person in academia on Earth, including everyone in college admissions. But the text was also proof that her mom wasn't BIG pissed at her anymore. Now she was just moderately annoyed and waiting to chew her out in person, not angry enough to give her the cold shoulder. The question was her olive branch. Things were going to be okay between them.

She wondered when they were really going to talk about Sable, then instantly stopped the thoughts in their tracks.

"Later. Just worry about that later." What had happened couldn't be undone, not that she wanted it to, and there was only forward. Sable was gone and Xeni didn't have a time machine. She wanted answers, but they could wait. She sent a text back.

> *Happy to.*
> *Tell her to text me and*
> *we'll set up a time to start.*

Thank you baby.
Call Dante and say hello. XM

> *I'll call you both tonight. XP*

Xeni slipped her phone in her pocket and was headed toward the laundry room to throw her clothes in the dryer when the doorbell rang. The only person she was expecting was Mason and he was just now finishing up for the day at the cafe. They were going to have dinner and see just how long they could pretend sex wasn't also on the menu for the evening. She walked to the front of the house and stood up on her tiptoes to peek through the transom window. A tall, slim older White man with graying hair and a mustache stood on the front porch. Behind him, Xeni saw a green taxi idling at the end of the driveway. She didn't even know you could catch a taxi this far out, but at least the driver could act as a witness if this visitor turned out to be a murderer.

She cracked the door and peeked her head through, taking in his dark blue suit and his freshly polished wingtips. He smelled faintly of self-importance. "Can I help you?"

"I'm looking for Sable Everly." The thick Scottish accent that flowed from his mouth immediately set her on edge.

"Sable isn't here at the moment. Is there something I can help you with?"

"Who are you?"

Heat flashed over her face. "Who are *you*? And how can I help you?"

"My name is Jameson McInroy and I'm trying to figure out why my son had Sable Everly wire me nearly forty-thousand pounds."

20

Mason was looking at the ferry schedule from Woods Hole to Oak Bluffs when his phone started ringing in his hand. XENI CALLING... scrolled across the screen. He ignored the sudden release of endorphins and hit ACCEPT. He'd planned to leave for her house as soon as he pulled on his sneakers, but he was happy to talk to her anytime.

"Hello, my love," he said as soon as he hit accept. "What can I do for you?"

"Your dad is here."

"What?" Mason knew he'd heard her wrong.

"Your dad is sitting in my living room. He's here about the money and he said he won't leave until you come here. I'm trying to keep my cool, but tell me what you want me to do."

"Are you okay?"

"I'm fine. He's pretty fucking rude, but I think we've come to an understanding."

"Love, I'm sorry. I'll be right there."

"Drive safe, but yeah, please hurry. I'm not gonna call the cops or anything. I just don't want him in my house."

"I'm on my way." Mason ended the call and scrambled to finish getting dressed. He rushed down to his car and spotted Silas walking back to the barns from the cannery.

"Eh!" he called out to him, as he jogged across the parking lot.

"Hey, what's up?"

"My father is here."

"Where?" Silas's shock registered as a slight frown, but Mason knew his cousin was just as confused as he was.

"He's at Xeni's house right now." Mason started walking backward toward his car. Silas followed. "I don't know what the fuck he's doing there, but I need to go and get him away from her."

"You want me to come?"

Mason paused a moment, considering it. Would bringing backup make matters better or worse? His father was his problem, not Xeni's. He needed to get the old man out of her house. But he also knew his father and how stubborn he was.

"Yeah, come along then."

They both jogged back to his SUV and climbed in.

"How did he get that address? Why didn't he just come to the farm?" Silas asked as Mason did his best not to speed through town.

"The bank transfer, I'm guessing. It came from Ms. Sable's account. You know my dad. If he wants information, he'll get it and use it to his advantage." Many scenarios ran through Mason's head, but at the moment all that mattered was Xeni. He was pretty sure his father wouldn't hurt her, not physically, but he could hear the stress in her voice over the phone. His father didn't know how to communicate without the brash, hurtful words that were only used by the most self righteous of elitist assholes. Mason knew he'd be apologizing for months for whatever his father had managed to say in a few minutes.

As soon as they pulled into Ms. Sable's driveway, the front door sprang open and Xeni stepped out.

"Stay in the car," Mason told his cousin.

"No problem."

Mason rushed over to Xeni and pulled her into his arms. "Okay?"

"No. I—do you want to talk to him? I mean, I really, really don't want to, and I can still call the police. I just don't know how trigger happy there are around here."

"No need for the cops just yet. I brought Silas just in case. Let me go speak to the bastard."

"Okay." Xeni gripped his hand. "I'm coming with you."

Mason nodded, then led her back into the house. The last bit of denial he'd been clutching on to vanished when they stepped into the living room. It had been years since he'd laid eyes on his father. The man had aged, and not well, but he still carried the same imposing presence about him. The danger of Jameson McInroy was his determination, his resolve. When he'd made up his mind, nothing would stop him from getting what he wanted and if you tried, you'd pay.

"Dad," Mason said.

His father stood, his eyes narrowing at the sight of Xeni's fingers grasping on to Mason's clenched fist.

"Suppose I should have known."

"Known what? What are you doing here?"

A red streak flashed over his father's face. "I'm here to ask the questions!" he shouted. "It would have taken you another two decades to pay me what you owe me. And now forty thousand pounds magically appears in my account, so I knew I had to come see for myself. I knew you were averse to hard work, but I never thought you would stoop to conning money out of a dying woman and her relatives.

"What did he tell you?" he asked Xeni. "That he's a true musician? He just needs someone to understand his art?"

"I didn't give him the money. The money was his," Xeni practically growled as she held his hand tighter. Mason glanced at her, his chest swelling with pride. He knew if he let go of her hand, she might catapult forward and rip his father's head from his shoulders, if Mason didn't do it first.

"I followed your terms to the letter," Mason said. "You've been repaid in full. There was no reason for you to come here and there is no reason for you to speak to Xeni this way."

"You are going to return that money and then you are going to return home with me tonight and get a real fucking job. And you will pay me back, you lazy shit."

"I'm not paying *you* back. I'm paying Moira's father back for the money *you* borrowed for a wedding *you* arranged. This is your problem, Dad. Your fault. Your debt. Your scheme failed and you want to make me pay for it. Well, I won't. You have your money. It's done. Leave it."

"Scheme. Wanting my son to grow the fuck up and stand on his own two feet. That's a fucking scheme?"

"Grow up to be like you? How much money do you still owe Uncle Seamus—"

"That's none of your business."

"Right. Well, this debt is and it's paid. Tough if you don't like the way I got it done. I am standing on my own two feet. I have been for years. You just don't like the way it looks from your high horse."

XENI

"You call this standing on your own two feet? You've never stood on your own two feet. You rely on your cousin and now this woman. She told me her aunt just passed away. How long did you wait before you started fucking your way into her pockets? Did you sleep with her aunt too, huh boy?"

"Wow," Xeni said with a shocked gasp. Mason felt himself slowly tuck her body behind his as he took a step forward. He didn't want to break anything in the house, but his father was asking to be shown the exit, through the nearest window.

"I'm not using her for anything. She's my wife and her aunt was my dear, dear friend. A mentor and a better role model than you'll ever be. This town is my home and I am not going anywhere," Mason said very carefully. "You, however, are welcome to leave."

His father tilted his head so he could get a better look at Xeni. "You married him? Maybe you're not as smart as you look."

"Get out," Mason seethed. "Get out right now. Find your way back to the airport and take yourself back to Scotland. You are not welcome here."

"You—you think—Christ." Mason watched as the color suddenly drained from his father's face. He sat, like a boulder was dragging him down, square in the middle of the couch. Mason rushed over to him.

"Dad?"

"Shit," he heard Xeni say. "I think he's having a heart attack."

———

There was a newly constructed Marriot right across the

street from the Kinderack County hospital. Xeni didn't go inside, but the place was practically dead on a Tuesday night and she felt better pacing in the soft ambient light of the outdoor waiting area than trying to hold herself still in the painfully bright lights of the hospital waiting room.

She'd never say it out loud, but she was actually conflicted about whether or not she wanted Mr. McInroy to pull through. For Mason's sake, she desperately wanted him to be free of the way his father had decided to treat him. And it absolutely was a decision. Every Everly came with a slick mouth, but she couldn't imagine anyone in her family talking to her the way Mason's father had spoken to him and to her.

It had taken half a second for Xeni to realize he wasn't snapping out of whatever made him collapse. She'd run outside and grabbed Silas. Thanks to his quick thinking, he and Mason had carried Mr. McInroy out to the back seat of Mason's SUV. It would have taken a while for the ambulance to get out to them and back to the emergency room.

Xeni had followed in her car, but by the time she'd arrived, the waiting game had already begun. Tense minutes turned to hours. A doctor had come and gone and come again to get Mason. It was, in fact, a heart attack and the doctors needed to keep him overnight. Since Xeni was now technically family, she was allowed to go back with Mason to see his father, but she didn't think the three of them being in the same room was a good idea. She'd sat in the waiting room with Silas for a while. His calm stillness should have helped her relax, but instead that need to climb out of her skin seemed to be clawing at the base of her neck.

She'd moved from the sidewalk in front of the hospital down to the corner by the traffic light and back again, then finally over to the hotel. She thought maybe she should just go back to the house. There was nothing she could do and she couldn't console Mason while he consoled his father, but she knew better than to just bail. Mason wasn't just her husband, he was her friend. She wasn't leaving until he told her to go.

Xeni checked her phone for the hundredth time, closing it every time her fingers automatically went back to the conversation Shae and Meegan were having in the group chat. Her brain couldn't handle their light and casual talk right now, not when she felt like this.

A shadow in the hospital entrance caught her attention. She looked up and saw Mason step through the sliding doors and out into the night. She checked that it was safe to cross and ran across the street, stopping short right in front of him. Instantly she could feel the anguish rolling off him. She'd wait to touch him until she knew he wanted to be touched.

"Is there anything I can do to help?"

"No, not really."

"I'm sorry."

"It's not your fault that he has a bad heart." Xeni could only imagine how he felt. Mason was full of empathy and compassion, and she knew he couldn't turn that off, even for a monster like his father.

"I'm gonna have to take him home."

Xeni cringed at the idea of him trying to help his father up the steep stairs to his apartment. "Seems like Silas's place might be a little more spacious."

Mason's jaw tensed as he looked at the ground between them. "Home to Edinburgh, love."

"Right, duh. Of course."

"It'll be another two weeks, but—"

"Right, right."

"It's late. You should go home and get some sleep."

"Yeah, okay. Are you sure you don't need anything?"

"I'm going to head back with Silas in a bit to get a change of clothes and then come back here. I'm sorry I can't go to the vineyard with you."

"Are you kidding? Don't even think about it. Be here, okay? You've showed up for me. It's more than okay that you need to be present for yourself."

"Yeah."

"Is it okay if I hug you?" she asked. It wasn't a purely selfish request. They were both off and she knew if she could just hold him for a second, it would help them both reset.

"Come here."

Xeni closed the small distance between them and walked into his open arms. She rested her head against his chest, pressing herself against his soft stomach. Warmth from his strong arms seeped into her as she let out a deep breath. She felt him relax as he lightly rested his chin on the top of her head.

"I love you, you know," he said quietly. Xeni knew exactly what he meant. He wasn't *in* love with her, not in that way. But in a short time, they'd both come to mean something to each other. Something important. They knew this wasn't meant to be anything more, but what happened between them mattered.

She stepped out of his grasp, then gave his arm a little squeeze.

"Keep me posted when you can. Okay?"

"Okay. I should go back inside."

"Listen. The upshot is that he isn't dead. Two dead parents inside two weeks and we'd have to answer to the local constable," she joked. It worked. Mason cracked a tiny smile.

Thankfully, Xeni's legs carried her to the car and somehow she made it back to the house safely. When she stepped inside and looked around at the boxes stacked against the wall, something in her finally cracked. She pulled out her phone and called the only person she knew would make things right.

———

Xeni had never been so grateful for the time zone difference in her life. Her mother let her blubber utter nonsense into the phone for a whole minute and a half before she offered to be on a red eye out of LAX to New York.

She thought her nerves and the need to get a text from Mason would have her up all night. But after she'd booked her mom's last-minute flight and confirmed that she'd made it to the airport on time, she'd collapsed on the couch and cried herself to sleep. The sound of the doorbell chiming the next morning woke her up. Xeni stumbled to the door and found her mom standing on the front steps. She'd never been so happy to see her in her whole life.

"Oh, my baby girl."

Xeni fell apart all over again as she let her mom gather her into her arms. "I'm sorry," she said through her tears.

"For what? We're all having a hell of a time. Come on." Her mom pulled her inside the house. "Well, this is a nice place."

"It's ours now," Xeni sniffled.

Her mom turned to her and looked her up and down.

"You go get washed up. Take a nice hot shower and wash your hair. There a kettle?"

"Yeah, she has a real fancy one."

"I'll make us some tea and then I'll braid your hair."

"Okay. Thank you for coming, Mommy."

"Anything for you, my baby girl."

Xeni checked her phone when she got out of the shower. It was almost dead, but there was enough juice to see that Mason hadn't texted or called. She thought about texting him, just to see if he was okay, but reconsidered it. He had enough going on and didn't need her hovering. She'd check back around lunch time.

She got dressed, then grabbed her comb and all the hair products she'd brought with her and headed back to the kitchen. Their hot tea was waiting, but her mom wasn't in the room. Xeni found her in Sable's office. She was looking at the gold records.

"I was going to ship those home," Xeni said.

"Good idea. You should have them. Sable sure had a gift."

"You all do. I wish I could sing like you."

"You can. You just didn't spend hours and hours of your life rehearsing, but you have the gift. You're an Everly."

"I—"

"She told me first that she was pregnant with you. She knew mama and daddy and our manager would kill her, but she told me and then she told me she was going to give you away."

Xeni slowly sat down at the desk, like any sudden movement would end her mom's confessional right then and there. When she spoke, she was careful to keep her voice calm and neutral. She wasn't accusing her mother of anything. She just wanted to know the truth. "What happened?"

"Sable was selfish, but so was I. We both should have told you a long time ago. I just didn't want you to get hurt because the whole truth wasn't pretty, Xendria."

"I know, Mom."

"I wasn't about to tell a twelve year old that her aunt who had just finished doing a Divas of The Eighties reunion tour, Sable Everly, was her real mama."

"I don't think—I don't think of you as any less of my mother. I just wanted to know why."

When her mother's only response was a sad tilt of her head, Xeni knew there was nothing more to be said. She had already made the choice. Joyce Everly was her mom and had been her whole life, no matter what her original birth certificate said. She would always be grateful to Sable, for the joy and the memories and her mere presence as someone Xeni knew she could reach out to, but her mother had done the real work every day and if that wasn't proof enough, she'd hopped on a plane, no questions asked to be by Xeni's side.

Her mom turned and looked at her. "This the ring?" Xeni looked down and realized the bright diamonds were in full display.

"Oh. Yeah."

Her mom came over and gently lifted her hand. Her own hand was starting to age. The dark brown skin creasing more and more, but Xeni was still familiar with those hands. The hands that had held her and wiped away her tears, rubbed her shoulders after a tough day at school, handed her the last piece of candy from her purse. Joyce Everly wasn't perfect, but she'd been a damn good mom.

"What do you think?"

"It's gorgeous," her mom replied, the expression on her face letting Xeni know she wasn't lying to protect her feelings. She patted the back of her hand, then started back toward the kitchen. "Come sit down, have your tea. You can tell me about this Mason boy and his jackass of a daddy."

21

That Saturday morning, Mason left the hospital his father had been transferred to in the city and drove back up to the farm. While Kinderack County had one hell of an emergency staff, they weren't equipped to deal with the angioplasty procedure his father needed. Xeni had been kind enough to put him in touch with her friend Sloan, who it turned out was one of the best heart surgeons in the country. While his father's physicians in New York were fully qualified, Sloan had a better bedside manner, even over the phone. She thoroughly explained the procedure and did her best to answer all of Mason's questions. Some of the information wasn't new, but he appreciated hearing from an expert close to someone he trusted.

His father came through the procedure just fine. When he made a point to criticize how long Mason's beard had gotten, he knew he'd be back to his old asshole self in no time. He left the old man to his breakfast and the patient nursing staff, and got on the road. He had to get back to say goodbye.

He and Xeni had come to an unspoken agreement that it

would be easier for them to communicate via text. Her mom had come to town while he'd been busy with his bedside vigil. From their short correspondence, she'd let him know that her mom had accompanied her on a quick overnight trip to Martha's Vineyard. They'd arranged for short-term care-takers of both homes while they figured out what to do next. She'd checked in, asking after his father's health even though the cruel bastard didn't deserve her kind consideration or well wishes, and then she'd let him know it was time for her to go. She was leaving a day early.

He parked beside her car outside of the cannery and shored up his nerves. Weeping like a child, loud enough for the whole county to hear, wouldn't convince her to stay.

He stepped inside and found her with Liz, Maya and Ginny. Silas was wandering down the aisles. Sad goodbyes were not his scene.

"Late to the farewell party, I see," Mason said as the door closed behind him.

"Just sending your girl off with some of that good stuff," Liz said.

"This family jam is crack. And you said you guys ship?" Xeni asked.

"We sure do."

"Okay. I'll be ordering by the case."

Silas stepped to the counter and tossed down a green McInroy Farm t-shirt. "All that on the house," he told Ginny.

"Silas, no. I'll pay for everything," Xeni pleaded.

"Too late, you're a McInroy," Silas said.

"Yup," Liz added with a smile.

"Seriously, I hate you guys. I cannot keep crying." Xeni shook her head. Then she went back and grabbed two more t-shirts. "These are for my parents and I'm paying for them."

"Fine," Ginny laughed. "Buy two, get ten free deal." Ginny totaled her items up and handed them off to Maya, who packaged everything neatly for her. Then they all came around the counter and swarmed Xeni.

"You are welcome here anytime," Liz said.

"I'll be back to see about the house. I just have no idea when."

"I'll be less pregnant then. We'll get fucked up."

That brought the smile back to Xeni's face. "I can't wait. I should go. Thank you guys for everything, really."

She turned then and nodded for Mason to lead the way as the others said loud goodbyes.

"Don't fuck this up, Mason," Ginny called after them.

"Thank you, Genevieve," Mason said, rolling his eyes. "Very helpful."

They stepped outside into the morning sunlight and walked back over to Xeni's car. She set her parting gifts in the back seat, then turned to him.

"You didn't bring your mother. I thought you'd want to show her the cannery."

"Maya, Ginny and my mom in the same room is a recipe for disaster. I know how to exit gracefully. My mom, not so much. We'd be here all day."

"I can understand that."

"Plus, I'm not sure introducing you guys right now is the best idea. You're under enough pressure."

"I appreciate the consideration."

"You know I got you," she teased. "How's your dad?"

"They are discharging him Monday. He'll stay with Silas and Liz until it's safe for him to fly."

"I'd offer my place, but it's kinda far from the farm. And he'd probably hate to accept the offer."

"I know he would. We fly to Edinburgh in two weeks. I don't think I'm coming back," he said.

"Ah—oh." Mason could see the pain in her eyes as her gaze dropped to his chest. She looked up again and fought to plaster a smirk on her face. "Oh, so you're *dumping* me, dumping me."

"I wouldn't look at it that way. More like I'm saving you from myself. I have a lot to figure out and I can't ask you to wait around for me. And why would you want to? You're rich!"

"Har."

Mason swallowed and told her the rest of the truth. "This? My life? This isn't happiness. I don't want this for you."

"I don't want this for you either," she replied.

"My mom's leaving him. She hasn't told him yet, but I need to be there."

"He wouldn't, like, hurt her, would he?"

"I don't think so, but I have to be there."

"I get it."

"I think if anyone would understand how complicated this all is, it's you."

"No, I do. I do. Hell, my mom's here. I mean, you know how I was feeling about her this time last week. I get it."

They were both silent for a moment. Mason couldn't help but wonder and hope if the same words running through his head were running through hers. *We can make it work. Long distance isn't impossible. If we love each other... if.*

If might have been enough if his father hadn't been right about one thing. It was time for Mason to grow up. He couldn't spend forever dreaming of music stardom while flipping burgers at his cousin's farm, and he couldn't abandon his mother to chase whatever future he wished he and Xeni could have with each other. His soon-to-be ex-wife deserved better than what he had to offer and the fucked up package it came with. He hadn't earned the support he'd need from her in the coming months. He had to walk away now.

"Well, I'll make sure I talk to Mr. Barber about the divorce papers," she said before a big smile spread over her face. "I'll make sure they're served to you in the most dramatic fashion. A guy in a clown suit. The works."

"I prefer strippergram."

"Done."

"I've never met anyone like you," Mason let slip.

"What is wrong with you? You can't break up with me and then say some shit like that."

"Sorry, let me try again. You're a feckless hag and I hope your luggage gets lost on the way home."

"Much better. Bring it in, champ."

Xeni gathered him close like he wasn't twice her size and he made sure to soak in the moment. He knew it would be the last time he touched her.

"I'm not gonna kiss you," she said when she stepped back.

"Good thinking."

"Bye, Mason."

"Goodbye, Xeni."

He watched her as she climbed into her car and waited until she pulled down the rock paved parking lot and back out onto the main road. Just before she turned, his phone vibrated in his pocket. He looked at the preview of the text staring back on the screen.

. . .

Your father is wrong. You are amazing.
And I've been proud to call you mine.

Mason almost went diving for the proper gif response, the perfect image to relate the depths of his heartbroken despair. Instead, he slipped his phone into his pocket and went inside to change. If he responded to her text, he knew he'd never stop responding to her texts again.

Xeni took one last look at her rings, then let out a deep breath and rang Keira's doorbell. It was time for their weekly viewing of *A Match Made In Paradise: Australia*. She taken both rings off that morning before she went to school to meet her students. She was jet lagged and beyond dehydrated, but the little ones had been a welcome distraction. It was hard to think about her shattered heart while chasing after a bunch of six year olds.

The door swung open and Keira's husband, Daniel, with his ridiculously hot face, welcomed her inside.

"Odd question, but how was it?" he asked as she followed him to the kitchen.

"Weird."

"Weird?"

"I'll give you the whole story when everyone gets—" Shae, Keira and Erica were already screaming and rushing at her before she could finish her sentence. She could spot Sloan hanging back on a kitchen stool as she tried to survive the onslaught of hugs. She'd already seen Meegan at school, who was currently busy trying one of Shae's cupcakes.

"Welcome back!" Keira said.

"Ugh, I missed you," Shae said, squeezing her tight.

"I brought you apple butter." Xeni reached into her tote and pulled out the jar she'd brought from the farm.

"She brought me jam. I had some when I got home, right out of the jar. It was a-maze," Meegan said, pretending to drool.

"Uh, excuse me," Shae grabbed her hand and turned it over, examining her rings. "What's all this?"

"Oh, pretty! Was it your aunt's?" Keira asked.

"Uh, no."

"I repeat, excuse me," Shae said.

"I have a lot to tell you guys."

Erica came around the counter and grabbed her hand. "Bitch, are you married? I see that band."

"Let's wait for Sarah and Joanna to get here and I'll explain."

"Oh. My. God. You're married," Shae spun away dramatically.

"Hi Sloan," Xeni said, trying to ignore the flailing of her other friends.

"Hey," her friend laughed.

"Did she know?" Meegan yelled.

"What are you talking about?" Xeni casually shrugged off her jean jacket.

"Yeah, you seem awfully calm, Sloan. What gives?" Keira said.

"My role in this was strictly medical."

The doorbell rang, giving Xeni the out she needed. "Just wait, like, five whole minutes and I'll tell you all everything."

"I can't believe you told Sloan when I, your best friend, am sitting right here. I am hurt," Meegan said.

"I'm her best friend," Sarah said, walking into the kitchen. She handed Keira a bottle of champagne.

"No, me," Joanna said, walking into the kitchen behind her. "Who are we talking about?"

"Xeni. This ho went and got married," Shae said.

"Why doesn't everyone grab a drink, we'll watch the first half of the episode and then I'll tell you what happened," Xeni said, knowing it would never work.

"Or you tell us what happened right now," Meegan replied. "I can't believe you did this to me. Now I'm the only single one left. We were supposed to die together, old and bitter in each other's arms."

"Oh, we still will. Let's get lit and I'll tell you all about it."

An hour later, Xeni had gotten the whole story out. She told them the details of her birth, her extensive inheritance, Sable's zany scheme to get her and Mason together and how that had fallen apart. The girls had listened intently, asking all the right questions, saying all the right things that she'd wanted her friends to say.

"So, you guys are going to dissolve the marriage in a few weeks?" Shae asked.

"Yup. He's staying in Scotland."

"I mean, you're a rich bitch now. You could go after him," Erica suggested.

Xeni shook her head. "We didn't end things like that. I would be in the way, but I think—I mean, I get it. Sometimes you only have room in your head to process so much, and with his parents and shit? I think he's at his limit. My going there wouldn't be romantic. It would be selfish. Plus, I am not in a good place."

Sloan reached over and squeezed her hand. "It's okay to be feeling a lot of things right now. I mean, you didn't just have a wild and wacky teen adventure. You lost someone close to you, then you found out some serious family secrets and fell for someone all at once. And the money, too? It's a lot to process."

"Yeah, maybe don't up and run off to Scotland," Sarah said.

"I won't. Seems like now would be a great time to start seeing a therapist." Xeni paused, noticing that Meegan had fallen silent, her lack of poker face telegraphing her obvious distress. "Meegs, what's wrong?" Meegan shook herself like she'd been caught and schooled her features.

"Oh, nothing. Just thinking. Go on."

"That's it. I wait until the thirty days are up, sign some divorce papers and get on with my life," she shrugged.

"Let me see the pictures again?" Joanna asked. Xeni handed over her phone.

"Jesus. You guys look so cute together."

"Salt the wound a little more, dear. It feels so good."

"Sorry."

"You really like him, huh?" Keira asked.

"How'd he measure up to the list?" Sloan asked.

Shae pointed at Sloan. "That's what I wanna know."

"Conservatively? A nine out of ten, so I guess I'll just have to hold out for that perfect score," Xeni said, lying through her teeth. He'd been all tens, across the board.

"Wow. It was the street magician thing, wasn't it? He felt short there," Shae teased.

"Nope. He did magic tricks."

"Damn."

Joanna laid her head on Xeni's shoulder. "Well, you know we're here for you. You've helped us through our heartache. We got you."

"Yeah."

"We sure do." The girls agreed.

"Thanks. It was a whole week, so I'll give myself a few days to mourn and then get back to being my fabulous self. I'm sure there's a prince of some remote kingdom somewhere who needs my money to help revive their economy."

"Are you going to quit teaching?" Meegan asked.

"No, not yet. No drastic changes. I haven't even properly grieved Sable yet, not as my mother. I'm waiting for those emotions to club me over the head. No need to throw an abrupt career change into the mix."

"Good idea," Sloan said.

Almost on cue, a wave of exhaustion hit Xeni. She'd just poured so much of herself out on the table and talking about Mason and her family made her realize all over again just how sad she was. There was no other way to describe it. Sadness had settled in the pit of her heart as Keira finally pressed play on the silly dating show. All she could do was wait for the pain to pass.

22

March

Mason sorted through the post, relief washing over him. It had been the same almost every day for the last six months. He spent his afternoons instructing the local youths through music lessons and then he waited for the divorce papers and they never came. He and Xeni had only texted a few times since they'd parted ways. Mason liked to think she was struggling the same way he was, heartsick and lonely, refusing to move on. He'd even refused to take off his ring. He wanted the best for her, and he could admit to himself that he hoped she hadn't found someone new. Not yet.

"Anything for me?" his mom asked.

"Yes. Here you go." He handed her a small package from her favorite paper company. Fancy stationery and calligraphy kits were her new hobbies, now that his father was out of the picture.

When they'd returned to Edinburgh, she'd agreed to take care of his dad until he was back to his old asshole self. As soon as the doctors cleared him to go back to the office, she started showing him listings for one-bedroom flats close to his work. She kept the house.

Mason struggled with the fact that he'd left his mum alone to deal with his father for all those years. Since he'd been back, though, he and his mum spent a lot of time talking, finding the space they needed to redevelop their relationship as mother and adult son. She'd admitted there were things she couldn't have told him when he was in his twenties, things she hadn't wrapped her mind around. When his father had announced his plan to go to the States and bring Mason back, she'd known nothing about the man was going to change.

His father functioned on control and she wanted no part of it. At first, Jameson didn't want to let her go quietly, but eventually he did move out and agree to her terms, uncontested. Mason had a feeling it had to do with his health, but he didn't ask. He was just glad his mum was happy and moving on with her life. Every day that went by, her strength to start over made him wonder what he was doing with his own future.

Shaking himself from his thoughts, he turned to find his mum looking at him, one eyebrow arched high. "You want some tea?" he said.

"I asked you a question," his mum said with a smile.

"What was that?"

"Did you hear from Xeni?"

"No, not yet."

"Hmmmmm."

"You have any wisdom to share, I'm all for it."

"You have to ask yourself, what do you want?" she said. "It's plain as day how you feel. It's written all over your face, every day those papers don't come. I know that you said you both need time, but it's not like you to leave things like this. You both deserve closure. Good or bad."

He thought for a few long moments. So long that his mum took a seat at the kitchen table and waited. Mason knew he was stalling. As long as things were quiet on Xeni's end, he didn't want to risk the conversation that might end it all for good. He was afraid, but that was no way to live.

"I'll call her," he finally said.

"Good. I'll take that tea now." Mason put the water on, then checked the world clock on his phone. She was just starting her day. He swallowed his nerves and sent her a text.

Hey, love. When's a good time to call?

He added a gif of Homer Simpson dialing a touch tone phone.

An hour later, she responded.

I'm free to have an uninhibited emotional breakdown at four p.m. my time. Is that too late?

He responded with the gif of former American football player Shannon Sharpe saying, "That ain't no problem."

Ha! Talk then.

It had been cloudy and wet all week, but there was finally a break in the rain.

"Do you need moral support?" Sarah asked.

"Can you please put the call on speaker so I can hear everything?" Meegan asked.

"No. And fuck you, no." Xeni's hands were trembling as she reached in her purse. She couldn't find her damn keys and she was supposed to talk to her husband on the phone in ten minutes. "I'm going to get in my car, drive to Trader Joe's and take this call. Then I'm going to walk inside Trader Joe's and buy a case of three-dollar wine. I may call both of you later and see if you want to work through the case with me."

"You know I'm game. I'll swing by Sweet Creams just in case and ask Shae to load me up," Meegan said.

"Antonio is bugging me, so you can count me in," Sarah added.

"Everything okay?" Xeni asked as her key magically appeared under her wallet.

"Yeah, he just wants to move in together and I don't want to. We'll figure it out."

"Tell Antonio it's fancy as hell to maintain separate residences. Okay, got my keys. Definitely come over tonight."

"We will."

Meegan and Sarah headed across the Whippoorwill parking lot as Xeni climbed in her car and prepared to meet her doom. Was she being dramatic as hell? Yes. She'd spent the last six months getting her life in order. She'd found a wonderful therapist. She'd moved. Helped her step-dad prepare for his retirement, argued with her mother about hers and made decisions about the future of her career. She'd tried yoga. She'd given up yoga. She'd even given herself a break and gotten an outstanding massage at Burke Williams. The only thing she hadn't done and absolutely needed to do was get a divorce.

She knew her family was starting to worry. Okay, so she was still wearing her rings. They were just so pretty and they brought her a level of comfort she couldn't explain. Her parents wanted her to get to grips with the fact that she was hanging on to a marriage to a man who lived eight thousand miles away and had no plans to ever see her again. She'd prayed on it. Done some light witchcraft. Done some intense witchcraft that she'd had to undo for fear that she'd accidentally started courting a demon. Cried a lot and ate most of her feelings. Finally, she'd decided to give them a year. Something about that felt right. If she couldn't get up the courage to contact him and if he maintained radio silence in all the time, she'd have her answer. The lingering feelings that refused to go away would have to be bottled up and cast into the sea.

Apparently Mason had made up his mind a little sooner.

The rain started up again and traffic slowed to a crawl. No one in L.A. could drive in the rain. Xeni watched her dashboard clock, hoping by some miracle that Mason wouldn't call her while she was trying to operate a vehicle. A few blocks later, though she could see the Trader Joe's up ahead, she was still stuck. Her dash display suddenly lit up.

MASON...INCOMING CALL

"FUCK!" She pressed the phone icon on her steering wheel and prayed she didn't throw up on herself. "Hey you," her voice wobbled in the most embarrassing way.

"Hello, love. How are you?"

"Jesus, did your accent get thicker?"

"I'm among my countrymen."

"Clearly. I didn't sign the papers yet," she blurted out.

Mason's deep chuckle coming through the surround speakers only made things worse. She'd missed him so damn much and so did her body. Her thighs instantly clenched.

"That's what I was calling to talk to you about. I was hoping we could talk in person."

"Oh yeah? Where? And when?"

"I was thinking next week. Turns out, a bassist I used to play with lives in Los Angeles. Place called Silver Lake?"

"Of course you know a bassist who lives in Silver Lake."

"I don't know what that means, but he said I could stay with him. I thought it would be a good time to hash things out in person."

"Hold on one sec. I'm driving," Xeni replied. Too many things were running through her mind, like how he was going to fly all this way to make sure she signed the paper once and for all. Her stomach lurched at the thought. He was probably seeing someone else. The light changed and Xeni finally pulled into the Trader Joe's parking lot. "Okay. So, next week." Xeni grabbed her phone and pulled up her calendar. She knew then that the universe was definitely fucking with her. "Yeah, I can do next week."

"I should have made this clear right when I called—"

"Made what clear?" Xeni really didn't want to be sick in the Trader Joe's parking lot, but she was real close.

"I don't want a divorce."

"Oh! Okay, well, I don't either." She thought it would be a relief to admit the truth out loud, but a whole host of other questions started bouncing around her head. Being married didn't mean he was in love with her. She knew how that might sound to some people, but she and Mason clearly didn't have a conventional relationship, if they had a relationship at all.

"That's something we have in common."

"Um, do you need me to get you from the airport or anything?"

"No. I won't be fit for human eyes after a transatlantic flight. I'll pull myself together and then I can come to you."

"Okay. We could meet at my house? I got a new place. And we can talk in private?" *That way if we come to the conclusion that we really do need to get a divorce, I won't be weeping in the middle of a restaurant*, she almost added.

"I would love to see your new place," he said. Xeni eyes started to sting. Why was longing even a thing? Why did she still feel this way about him after all of these months? Could she even make it a week? Taking this call was a mistake. She wanted to see him now. She needed to get off the phone.

"Great. So, you wanna say next Friday night at seven? I'm not sure when you get in."

"Friday night sounds perfect. Just let me know your address and I'll get myself over there."

"Okay. Well, I'm going to go get wine drunk for the next six days. See you soon!"

His deep laugh came through the speakers again. "See you soon, love."

Xeni ended the call and sank back against her seat. Then she opened her phone again and went right to the group chat.

Xeni: all hands meeting at my house tonight for all who can make it.

Meegan: YOU TALKED TO HIM???
Joanna: What? What's going on?
Xeni: My husband is coming to town.
Shae: Holy shit. I'll be there. And I'm bringing a whole ass cake.
Xeni: Good. I'm gonna need it.

23

_____

The Vernal Equinox

Xeni stood in her bedroom, looking at herself in the mirror. It was a little cool out for the short sundress. Also, it was night time, but whatever. The yellow floral pattern looked amazing against her dark skin and the cut of the dress made her ass look amazing. She leaned forward and adjusted her tits in her bra. She wasn't panicking. Nope, she was totally cool and calm. And who wouldn't want to look good for a house guest and potential gentleman caller?

She'd spent the week discovering which breathing exercises worked best and she'd spent the afternoon trying to figure out how many bouquets of fresh flowers telegraphed "I'm trying to pretend I'm happy, healthy and completely balanced. Everything is fine".

The doorbell rang.

"Let him talk. Just let him talk and then you can say whatever unhinged shit that wants to come flying out of your mouth." She breathed. "Coming!" Xeni power walked through her new Spanish style home. Rounding the corner to the front entrance, she could see Mason's towering shape through the stained glass transom in the front door. She opened the door and let fate in.

"Hey!" she said a little too loud. He looked better than she'd remembered. Tall, thicc as hell, and that beard. He looked comfortable in his cool weather clothes, the dark jeans hugging his thighs just right and a light Henley under a dark blue Carhartt jacket. And of course, his green McInroy Farm hat. He had a small potted succulent in his hand and a bag hanging off one shoulder. Xeni hoped it was filled with condoms.

"Come in. Do you mind taking off your shoes?"

"Oh sure."

"Here, I'll take that for you," she said, taking the plant from him.

He was still wearing his ring.

"That's for you. A little housewarming gift."

"Thank you." Xeni stepped back and gave him room to set his bag on the bench. He shed his boots and tucked them under the bench next to her shoes. She wasn't thinking anything weird like how his boots belonged there or anything. She didn't take note of how he looked shrugging out of his jacket either or how it looked good suddenly hanging next to her raincoat. These were not things that crossed her mind. Not at all.

"This is a lovely neighborhood," he said, closing the door behind him. "Seems very cozy."

"Thanks. The area is called Leimert Park, mostly Black and Brown people live over here. My parents are just a five-minute drive away. Close, but too far for my mom to walk over here. Boundaries and shit, you know."

"I do. Been living with my mum the last few months. Been great to reconnect, but—"

"You're a grown man and you'd love your own space."

"Something like that."

"Well, come all the way in and I'll give you the tour and then we can talk about calmly and rationally about our future. Aahahahah!" Xeni laughed.

Mason shook his head, not bothering to hide his smile, and followed her farther into the house.

"I was in a nice one-bedroom closer to the school before, but I've always wanted to live over here. This place popped up, nearly remodeled and I had to grab it," Xeni beamed, adoring the painted tile that covered her backsplash. She set the plant on the island so she didn't drop it by accident.

"I wanted to bring you a St. John's Wort plant, but I didn't realize it was basically a bush. The woman at the gardening store suggested a succulent might be more practical."

"I appreciate that. I don't have much of a green thumb. Don't let the roses fool you, I just bought them. Um, my friend Shae made us these amazing tarts." She motioned to the spread she'd set out on the counter. "And I figured we could order in. There are a bunch of great places nearby we could have delivered."

"If you have any suggestions for Mexican food, my friend said I needed to try more real tacos. He also suggested we go to a Korean BBQ place."

"We can do both of those things." The idea of doing a whole culinary tour of L.A. with Mason made her ridiculously happy. So did the idea of him sticking around long enough that she could take him to the beach and Disneyland and… "There's a place nearby called World of Tacos. Why don't I show you around and then we'll order?"

"Perfect plan."

"So, this is the kitchen slash dining room. You saw the living room on the way in. Bedrooms are this way." She led him to the back of the house and pointed out the guest bedroom and her office. She could feel him as he walked behind into her master bedroom, ignoring the way just being around him caused her body to ignite.

"Bathroom's through there and the French doors lead out to the back yard. It took about three months for me to stop being afraid of someone just busting through here while I'm sleeping, but I have an alarm system and the fences are pretty high. I might get a dog, though. Everyone in this neighborhood has a dog. The barking works."

Mason looked around the room. "That's a big bed for one person."

Xeni nodded slowly. "I have noticed that."

"And that's a very interesting chair." Mason tipped his chin toward the oversized ladder-back chair sitting in the corner.

"It's a sex chair," Xeni blurted out.

"A sex chair for a sex witch," Mason joked.

"Pretty much."

He walked over and examined it more closely. "May I?" he asked.

"Yeah, of course. Make yourself comfortable," she replied, her voice squeaking a little bit. Mason took a seat. Heat flashed over Xeni's whole body at the sight of him sitting there. She'd pictured it more than a hundred times and none of her fantasies had come close to the real thing.

"Has the sex chair gotten much use?" he asked.

"Uhh… solo use? Yes."

Mason glanced up at her before he ran his fingers over the wide set arms. "Is that mirror always there?"

Xeni swallowed and considered taking a seat on the bed before her knees gave out. "Yes."

"So, what you're telling me is that you sit in this chair and masturbate every night while looking in that mirror."

"Well, not every night. Lesson plans take up a lot of time, even for kindergarteners. But yeah, sometimes, I guess."

"I see." Mason leaned forward and pulled a piece of paper out of his pocket before making himself comfortable again. "I finally saw Practical Magic."

"Oh yeah?" Xeni laughed. "What do you think?"

"Stellar performance by Sandy Bullock and that Aidan Quinn's a total babe."

"He is," Xeni laughed even harder.

"It inspired me to make a list of my own. I asked my mom about homegrown witchcraft and love spells, and after she lectured me about feminist struggles across Scottish history and midwifery and not toying with curses and Catholicism? This is what I came up with." He made a big show of clearing his throat. "What I Want From Life: A Comprehensive Accounting, by Mason McInroy, Age Thirty Six."

Xeni bit her lip, not sure whether to laugh or cry.

"Actually, why don't you come over here and read it yourself."

Xeni crossed the room and took a seat on Mason's lap. She stopped herself just shy of settling into his warmth, perching herself carefully just above his knee. She needed to know first. She needed to be sure. He handed her the piece of paper and Xeni was shocked to find there was no list at all. She read the words on the page, a few fat tears running down her cheeks.

"Go ahead and read it out loud," he said quietly. His fingers brushed her skirt aside and settled on her thigh. With his other hand, he took her fingers in his and jostled her rings a bit, letting her know that he'd seen them just like she'd seen his.

"I want Xeni Everly-Wilkins to remain my wife from here forward. With her by my side, the rest will take care of itself," Xeni managed to say.

"I hate doing dishes," Mason said. "But I scrub a mean toilet and since I'm no longer cooking for a living, I'll happily do the cooking for you."

"That all sounds amazing, but what the hell is this?" Xeni pointed to the crude drawing at the bottom of the paper.

"I was thinking about surprising you outside of your school with my bagpipes, but then I remembered how much you hate surprises so I thought I'd draw a little something. That's me there, playing for you, and that's you up on the balcony."

"What balcony?"

"I don't know. It seemed very romantic at the time. Can you just appreciate the effort here? I cook, sing and play seventeen instruments, and my dick is a foot long. Sorry I'm a terrible sketch artist. I can't be everything for all people, Xeni."

"I guess. Come here." Xeni cupped his cheeks and pressed her lips to his. What was meant as a sign of gratitude, a 'welcome home to me,' quickly morphed into something else as his tongue slid into her mouth. She shimmied closer, wrapping her arms around his shoulders. She pulled back just as she started to feel his erection pressing against her thigh.

"Is this why you came to me on the first day of Spring?" she breathed, searching his face. She reached up and smoothed an errant hair in his mustache to the side. "'Cause, whoa, bruh. This is intense."

"It was that or next Wednesday on the new moon. I figured if all things went well tonight, we could work on some affirmations together."

"My god," Xeni groaned. "Take me now."

"Is that a yes? You'll stay married to me?"

"Yes. Absolutely yes. I'm not changing my name though."

"I wouldn't dream of asking."

Xeni kissed him again, unable to keep her hands off his face, his chest, his arms. His hand slid high up her skirt, taking a firm grip of her ass. Mason took the piece of paper from her hand and let it slide to the floor before he lifted her and moved her between his legs. His mouth found the side of her throat as he spread her thighs and pushed up her skirt.

"Open your eyes," he whispered.

Xeni did as she was told. A desperate whimper slipped from her lips when her gaze caught his in the mirror. His other hand went to her breast and pulled her dress and her bra to the side, exposing her hard nipple. He grazed his thumb over the tight tip twice, then three times.

"Spread your legs a little more for me, love. That's perfect." He pushed his fingers inside her underwear. She knew he could feel how wet he'd made her with just a kiss. "Is this how you do it?" he asked. "You watch yourself like this?"

"Yes," Xeni breathed as he pushed two fingers into her aching cunt. "But this is much better."

EPILOGUE

June

"Babe. Fuck, fuck, fuck. Babe. We have to stop."

"Not until you come," Mason groaned behind her.

Xeni had stepped into the bathroom to finish her makeup and, the next thing she knew, her amazing husband was fucking her from behind as she gripped the edge of the sink.

Thanks to Sable, the two of them had done everything backwards, but every morning Xeni woke up and looked at the man beside her, she knew things were exactly how they were meant to be. Mason McInroy was the love of her life and she couldn't imagine being without him.

"Okay. I don't want you to stop—oh my god. But babe, our moms are going to be back any second."

Today they were throwing their third party of the summer. There had been an engagement party for Sarah and Antonio. Turned out all his nosing around about moving into together had been a warm up to a proposal. He'd done the grand gesture at the Third Street Promenade, string quartet by the singing fountain, the whole thing. Sarah didn't want to shack up with him, but marriage was a different story. Xeni was happy to offer up her massive back yard to celebrate their love.

When school let out, there had been a small going away party for Xeni and her former fellow teachers. She'd completed the school year before handing in her resignation. For months, she'd been thinking about what she wanted to do next, how she could put her money to work. After her cousin announced she was pregnant, she'd realized the answer was right in front of her.

Things were in the early stages, but she was starting a program to help Black and Brown pregnant people and new parents in L.A.. Her first step was to complete her doula training. She and Mason had come to a decision. They might take in some older children or teens down the road, but no babies for them. Xeni plain didn't want to get pregnant again, but she still wanted to do something to help the next generation and their parents. When she'd talked more to Mason about her feelings, she'd felt more secure in that stance.

Plus, they were too busy fucking all over the house to let an infant interrupt the fun. Mason's mom, Marjorie, had only been staying with them for a week and she'd already put a damper on their sex schedule.

They had maybe ten minutes before their moms came back from the store to help set up for her cousin Rosia's baby shower.

Xeni's head dropped between her shoulders as another plea died on her lips, her pussy clenching around his hard cock. Okay, maybe they didn't need to stop. Not yet. Just a few minutes more.

"Baby, I'm gonna come," her moan echoed off the bathroom tile, just Mason reached around and firmly pressed her clit. He ground into her, pulling her back tight against his hips as the orgasms rolled through her. Through her own haze of pleasure, she could feel his erection pulsing as he came inside of her.

He gently pulled out and smoothed his hands over her lower back. "Don't move yet." Like she could. Lights were still bursting in front of her eyes. She peeked over when she heard the sink beside her come on. A second later, he was cleaning her up with a wet washcloth.

"Good looking out," she said.

"Anything for you."

Xeni let out another deep breath before she stood. She grabbed her lotion to restore the baby softness to her butt and inner thighs. Then she went looking for her underwear, which had apparently landed by the foot of the bed when Mason had tossed them over her shoulder. The doorbell rang just as Mason pulled on a fresh shirt. He grabbed his cologne off the counter and gave himself a spritz.

"Good?"

"You're good. You don't smell like you've just been plowing me in the bathroom."

"Scent of Xeni is gonna be the title of my first studio album," he said with a wink as he went to the door. A few seconds later, she heard her mom's muffled voice. Mason had planned to teach music lessons here, but after word of his musical skills had gotten around to her family, two of his aunts had put him in touch with musician friends of theirs who got him some work playing the trumpet, flute and oboe on a few studio tracks. Seriously, who the fuck was her husband? But it wasn't the Everlys who got him the break he'd been hoping for.

In all their years of friendship, Meegan had failed to mention that international mega popstar and producer Duke Stone was her cousin. She'd put Mason in touch with him, just as a favor neither of them thought would go anywhere and it took a whole two minutes at the piano for Duke to fall in love with him. He'd hired Mason to record on his next album and if all went well, Mason would be on Duke's next tour. Duke had some ideas for him and his bagpipes. Xeni was gonna miss him like crazy if they went on the road, but the look on his face when he told her the news? She knew every minute they were apart would be worth it. Mason had never been so happy. Well, except when he was with her.

She finished up her mascara then triple checked herself in the mirror. Out in the bedroom, she grabbed at her phone and stopped just a moment to straighten the framed letters by the bedroom door. The letters they'd received from Sable and Mason's comprehensive list of what he wanted out of life, all a reminder of the reasons they belonged together. There had also been a small picture of Aidan Quinn, but Xeni had made Mason take it down.

"Where's Marjorie?" she asked her mom when she stepped into the kitchen.

"She's outside talking to your neighbor."

"Left or right?"

"The woman on the right, who's the selling honey."

"Oh, Miss Veronica. Her husband loves Mason. He always asks him to come and play guitar for his dogs," Xeni laughed.

Her mom just shook her head.

Xeni looked around at the cases of soda and beer piled on the island. Shae would be dropping off the gender reveal cake Xeni had bitten her tongue about in an hour. "What's left in the car?" she asked her mom. Enough food to feed the whole block would arrive with the rest of her family.

"There's ice in the trunk," her mom replied.

"I got it," Mason grunted, carrying a metric ton of ice under each arm. He ducked below the OH BABY banner hanging just inside the door, before he set them on the counter.

"Anything else?"

"Just the fruit, dear. I got it right here," Marjorie said as she made her way in behind him, carrying a massive fruit platter. "Oh, that Veronica is just lovely and she's so happy to have you two for neighbors."

"She's great," Xeni agreed. "Let me take that for you."

"You know, if you two aren't going to give us any grand-children, you should at least get a cute little dog," Marjorie said, handing over the fruit.

Sloan's husband had just convinced her to get a puppy, and with twin ten year olds running from responsibility and a toddler who had just learned to walk, she said she'd never known such regret.

Xeni looked over at Mason, who looked back at her and winked. "Not much like a child, Mum," he said. "But the discussion is on the table."

THE END

MORE LOOSE ENDS

Hello Reader!

Thank you so much for checking out Xeni and Mason's love story. Mason appeared in Sanctuary by complete accident, but Xeni's role in Sloan's life was very deliberate. There was no way I could leave her out in the cold. Mason came back around, tapped me on the shoulder and let me know he was the perfect man to make her happy. I have to agree.

Up next is my poor baby Meegan. She's way overdue for some loving. Keep your eyes peeled for her Christmas time, fake dating, BDSM story. It'll be a rocking good time.

Xoxo - Rebekah

ACKNOWLEDGMENTS

I must thank Alison from Mom's Apple Orchard. Our visit to the farm has inspired five books now. I'm sure it will inspire many more.

I must thank my supportive friends and family. My agent and of course, my dog.

I must thank my darling friend Emmy, for letting me ask you weird questions about Scotland and the mail.

Thank you to piper, David James Winter. Talk about right place, right time.

Most importantly I have to thank you, the reader. This is for you.

If you're interested in more groovy bagpipe tunes, please check out the life and work of jazz bagpiper, Rufus Harley.

ABOUT THE AUTHOR

Rebekah Weatherspoon is still exhausted, but optimistic.

Be on the look out for Rebekah's next book, A COWBOY TO REMEMBER. This Sleeping Beauty inspired contemporary Western will be out early 2020 from Kensington Books.

Come on by and get to know more about Rebekah on her Facebook, Twitter, or Tumblr. You can find more stories by Rebekah at rebekahweatherspoon.com

www.rebekahweatherspoon.com
author@rebekahweatherspoon.com

COPYRIGHT